CHOKE HOLD

A TOM ROLLINS THRILLER

PAUL HEATLEY

INKUBATOR
BOOKS

Published by Inkubator Books
www.inkubatorbooks.com

Copyright © 2024 by Paul Heatley

Paul Heatley has asserted his right to be identified as the author of this work.

ISBN (eBook): 978-1-83756-488-0
ISBN (Paperback): 978-1-83756-489-7

CHOKE HOLD is a work of fiction. People, places, events, and situations are the product of the author's imagination. Any resemblance to actual persons, living or dead is entirely coincidental.

No part of this book may be reproduced, stored in any retrieval system, or transmitted by any means without the prior written permission of the publisher.

For Aidan

1

Tom Rollins is in Texas.

Just a couple of days ago, he was in California. San Francisco, to be precise. It was the longest day of his life. A black-ops team sustained a bombing campaign against the city as part of a false-flag operation, and they tried to use Tom as their fall guy. That didn't work out too well for them.

Tom's face was plastered across the news for a couple of days. National news – maybe international, too. At first, as a wanted man, blamed for the bombings. Then, corrections were made. His face was everywhere, and now they were telling people to leave him alone. No longer was he to be apprehended on sight. No longer was he a wanted man. Tom has noticed the side-eyes he's received the couple of times he's had to stop for gas. People looking him over, either recognising him outright, or sure that they've seen him someplace before, but unable to place why. The further he got from San Francisco, however, the less people seemed to pay him attention. Sure, when he stopped for gas in New

Mexico – his home state, coincidentally – people still looked his way, but there weren't so many of them.

He's feeling the effects of his time in San Francisco. When it was over, he expected to spend a few days lying in bed, healing and recovering with his new friend, Nina Perry. Unfortunately, that wasn't to be. An old friend, Cindy Vaughan, got in touch. She needs his help. Tom left the city straight away. He didn't have time to say goodbye to Nina. He had to settle for sending her a message, explaining the situation. She messaged back, wishing him well.

The online map says it's a twenty-hours-and-thirty-minutes' drive from San Francisco to Lubbock, Texas, but this is on the assumption that a driver does not stop for either food, gas, or rest. Tom has done his best to ignore all three of these necessities, but he's only human, and the car is not so focussed as he.

While driving, Tom has done his best to ignore the various aches and pains that plague him. Jumping into his Ford and driving halfway across the country has not been conducive to his health. His back aches. His head hurts. His limbs feel heavy. But only when he lets them. While he drives, he compartmentalises. Packs the pain away and doesn't think about it. It does its best to inch its way in, but he focuses on the road. On the journey. On Cindy, and what is waiting at the end for him.

So far, she hasn't told him much. She didn't want to speak too long on the phone, no idea who might have been listening in, or how. There wasn't much time for them to talk and to exchange details. Tom understood. He'd heard enough. He could hear the strained tone of her voice, too.

It's been a straightforward journey, for the most part. When he first set out, he was busy. He had to make a lot of phone calls. People had seen the news. They'd been trying to reach him. Tom saw the timestamps on their calls and their messages, and saw that most of them came before the truth of the bombings came out. He was pleased to see that his friends and family never doubted him. That even before it was over, they could guess the truth. They offered help. They knew he wasn't responsible. He's spoken to Zeke Greene. He's spoken to his father. He's even spoken to Hayley. It was nice of her to reach out.

He felt guilty passing through New Mexico, knowing he wasn't far from his dying father. When they spoke, Tom promised he'd visit soon. Other than the occasional cough, his father sounded well on the phone. He wouldn't let the lung cancer take him without a fight.

The land either side of him is flat, stretching out as far as he can see. The fields are green, but the sun is drying them yellow, patches of dead growth spreading ever outward. He reaches a small town. He doesn't see a name for it. He can see life inside some of the buildings, and there are other vehicles passing, but there is no one on foot. It looks like a ghost town. The ground is dried out and cracked, and the whole town looks bleached under the hot Texas sun. It doesn't take long for Tom to come out the other end of it.

Tom concentrates on his breathing, doing his best to stay calm and to ignore the pain. He's slept once on the journey, early this morning, and only briefly when his eyes became too heavy to continue. He found a quiet spot under a tree and curled up on the backseat for a few hours. He awoke with a start, and quickly resumed the drive.

It's early afternoon now. He hasn't heard from Cindy since they spoke on the phone. He hopes this is a good sign.

He passes a farmhouse on his right. It's quiet. It's hard to tell if it's still in operation. A sign a little further down lists how many miles until Lubbock. Tom still has a couple of hours to go. He thinks of Cindy. Thinks of how she's in trouble. Potentially in immediate danger. He grits his teeth and drives on.

2

Cindy Vaughan sits cross-legged at her computer. She's wearing her boots and her jacket. She's ready to up and go at a moment's notice. She breathes deeply and stays calm as her fingers dance across the keyboard. Ordinarily, when she works, she listens to music. Right now, she's in silence. Chris is not as calm as she is. She doesn't think music would help him, and especially not *her* kind of music.

Chris Parton paces the floor of her apartment. His breathing is not deep and controlled. It's short and shallow. He bites his bottom lip. Occasionally he pauses, goes to a window with his fingers laced atop his head, flattening his sandy blond hair, and then he resumes pacing. He's tall and has an athletic build, like he runs, or swims, or both. Currently, his brow is regularly furrowed, creasing his features. In more peaceful times, he likely gets a lot of attention from the opposite sex. Right now, that's the furthest thing from his mind, and it shows.

"How much longer do we stay here?" Chris says.

"Until Tom arrives," Cindy says. "Why don't you take a seat? Pacing isn't going to help anything."

He pauses momentarily. "Am I annoying you?"

"No, but I can see that you're annoying yourself."

He manages to stand still, but he looks just as antsy as when he's in motion. "How much longer will he be?"

"He was coming from San Francisco," Cindy says. "It's not like we're just down the road. But trust me, he'll be here soon."

"How long is it from there to here?"

"Over twenty hours."

"And he'll have had to stop to rest, right? So he'll probably be a few more hours. Hell, it could be tomorrow."

"Trust me on this, Tom is a machine. He'll get here a lot sooner than you expect. He won't be far now."

Chris bites his lip. He forces himself to sit down. His right knee bounces as he stares thoughtfully off to the side.

Cindy can understand his consternation. She'd be the same, but it's not her first time being chased. She's spent a lot of time with Tom Rollins, and there's never a dull moment in his company. Even before she first met him, she'd done her fair share of running. Since she saw Tom last, nearly two years ago, she's started attending self-defence and karate classes. Two sessions a week. She never misses a lesson. She's had an opportunity to put them to use once, a few months back, when she was coming home from seeing a band play at an underground club and someone attempted to mug her. Well, she thinks it was an attempted mugging. It could have been an attempted something worse.

It was late, and dark, and Cindy knows she looks like an easy target – she's short, and her loose-fitting T-shirts disguise the muscle she's been gaining since she started the classes. The guy was about twice her size. Didn't even bother pulling a weapon. Grabbed at her arm and demanded her cash and cell phone and anything else of worth she had. She kicked him hard between the legs and jabbed her knuckles into his exposed throat, and then, using the arm holding onto her, she flipped him over her shoulder onto the hard concrete. She left him winded. When he tried to push himself up, she kicked him in the face, breaking his nose.

Chris twists on the sofa and looks out the window behind him, down to the street below. Cindy's apartment is seven floors up. "See anything?" Cindy says.

"Just cars," Chris says. He knows what Tom looks like. Cindy has shown him a picture, and they both saw his face on the news. From up here, though, it's doubtful he'd be able to spot him. Plus, if Tom doesn't want to be seen, he won't be.

Outside, the sun is going down and the sky is dimming. Cindy's apartment is on the side of the building facing west, and she has views of the setting sun every night. It casts an orange light in her apartment, making everything glow.

She glances at her computer. In the right corner of her screen there is a live feed. It shows the lobby into the building. When she moved in here, she made sure to plant a secret camera down there, concealed in a top corner of the lobby where no one could easily spot it. It points toward the door. She can see everyone who comes and goes. She keeps it on a live feed, twenty-four seven. Past experiences have made her cautious. People looking for her in her apartment are the whole reason she moved here a few years ago. She hates the fact that it could be happening again.

Chris turns away from the window. He rests his neck on the back of the sofa and stares at the ceiling. His hands open and close on his thighs, making fists. He wants to get moving. He needs to be proactive. Every second they wait he feels like it's a second wasted. Cindy understands, but they need to be cautious. If they rush off, knowing they're already being followed, they're liable to get themselves killed.

She spots motion on the live feed. Two men entering the building. She snaps a shot of their faces and enhances the image. She doesn't recognise them. She's familiarised herself with the faces of everyone who lives in this building, as well as their regular visitors. Their friends, their families. She doesn't know these two men. She's never seen them before.

They could be workmen – it's not unusual for workmen to turn up. But it's after eight, and unless it's an emergency call she doubts it. She rises from the computer and goes to the window, standing next to Chris while she looks down below.

Chris notices the change in her demeanour. "What is it?" he says.

Cindy spots a van below, parked outside the front of the building. A nondescript white van. A workman's van. No one else gets out, but that doesn't mean it's empty. It could be nothing, but it could be everything, and she's not willing to take any chances.

"I don't know yet," she says. "But be ready." She crosses the room, returning to the computer. She checks the whereabouts of the men. She has cameras in the stairwell. She has a camera in the elevator. The elevator is currently out of order. Whatever the men are here for, they've not come to fix that. They're coming up the stairs. They wear all black – jeans and shirts, thick jackets over the top that could easily conceal weapons. They're big guys. The same kind of guys Cindy and Chris have noticed following them for the last few days.

Cindy doesn't monitor their ascent. She needs to prepare. There isn't much time. She goes to the kitchen and lights the stove. She places a frying pan on it, heating the underside. Next, she goes into a bottom drawer of her desk and pulls out a spool of Kevlar trip wire. She heads to the front door, glancing at her computer screen as she goes. The men are in better shape than they look, and they're making quick work of the stairs. They're two floors away. They'll be here soon.

"What are you doing?" Chris says, watching her with alarm.

"Go into the bedroom," she says. "I'll be right there."

Chris frowns, not understanding, but he gets to his feet and does as she says.

While he goes to the bedroom, Cindy sets the trip wire in front of the door. She opens the door and swings it wide, making sure the wire is out of reach of its opening. She closes the door and re-locks it, putting on the chain, too, then goes back to her computer. The men are one floor away, and gaining. If they're coming here, it's not going to be long before they arrive. She picks up the laptop, keeping it open, and carries it through into the bedroom with Chris.

Cindy's apartment isn't large. She can afford a bigger place, but she doesn't *need* a bigger place. It's just her, and occasional visitors. She's happy with what she has. The living room is open-plan, connected to the kitchen. It's fifteen paces from her front door through to the main bedroom – her bedroom – door. It's to the right, off the kitchen. There's a smaller spare room directly off the kitchen. She keeps spare computer parts in there, and currently a pile of clean clothes she hasn't gotten around to folding and putting away. The bathroom is next to the spare bedroom.

Chris is standing in her room, close to the door, waiting for an explanation. Cindy places the open laptop on the bed and points at the live feed. "I don't recognise those men," she says, pointing. "And all things considered, that concerns me."

"You think they could be coming for us," Chris says. It isn't a question. He understands fully.

Cindy nods. "I don't want to take the risk. We'll find out soon enough." They watch the screen as the men reach the seventh floor. Cindy's floor. They come out into the hall and make their way down, checking door numbers as they go. They're not carrying any tools. Cindy doubts more and more that they're workmen.

"When they knock, we don't answer," Cindy says. "It won't take long – they'll break the door down. When that happens, follow me. We head for the stairwell. We leave out the back. If there's anyone else in that van they came in, we don't want them to spot us – same reason we're not leaving via the fire escape right now."

Chris sees their heavy jackets. "Do you have a gun?" he says. He's had the same thought she did.

"I need to add that to my grocery list," Cindy says. She goes to her dresser. She picks up a tin of deodorant and tucks it into her back pocket. From her bedside table drawer she pulls out a lighter. Cindy isn't a smoker. She has no need for a lighter. A friend left it behind six months ago. A zippo. They haven't been back for it since. Cindy has kept hold of it for them. Now, she needs to use it. She slips it into her front pocket, then stands beside Chris, next to the ajar bedroom door. On the screen, the two men are only one door away.

"What about the pan?" Chris says.

Cindy doesn't answer. There's no time. He'll see soon enough.

There's a knock on the door. Three hard thuds with the side of the knocker's fist. A pause, and then the man calls through, "Maintenance. We've had reports of a gas leak. Anyone home?"

Another pause. Cindy watches the camera. The knocker turns to the other man, nods, and then steps aside. The second man crouches at the door and picks at the lock. Cindy can hear his tools scraping around, working at the mechanism. She sees the other man looking up and down the hall, keeping watch.

He gets the door unlocked and attempts to push it open. The chain blocks him. Cindy can hear their lowered voices. "Chain's on," one of them says. "They're here."

The knocker pokes his face through the gap and calls into the apartment. "Open up – we just wanna talk with you."

Cindy glances at Chris. Neither of them responds.

"This ain't gotta be difficult," the man says. "Just come and open the door. You really don't want us to have to huff and puff and blow it down, now, do ya? You ain't got a big home here, and it's not gonna take us long to find you."

Cindy braces herself. She peers through the crack in the door toward the kitchen. She can see smoke rising from the hot pan atop the stove.

"Let's just break the fucking door in," one of the men says. He's not quiet about it. "It's just a chain. It ain't gonna take much."

Cindy looks at the feed. The man who picked the lock takes a step back. He readies himself, then charges the door, ramming it with his shoulder. Cindy shuts the laptop and prepares. She's already moving as the door breaks open.

The man bursts through into her apartment, takes a stumbling step forward and hits the tripwire. He lands flat on his face. The second man follows close behind him, looking down, trying to see why his partner has fallen.

Cindy grabs the pan from the stove and charges. She clears the fifteen paces in no time at all, and slams the hot bottom of the pan into the face of the man still standing. He screams as it scalds him. Cindy hears his flesh sizzle upon the burning impact. Sees how as he goes down and the pan follows through, bits of his skin have clung to it and been torn away from his left cheek. The opposite side of his skull cracks against the doorframe and he falls out into the hallway. Cindy pushes him aside as he goes down, stepping over his body.

The first man, still on the ground, recovers himself, pushing himself up as Chris attempts to follow Cindy out of the apartment. He grabs at Chris's legs, preventing his escape.

Cindy drops the hot pan and spins, pulling the deodorant and lighter from her pockets. "Hey," she says.

The man looks up. Cindy hits the flame and sprays the deodorant. The blast hits the man straight in the face. His hair catches fire. He screams, but the flame goes into his mouth and he doesn't scream for long. He pushes himself up off the ground but Cindy follows him with the makeshift flamethrower and he falls back, flailing, his head aflame. He throws himself over Cindy's computer desk and pats frantically at his skull, trying to beat out the fire.

"Jesus Christ," Chris says, eyes wide.

Cindy looks toward the bedroom. To her laptop. The

burnt man on the ground is blocking the way. Behind them, in the hall, the man she hit with the pan is stirring. She thinks of the van parked outside. There could be others coming. They don't have time. They need to go.

She grabs Chris and drags him out of the apartment. They run, heading for the stairwell. Anything left behind can be replaced. What's important is staying alive. Everything else can be dealt with once they get clear.

3

It's dark when Tom reaches Lubbock. He drives straight to Cindy's building and finds a parking spot on the opposite side of the road. He doesn't get straight out of the car. He looks around first, checking the area. Other than the occasional car passing in front of him, it's quiet. He checks the parked vehicles. There's a van parked down from the front of Cindy's building, pointing his way, but he doesn't see any signs of life there. No one in the front, and no movement in the back.

He pulls out his cell phone and calls Cindy. There's no answer. He frowns at this. He leans forward and cranes his neck, looking up toward her apartment. The lights are off. If she's gone out, she won't be gone for long. She knows he's coming. She knows he'd get here as fast as he could.

But, if she *has* gone out, she would have taken her cell phone with her.

Tom doesn't like it. He gets out of the car, taking his time. He pops his spine as he straightens, twisting left and right. Still, he keeps the pain compartmentalised. Pushes the aches clear of his thoughts, as if they don't exist at all. He reaches into his backpack in the passenger seat footwell and pulls out his Beretta. He keeps what he's doing low, so no one will see his weapon through the windshield. He checks it's loaded, then tucks it down the back of his waistband, concealing it under the tail of his jacket.

Alert, Tom crosses the road to the building. He rings the buzzer for Cindy. He waits. There's no answer. He pushes it again, but still nothing. He takes a step back, thinking. More and more, he doesn't like this. He's on high alert. He turns right and makes his way down to the corner of the building, watching the sidewalk and the road as he goes. He looks toward the nearby buildings, too. Nothing sets him off. He doesn't spot anything suspicious. He turns left at the corner and makes his way down the side and around the back of the building, performing a sweep for anything of concern.

He doesn't see anyone else hanging out around the building. Sees no signs of forced entry at the rear door, or any of the windows. Sees no signs of surveillance, either. Tom goes around the building and reaches the far corner. He pauses, checking the nearby vehicles once more. There's no one around. Again, he calls Cindy, but still there's no answer.

By this point, Tom is certain that Cindy is not at home. He needs to get inside, though. He needs to get into her apartment, check it for signs of where she may be. Check it for signs of struggle.

He's hoping that nothing will be wrong. He's hoping that he'll get inside and he won't find her there, not now, but that everything is where it's supposed to be, too. Because if she's home, and she's not answering, that's not good. And if the place has been tossed and tables and chairs have been overturned, that's not good, either. She could be hurt. It could be worse.

Tom thinks about how to get inside. He could climb up the fire escape, but it's on the front of the building, and he doesn't want to be seen climbing up. Someone could call the cops, mistaking him for a thief or a creep. Around the back is probably his best option. Breaking the lock on the back door, which he knows is not alarmed and leads into the stairwell.

Before he turns, he spots a small group of four crossing the road. Two guys, two girls. They huddle close together, laughing about something. They're young, look like college types. They're not threats. They're not anyone Tom needs to be concerned about. They're heading for the building. One of the girls is pulling out her keys.

Tom waits a beat, and then walks toward them. He takes his time, waiting for them to get the door unlocked and to step into the foyer. They're all too wrapped up in each other, in their laughter, to notice Tom right behind them, keeping the door from falling closed and locking him out.

He waits, putting some distance between himself and the small group, then looks back over his shoulder, making sure no one is following. Confident that no one is, Tom steps inside.

4

Tom reaches Cindy's apartment and knocks on the door. There's no answer. It doesn't take him long to notice the boot print on the door, though he sees no signs of splintering around the frame. He frowns at this. Wonders if someone knocked at the door, and when Cindy answered they might have kicked it open. He doesn't like it. He's concerned what he might find when he gets inside.

When he breathes in, Tom can smell burning, and a hint of overcooked meat beneath it. He smelt it as soon as he exited the stairwell and stepped into the corridor. It's at its strongest outside Cindy's apartment.

Tom tries the door handle. It's not locked. He reaches back and places his right hand on his Beretta as, with his left, he slowly pushes the door wide.

The apartment is empty. Tom steps inside. The smell of burning is stronger. He keeps his hand close to his gun, but he doesn't pull it out yet. He sees no reason to. The apartment is still. There are no signs of life.

There are, however, signs of battle. Cindy's computer

desk has been swept clear, the items that were on top – a couple of books, some empty soda cans, a small stack of CDs, and a magazine – have been knocked to the ground and scattered. Close to this, there is a large, round black mark burnt into the carpet. When Tom kneels to inspect it closer, this is where the burning meat smell is at its strongest. Close by, amongst the items scattered from the desktop, Tom spots a cell phone. He picks it up and inspects it. The phone is locked, but he can see the home screen. It's an old picture. Cindy when she was younger, and her sister, Erica, when she was still alive.

Tom pockets the phone and straightens, frowning. He looks around the rest of the apartment. The spare room is empty, save for a pile of clothes stacked on the bed. The room has not been searched. It was harder to tell if the living room area had been looked through, due to the mess. Tom moves on. In the main bedroom, the first thing he spots is Cindy's laptop, lying flat on her bed. He opens it, but this too is locked. He keeps hold of it. He'll take it with him, same as her cell phone.

He spots her dresser at the foot of the bed. Photographs are stuck to her mirror, tucked into the frame around the outsides. Tom sees one he recognises. A picture he's in. He leans closer to see it better. Zeke took it, on his porch in Louisiana. Tom and Cindy, the last time they saw each other. They both look tired, but they were happy because they were still alive, and, more importantly, so was Zeke's family. Tom has his arm around Cindy's shoulders in the picture, and Cindy is leaning into him, the back of her head on his chest.

Tom hesitates, and then he takes the picture from the mirror. Cindy isn't here. Her phone and laptop are. There is the smell of burning flesh in the air, and a black mark on the carpet where someone has clearly been on fire. Tom breathes deep, staring down at the picture. He doesn't want to admit it, and he won't believe it until he knows otherwise, but Cindy could be dead. He could have arrived too late. He slips the photograph into his pocket, next to her phone.

With the laptop tucked under his arm, he leaves the bedroom, and prepares to leave the apartment. It's a dead end. He needs to look elsewhere.

The apartment door opens. There's no knock.

Tom pauses, hand moving toward his Beretta. Two men step into the room. They're big guys, and they wear heavy jackets that could conceal any amount of weaponry, but their hands are empty. They stare at Tom, like they're not surprised at his presence. Like they expected him to be here.

"Who are you?" one of them asks bluntly, the taller of the two. The point man, getting straight down to business.

"Could ask you the same question," Tom says.

The taller man looks Tom over. His eyes flicker toward the laptop under his arm. He sniffs and clears his throat, then says, "We work for the building," but Tom doesn't believe it for a second. They wear dark clothing under their jackets. If they were workmen, Tom would expect coveralls, or at least a work shirt. There's no sign of tools, either. "There was an accident in this apartment – a small fire. One of our colleagues was injured. You might have seen it." He points toward the dark mark on the ground.

Tom says nothing. He watches the two men. He notices how the shorter one is staring at him, like he expects him to make a run for it.

The taller man speaks again. "We're looking for a Miss

Cindy Vaughan," he says. "I assume you know this is her apartment."

Tom says nothing.

The taller man clears his throat again. "Do you know where she might be?"

"No," Tom says.

"Why've you got her stuff?" the smaller man says, tilting his chin toward the laptop. "She send you to pick it up?"

"How do you know this isn't mine?" Tom says.

They don't respond.

"It's very important we find Miss Vaughan," the taller man says. "We need to talk to her about the fire. Now, the fact that you're in this apartment, Mr –"

Tom won't be drawn. He doesn't give them his name. "Was she here when the fire happened?" Tom says. The fact they're asking about her gives him hope. It sounds like they're looking for her. Like whatever happened here, with the fire and the kicked-in door, she was able to get away. The laptop and cell phone now appear to have been left behind in her escape, and nothing more sinister.

The taller man sucks his teeth. "We believe so, yes."

"You believe so? I thought your colleague was burnt. He would know whether she was or not, right?"

They don't answer.

"What caused the fire?" Tom says.

"That's why we need to talk to her. It would be very helpful to us if you could –"

Tom blows them off. "If I find her, I'll be sure to let her know you're looking." He starts walking, making his way toward the door and the shorter man blocking it.

The shorter man cuts his eyes toward the taller. "He ain't buying it," he says, showing his teeth.

"No," the taller man says. "He ain't. But I reckon he knows her for sure."

Tom drops the laptop onto the sofa. He doesn't want it to get damaged. He moves fast as the taller man reaches inside his jacket and cuts him off before he has a chance to pull clear whatever he's grabbing at. The taller man's eyes open wide, startled at Tom's speed. Tom balls his right fist and punches him straight in his exposed throat. The tall man stumbles back, gagging, holding at his neck.

The shorter man lunges for Tom, but Tom twists and buries his left fist in the centre of his face, crunching his nose. Before he can fall back, Tom grabs him by the back of the neck and punches him in the hinge of his jaw, knocking him out. The shorter man goes limp and Tom lets him fall.

The taller man has hit the wall, still gasping. He slides down to the ground, his eyes fluttering closed, slipping unconscious as oxygen struggles to reach his brain.

Both men are out. Tom looks them over, but finds little of interest. No identification. Each man carries a handgun, a Glock, as he suspected they might. He pops the magazines, putting them in his pocket to drop down the trash chute on his way past. He leaves the empty guns beside their prone bodies.

Tom goes back to the sofa and retrieves the laptop. He looks out of the window at the dark streets below, wondering where the two men came from. He didn't see anyone on his way around, nor coming up. They seemed to know he was here, though. They must have been aware of his entrance.

One of their cell phones begins to ring. Tom ignores it, but it makes him wonder if there are others nearby, lying in wait, calling to see how things are going. Tom's eyes return to the van parked below. The van he earlier spotted, but which was empty. When he leaves the building, he'll have to be careful.

Carrying the laptop, Tom leaves the apartment, closing the door behind him. He disposes of the Glock magazines, and heads down the stairwell. He leaves via the back door, checking the way is clear. He sticks to the shadows as he makes his way around the building. He heads down the street, clinging to the darkness, then, when he's sure no one is following him, he crosses the road and circles back to his car. He waits before he starts the engine. Watches the road, and his mirrors. He doesn't want anyone sneaking up on him. No one does.

When he's confident no one is coming for him, Tom starts the engine and drives, leaving Cindy's apartment building behind.

5

Tobin Klinghoffer makes it to Cindy Vaughan's building. He was in the gym when he got the call to tell him that someone had turned up, and that Jagger and Kent got their asses kicked.

"By one guy?" Tobin said.

He spoke to Jagger. Jagger's voice was raspy. It was a struggle for him to speak. "He hit hard," he said.

It's not the first time today two of Tobin's men have been beaten down by a target who shouldn't have stood a chance against them. Well, it's a learning curve. They'll know for next time. Tobin has plenty more men. His employers pay well, and numbers aren't an issue. And then, of course, there's himself. His men may have failed, but he has more than enough confidence in his own abilities.

He hasn't had a chance to shower yet, and he's uncomfortable in his clothes. He shifts in the driver's seat. He smells of sweat. It reminds him of when he was starting out in MMA and he spent endless hours in the gym. He'd finished his weights tonight and was laying into the heavy bag when his phone rang. His knuckles are flattened and calloused, and his shins are numb from years of bag work, but he feels the tingle left over from the impact of skin on leather.

He pulls up in front of the building. One of his men is waiting in the foyer and unlocks the door when he sees him approach. "They're in the apartment," he says, not waiting for Tobin to ask, craning his neck to look up at him. Tobin is tall – six foot five.

Tobin makes his way up, jogging up the stairwell. He's already been informed the elevator is out of service, and he doesn't waste time going to it.

The door into Cindy's apartment is not locked. Tobin walks straight in. Jagger and Kent are slumped on the sofa in front of the window, nursing their wounds. Davies and Carter are standing. Davies leans against a wall, and Carter is in the kitchen. They all look up at Tobin as he enters. Tobin sniffs the air.

"You all don't smell that?" he says.

The four men look between each other. They smell it, but they're not sure how to answer.

"None of you thought to open a fucking window?" Tobin says. "Get the stink out before the rest of the building smells it? Hell, smells might be the least of our problems considering the noise you assholes have made." He doesn't differentiate between who is at blame for what has gone wrong here. He's not happy with any of them.

Carter hurries to crack a window and clear the smell of Clegg's burnt flesh.

"I don't think anyone heard," Davies says. "Or, if they did, no one has come investigating. No one's called the cops.

We've been here the whole time, ever since the new guy left."

"Since he beat these two's asses, you mean," Tobin says, nodding toward Jagger and Kent. Jagger rubs at his throat. He swallows. Kent gingerly prods at his nose with the tip of a finger, and winces as he makes contact. His nose looks bigger than usual. Swollen. It looks broken to Tobin. He's seen, and given, and experienced enough broken noses. "Where were the rest of you when that happened?"

"He didn't look like a big guy," Carter says, turning from the window. "We thought Jagger and Kent could handle him no problem."

Tobin grunts. "After Cindy, you were willing to take chances?"

They don't have an answer for this.

"Speaking of Miss Vaughan," Tobin says, "how are Donkin and Clegg?"

Their silence is ominous at this.

"Spit it out," Tobin says.

Davies clears his throat and shuffles his feet. "Donkin is gonna be okay," he says. "He's gonna have some gnarly scars on his left cheek, but it's not like he was all that pretty to begin with."

Tobin doesn't laugh. He stares at Davies and waits for him to continue.

Davies shuffles his feet again. "Uh, Clegg...Clegg isn't so good."

"Clegg is dead," Carter says.

Tobin doesn't feel anything at this news. He grunts. "What happened?"

"The bitch blasted him in the face with a flamethrower or something," Davies says.

"I know that," Tobin says. "It wasn't a flamethrower – it was a tin of deodorant and a goddamn lighter. How did *that* kill him?"

"It got in his mouth," Davies says. "He breathed it in. Scorched all the way down his windpipe, was probably in his lungs. The deodorant created a layer, meant it hung around, kept burning. He couldn't breathe."

"It might've been the best thing for him, if we're honest," Carter says. "His eyes had melted. He was gonna be blind, and all kinds of fucked up. That was no way to live."

"Was his body dealt with?" Tobin says.

"We buried him out in the scrub," Davies says.

Tobin nods. "Donkin patched up and good to go?"

"He should be," Davies says. "By now."

"All right," Tobin says, turning his full attention to Jagger and Kent. "Back to the matter in hand. Our new arrival. The mystery man. You get a name?"

"He wasn't talking," Kent says, his voice muffled and nasal due to his broken nose. "Something about him was familiar though, but I can't put my finger on it."

Tobin tilts his head. "What do you mean? You've seen him before?"

"I don't know," Kent says. "Not in the flesh. But still, something about his face…"

Jagger is nodding along to this. "I know what he means," he says, his voice still straining. "From the TV, maybe?"

"What, like an actor?" Carter says.

Jagger shrugs. "I don't think so. I'm not sure."

"Let's put a pin in who he is for now," Tobin says. "So you all saw him come in, but you didn't see him come out?"

"That's right," Davies says.

"So either he's still in the building, or he's a sneaky motherfucker."

"He's a sneaky motherfucker," Carter says. "His car's gone. We saw him pull up in it, but we didn't see him go. Think he maybe drove off when we were making our way up here to check on Jagger and Kent."

Tobin grits his teeth, thinking things over. "So we've lost him?"

"I spoke to Daniels," Davies says. "They've followed Cindy and Chris, but they haven't seen any sign of this new guy. Wherever he is, he either doesn't know where they've gone, or he hasn't caught them up yet."

Tobin pulls out his cell phone. He brings up Daniels' number. Before he hits dial, he looks around and says, "Have you searched the apartment yet?" It's hard to tell, from the obvious signs of fighting, whether the place has been investigated or not.

"Uh," Davies says. "Not yet."

Tobin stares at him. "Why not?"

"We were waiting for you."

Tobin glares. He doesn't need this shit. He needs a shower and a change of clothes. "Do it now, while I call Daniels. See if you can find anything useful. See if there's anything that might give us an idea of how much they know." He shoots a look at Jagger and Kent, still on the sofa. "You two as well. Get to work."

The four jump to attention and begin searching the apartment. Tobin rolls his eyes and turns away from them. He hits dial. It doesn't take long for Daniels to answer. "Yo, bossman," he says.

"How are things out there?" Tobin says.

"They checked into the motel and they haven't moved since." Daniels sounds bored.

"No one else has turned up?"

"No. Why? You expecting someone?"

"Maybe. Keep an eye out. A male – that's all we have so far. I'll get Jagger and Kent to message you a description. He did a number on them and we figure he's likely looking for Vaughan and Parton now. Could be sneaky, so be aware of that."

"We could go in and grab them now," Daniels says. "Secure the area, have a nice surprise waiting for this mystery man when he shows his face."

"Who you got out there with you?" Tobin says.

"Just me and Neil."

"That's not enough."

"Not enough? I got a good look at her. It ain't like she's a big girl. A little punk. The guy didn't look up to much, either."

"We've already underestimated them once," Tobin says. "When you move in, I want more bodies on the scene. I've got people coming your way now, but here's what I want you to do – continue to sit tight. Watch the place. If they try to go somewhere else, follow them."

"Jesus, bossman, how long you gonna keep us out here? You say to wait until more bodies turn up, and now you're saying that when the bodies turn up we've still gotta *wait*?"

"We want to give our new arrival a chance to turn up," Tobin says. "Or, if they move on, we want them to lead us to him. We get them all in one go. And this new guy is dangerous, too. Do exactly as I say. That clear?"

Daniels sighs, but he doesn't protest. "Yeah, it's clear. Whatever you say, bossman."

"Good. When your back-up arrives, message me so I know they're on site."

"Got it."

"And if the man turns up, call me immediately. Call me if you see anyone that makes you suspicious. And keep a low profile out there. Make sure you're not seen."

"Of course," Daniels says.

Tobin hangs up.

6

Tom has driven in circles for a half-hour, making sure he isn't being followed. By this point, after taking nonlinear routes and abrupt turn-offs, he's confident he's not. He finds a quiet place to park up, over the road from the Buddy Holly monument. He kills the Ford's engine and lights and sits in darkness. He doesn't move straight away. He sits very still and watches the road and the pavement. Checks his mirrors. It's quiet. There's no one around.

Tom reaches to the passenger seat and picks up Cindy's laptop and cell phone. The phone has a fingerprint lock. He presses the button so it brings up the screen for the code. Six digits. He punches in numbers that on the keypad spell out CindyV, but no good. He knew it was a long shot. Cindy is smart. She wouldn't use anything obvious. He puts the cell phone down and opens the laptop.

Headlights illuminate the inside of the car from behind him, coming down the road. Tom freezes and watches in the mirror. The car is driving the limit. It passes him by and continues on its way.

Tom puts the laptop back down. There's no point trying to get into it. He won't be able to guess the password, same as with her phone. He needs to try and find her. It was a slim chance that anything on her laptop or phone would be able to lead him to her, but always worth checking.

The men back at the apartment building, claiming to be workmen, are clearly looking for her. This is good. It puts Tom's dread at bay, at least for a while. She's not dead. She got away. Now he just needs to find her, though he has no way of contacting her.

He blows air, momentarily fogging the inside of the windshield. He's going to have to find her the hard way. If she's fled, she'll know to lie low. She's possibly checked into a motel, likely on the outskirts of the city. She'll have used an assumed name. She'll know Tom was soon to arrive. She'll know he can't get in touch. There's a chance she could have left a message for him at the desk. She could have used an assumed name, but there would be no need to lie about who Tom is. Whoever the people at her apartment were, there's no reason to believe that they know who *he* is. Unless, of course, they recognised him from recent news reports.

Or, if Cindy has decided to be extra careful and not reveal his name, if she's left some kind of coded message, she'd be sure that it was something he'd understand. Something they'd both know. Tom doesn't know what that could be right now, but if he hears it he'll make the connection.

He pulls out his phone and searches the motels in Lubbock. There's a few very close to him, near to the monument. He's not surprised. They're closer than he would expect

Cindy to go, but he'll check them out first anyway, just in case. It's important to leave no stone unturned. If he passes any buildings that appear abandoned, he'll check these, too. Tom reckons her hiding out in a motel is more likely, as she knows he'll be looking. It'll be easier for him to find her, and for her to leave a message, but, again, he needs to check everywhere.

As he starts the engine, his phone begins to ring. Tom looks at the caller ID. It's not a number he recognises. He answers. It's Cindy.

"Tom, where are you?" she says.

"I've been by your apartment," Tom says. "I had a run-in with the welcoming committee."

"Shit. Are you okay?"

"I'm fine."

She breathes a sigh of relief. He can imagine her grinning when she asks, "And how are they?"

"They're sore. Whose number is this?"

"It's Chris's."

"Chris?" Whatever trouble Cindy is currently in, Tom assumes it has something to do with this Chris.

"You'll meet him soon. Where are you?"

"I'm at the Buddy Holly statue, trying to figure out how to find you. I have your cell and your laptop, by the way."

"You do? You're a lifesaver, Rollins."

"Where are you?"

"We're in a motel, but we're nowhere near Buddy Holly. You're gonna have to come south. I'll message you the address."

"Are you okay?"

"All things considered, yeah, I guess so. I mean, obviously none of this is *okay*, but physically I'm unharmed."

"Good. Send me the details. I'll be there soon."

7

Tom drives to the motel. He slows as he approaches, driving below the limit. It's late, dark, and he's not holding anyone up on the road.

The motel is on the outskirts of the city, off the 289. Close by is a row of restaurants, lit up, still serving, and there's a little more life there. A couple dozen vehicles in the parking lot. Tom drives by slow, looking into the vehicles. They have a clear view of the motel. Most of them are empty, but he spots a couple of cars parked next to each other, at least two occupants in each. There could be more in the backseats, hidden in the dark. The two vehicles look like they're talking with each other. It's hard to tell if they're watching the motel. Further down the line, Tom spots a couple more vehicles with people in. A young couple making out. A pickup truck turns on its lights and starts reversing. Tom blows air through his nose. It's hard to tell if the motel is under observation.

Tom leaves the parking lot behind and goes to the motel. In her message with the address, Cindy told him there was parking at the back, and he'd be able to climb in through their window. She says they've parked Chris's car around there, too, out of view of the main road. Tom drives around to the back of the motel as instructed, reversing into a space in case they need to leave fast. He parks in a corner, also out of view of the road, under a tree providing further cover. He looks around the parking lot. There's a handful of vehicles, all empty. He doesn't know which car is Chris's.

Tom brings his Beretta. He gets out of the car, and he feels the effects of the long drive, the brief fight, and the events of San Francisco catching up to him. He grits his teeth and compartmentalises. He looks at the motel.

Cindy has been watching for him. She waves to him from a ground-floor room, the window wide open. They have the lights off. Tom goes to her. She steps aside so he can climb in, and then she throws her arms around him.

"Jesus, it's good to see you," she says, letting go and looking him over. She sees the bruises and cuts on his face, not yet fully healed. "Is that from San Francisco?"

Tom nods.

"You look like you need to sleep, Tom."

"I can sleep when we get through here." He looks her over in turn. Like she said, she's physically unharmed. Her hair is cut jaw-length and choppy, and she's dyed it blonde. She's wearing a Jesus Lizard T-shirt. When she hugged him, she felt firm in his arms. Strong. She's never been out of shape, but she feels like she's been working out.

"Where's my laptop?" Cindy says. "In the car?"

"It's in the car," Tom says. "I have your cell here." He takes it from his pocket, along with the photograph he took. He hands them both over. "I wasn't sure if you were still alive when I took the picture."

Cindy smiles. "Well, that's very sweet, Tom. I'm glad you'd like to remember me if I was gone." She hands him the picture back. "Keep it. I have it on my computer. I can print out another."

Tom slides the photo back into his pocket while Cindy checks her phone.

Tom turns. He'd already noticed the third person in the room, but now he looks at him fully.

"Tom, this is Chris Parton," Cindy says. "Chris, this is Tom Rollins."

Chris nods and offers a hand. "I've heard a lot about you."

Tom shakes his hand. "I'm afraid I've heard nothing about you," he says. "But I have a feeling that's going to change soon." He looks toward the window at the front of the room. "Just maybe not here."

"What is it?" Cindy says. "Have you seen something?"

"I'm not sure," Tom says, crossing the room to the closed curtains. "The parking lot next door has too many occupied vehicles, and I don't like it." Tom opens the curtain just a little and peers out. Most of the vehicles have not moved, and he doesn't see anyone on foot. However, one of the cars with men inside has gone. "I think we should move on. Find somewhere else to lie low."

"Is someone coming?" Chris says.

"Not right now, but we don't want to take chances."

"But if there's no one coming, then why do we need to go?"

"Because if Tom thinks something might be wrong, then we need to trust him," Cindy says.

Tom is still looking out of the window. While he watches, the missing car from the parking lot comes back into view. It glides by the front of the motel. The two men in the front are leaning forward, inspecting the building. They don't see him, but they're looking right back at him. They're looking at the motel room. The passenger is on his phone.

Tom wonders, briefly, if they spotted his car at Cindy's building from wherever it was they were hiding. They knew he'd entered, that much was obvious. That was why they came up to confront him. It stands to reason that they saw what he drove up in. If that's the case, they likely spotted his car when he arrived *here*, too. Now that he's come, they seem to be making a move, as if they were waiting for him all along.

The passenger gets off the phone. The car stops moving. Both men get out. Like the two men back at the apartment, they're wearing heavy jackets. They're probably carrying concealed handguns like them, too.

Tom looks toward the parking lot, and the second car they were next to. It's gone. It's not with the first. It could be coming around the back. It would make sense.

"We need to move," Tom says. "Right now."

"What is it?" Chris says.

Tom steps away from the window. "Men I spotted in the parking lot are rolling up on us right now. Let's go. Out the back, go to my car."

Cindy is already at the back window. She doesn't climb straight out. Instead, she peers out, standing sideways, checking the way, careful not to expose herself. Her head snaps back toward Tom. She points toward her right, then holds up three fingers. Men are coming. Three of them.

8

Cindy has left the window open since Tom climbed in. Tom stands close by, and in the reflection of the glass opposite he can see the men approaching. They're getting close. He watches their hands. They're empty. If they're armed, which they likely are, their weapons are concealed. They don't want to make noise here. They want this to be quiet.

The three men stop. They're waiting for the men at the front to make a move. Tom gauges where they are. They're beneath the bathroom window. He wouldn't be able to get the window open without alerting them. He looks around the room. There's a bed, a television, and a chair in the corner.

Cindy is at the front window. She's taken Tom's place there. She gets his attention and mouths that the men are almost at the door.

Chris is against the wall next to the bathroom, where Tom motioned for him to stand. He waits for further instructions. He's likely never been in a situation like this. He doesn't know what to do.

There's a knock at the front door. The two men have arrived. Tom expects they anticipate one of two things to happen: either they answer the door, and the men stick guns in their faces; or they attempt to escape out the back and get grabbed by their friends at the rear.

Tom unplugs the television and lifts it from its stand. As he passes Chris, he hands him the keys to his car. He speaks in a low voice. "Be ready to run."

Chris takes the keys. "How will I know when?"

"You'll know."

Tom takes the television into the bathroom. It's a flatscreen and easy to carry. At the base of the window, he can see the tops of the three men's heads outside. He hefts the television, and then throws it through the window.

The glass shatters. The television lands on top of one of the men, clips another, and causes the third to step back, caught by surprise. Tom follows the television out, placing a boot on the edge of the bathtub to boost himself through the opening.

Behind him, as he goes, he hears the men at the front throwing themselves against the locked door, trying to break through. Tom lands on the ground and drives his left fist into the chest of the man who stepped back and avoided the worst of the crashing television. The man stumbles back with the impact, coughing hard. He loses his footing and falls on his ass.

Tom has already turned to the man the television clipped. He's holding the back of his neck. It's bleeding. The corner of the television has done a number on him. Tom doesn't have much sympathy. He punches him in the solar plexus, and then smashes his forearm across his face.

Chris climbs out of the main window. He turns and catches Cindy as she follows him out. Tom waves them toward his car. He won't be long behind them. He steps toward the man on his ass, still coughing, both hands on his chest. Tom kicks him in the face, putting him down, then turns back to the man the television landed on. The television is damaged beyond all repair. It bent upon impact with the man's head. He's pushed it off and it lies discarded on the dried grass amid all the shattered glass. The man is on his knees. He's been cut up, too. The raining glass has bloodied him. Tom places a hand upon his forehead and slams the back of his skull into the motel's wall. He goes instantly limp and collapses among the shards of glass and the broken television.

Inside the motel room, Tom hears the front door break open. He hears the footsteps of the two men racing through the room to reach the rear window. Tom doesn't hang around for them. There's no need. He runs toward his car. Chris has it running. He's pulled it out of its space and is ambling it forward, waiting for Tom to catch them up. Cindy is in the front. One of them has pushed the rear door open for him. Tom dives inside.

"Go," he says.

9

Tobin is getting out of the shower when his phone rings. The phone balances on the marble counter, next to the sink. The call is coming from Daniels. It's either good news, or very, very bad.

Tobin quickly grabs a towel and dries a hand and the side of his face and answers the call. As he does so, he notices that he has a couple of missed calls, unheard while he was under the water. "How'd it go?" Tobin says.

"Uh," Daniels says. He hesitates.

"Good or bad, spit it out," Tobin says.

Daniels takes a deep breath. "All right. It didn't go well." He gives Tobin a quick rundown of what happened. How two of them approached the front and three went around the back, and the next thing they knew the mystery man was jumping through a window and kicking their asses. "There was a television on the ground," he says. "From what I could see, and from what I've manged to gather from the others, he threw the TV out first, and then he jumped out after it."

Tobin is silent for a moment. He draws it out. "Anything else?"

"Yeah – they said this guy hits like a fucking train."

Tobin grunts. The water drips from him, spattering on the tile flooring. "It sounds noisy."

"It *was* noisy," Daniels says. "We had to kick the front door down."

"Have you gotten clear of the area?"

"Yeah, we grabbed the three and we high-tailed it out of there."

"But you lost the man and the others?"

Daniels doesn't answer this straight away. This is answer enough for Tobin. Daniels changes the subject. "We did it all by the book," he says, making excuses. "Exactly how you would've wanted it. I tried calling you a couple of times before we made our move, after we saw the guy arrive, but you weren't answering and I figured you wouldn't want us to let them slip away."

"How did you spot him?" Tobin says.

"We were parked over the road and we saw his car coming. He crawled by, checking us out, but we made sure we looked like we weren't paying any attention."

"So he was already looking for you?" Tobin says. "He checked the area. It didn't occur to you that he was going to be suspicious of five men spread across two cars, just sitting and talking?"

"Like I said, we moved in fast because we didn't want to give them a chance to get away. We didn't know whether he'd made us or not, but it wouldn't have mattered if we caught them. And from how fast they got out, it looks like they were about to move anyway. We could've either sat tight and let them go, or we could have tried *something*."

Tobin doesn't respond to this straight away. He considers what Daniels has said. They did everything right. They covered the front and the rear. Tobin is annoyed, and he needs to take it out on someone. Their targets have slipped through their fingers yet again.

Back when Tobin was training regularly, his coach told him he needed to learn to get his temper under control. It was one of his earliest lessons. Told him he couldn't let every little thing get to him; that if he allowed his anger to overwhelm and control him, he would always lose more fights than he'd win. *If you don't control your anger, then it'll always control you.* He'd recommended Tobin take up meditation. Tobin did not. He had no interest. He wanted to keep his edge, and his anger gave that to him. He just got better at putting it to work *for* him, instead of against.

So now, he doesn't lose his cool with Daniels. Instead, he says, "All right. We'll find them another way. Stay close to your phone. I'll call you if anything comes up. Be ready to move when it does."

He hangs up the phone, takes a deep breath, and finishes drying himself. He stares at his reflection through the condensation clinging to the mirror. He locks onto his eyes. Whoever this mystery man is, this seeming spectre, Tobin needs to deal with him, and fast. A challenge that Tobin looks forward to meeting head-on. Tobin has no doubts in his own abilities. So far the stranger has beaten down some of his lackeys – so what? It's not exactly a great achievement. Tobin is on another level. Tobin is trained, and he's dangerous. He's yet to have seen anything from this stranger that concerns or impresses him.

He heads through to his bedroom and pulls on his

clothes. All black. A tight T-shirt that clings to the contours of his torso's muscles, and a pair of jeans. Stretchy denim, so that if he kicks he doesn't have to worry about tearing the crotch.

He thinks about the Cindy problem while he dresses. Cindy and her friends. He thinks about the mystery man most of all. Tobin would like to get a good look at him. He'd like to know who he is, and why Jagger and Kent thought he looked familiar.

It's late, but he knows there's still a lot of work to do. He picks up his cell and places a call. Brad is the head of the tech department for their operation. When it comes to computers, he's their best man. He answers on the sixth ring. "Hello?" He sounds like he's been sleeping.

"Did I wake you?" Tobin says.

Brad coughs. A phlegmy smoker's cough. Tobin can hear him moving around. "Yeah, I guess so."

"Have you heard about the trouble we've had?"

"Uh, with Cindy Vaughan? I heard she got away. That was the last I heard. Has there been more?"

"There's been more," Tobin says. "A new player has entered the game. You can find out the details soon enough, but what I need from you is to find him for me. Get in the cameras and track him down. I'll message you the details of where we know he's been, and you see what you can do from there."

Brad sounds wide awake now. The prospect of an important task, of a challenge, has roused him. "Got it," he says.

"I need everyone working on this, Brad," Tobin says. "Make some calls. Wake people up. *Everyone*. And round the clock."

"Say no more," Brad says.

Tobin smiles. "Find this asshole for me, Brad. There's a bonus when you do."

10

When they got clear of the motel, Tom took over driving from Chris. First thing he did, he found a bar, and swapped plates with another vehicle in the parking lot, using his KA-BAR to undo the screws. After that, they circled for a while, Tom again making sure that they weren't being followed.

They find an out-of-business launderette and Tom parks behind it. They break in through the back door. Inside, it still smells of cotton and softener, though overlaid with layers of dust and must. Cindy says it's been out of business for four years now. Some of the washers and driers have been left behind, though they've been smashed up, likely by teens with nothing better to do.

The windows are boarded over, but there's a gap between the planks for Tom to peer out through. He watches the road for a while. It's a quiet area. There's no one around, either on foot or in a vehicle. It seems they're safe.

"What should I do about my car?" Chris says. "I left it

back at the motel. They probably know it's mine, right? Should we be concerned about that?"

"Is there anything important in it?" Tom says.

Chris thinks for a moment. "Nothing," he says. "There's a few nickels and dimes in the cupholder, but there's nothing else of worth."

"Nothing personal?"

"I had a bag of clothes, but we left them back at Cindy's place when we had to run."

Tom tilts his head at the mention of the bag of clothes. Like Cindy, Chris has a Texas accent. He assumed he was from the city, but if his home is nearby there'd be no need to carry around washing. "You're not from Lubbock?" Tom says.

"Amarillo," Chris says.

"What do you do in Amarillo?"

"I'm an accountant."

"You part of a firm?"

"It's just me."

"Maybe we should fill you in on the backstory," Cindy says. She pushes herself up onto a left-behind washing machine and sits there. "Tell you what brought Chris from Amarillo to Lubbock."

Tom nods at this. "That's a good idea." He stays by the window, occasionally peering out.

Chris looks at Cindy, not sure where to begin.

"Tell him about Louise," she says.

Chris nods. He turns back to Tom. "My sister, Louise – she's gone missing."

"Is that what this is all about?" Tom says.

"We think so," Cindy says. "We can't imagine what else it could be. I started looking for Louise, and then all these guys start turning up looking for *us*."

"How long ago did she go missing?" Tom says.

"Three weeks," Chris says.

Tom doesn't say anything. He can see from the look on Chris's face that he doesn't need to. He already understands. Three weeks is a long time. The outlook isn't good.

"I know how it sounds," Chris says. "But I can't give up on her. I need to know – I need to find her, one way or the other. I can't just leave her alone out there. I know that...I know that she could be...dead... But what if she's not? What if she's still alive, and someone is holding her captive? I have to do everything I can to find her." Chris pauses. He takes a breath, composing himself. "She's my sister, but it's more than that. There's only six years between us, but I practically raised her. I know it's stupid when there's not that much of an age difference between us, but I look at her like my daughter sometimes. Our father walked out on us when we were young. I had to step up. I had to be the man of the house. Then, when I was eighteen and she was twelve, our mom died. We were all we had left. And when you're that young, six years *is* a big difference. I had to be her parent. I didn't have any other choice."

"How old are you now?" Tom says. Chris looks mid to late twenties.

"Thirty," Chris says. "Louise is twenty-four."

"Do you have a picture?"

Chris nods and steps forward, reaching into his pocket. He brings out a photograph, folded in half, and opens it up. Louise Parton, in a field, the sun shining down around her, making her blonde hair shine. She's very pretty, her blue eyes sparkling. She looks just like her brother, but with long hair. His feminine flipside. They could almost pass for twins.

"Is this a recent picture?" Tom says, handing it back.

"Last year," Chris says.

"Does Louise have a boyfriend you know about?"

Chris shakes his head. "She's been single for six months. If there was anyone else, she would have told me. She tells me everything."

"Does she live in Amarillo, too?"

"No. She lives here, in Lubbock. She moved here to go to college, and she stayed. But we keep in touch. Video calls, phone calls. If we don't talk, we at least message every day."

"How did you know she'd gone missing?" Tom says. "Tell me about that."

Chris blows air. "So, about four weeks ago, she told me she was at work – she's been waitressing while she looks for something else – and she said she was approached by a woman who claimed to be a talent agent. She said Louise had great features. Great bone structure. She told her a lot of complimentary things. Asked her if she'd ever considered modelling."

Tom thinks of the picture. He could believe it.

"I told her to be careful. I asked her for information on this 'agent', and Louise sent me a picture of the business card she was given. I should've done more. I should've done more research. But I was busy at work, and it looked legit, but I've searched since and no such talent agent, or agency, exists. It was a fake name."

"What was the name?" Tom says.

"Does it matter? It was fake."

"It might be important," Tom says.

"It was Lola Knox," Cindy says. "I've searched, and there are, of course, some existing Lola Knoxes. A couple of them aren't all that far away. None of them are talent scouts, and none of them match the description we have."

Tom raises an eyebrow. "Do you know what this Lola Knox looks like?" he asks Chris.

Chris shakes his head. "I never saw a picture. Louise said she was early fifties, short hair, greying. I know it's not much to go on."

"It's better than nothing. What happened next?"

"Well, I still had my concerns, but I knew Louise was smart. She wouldn't do anything stupid. And she can take care of herself – I have to keep reminding myself that she's not the same little orphan she was at twelve. I have to give her space and let her live her life." He purses his lips and shakes his head, lacing his hands together behind his head. "When I say it out loud, I hear what a mistake I made. I should've said more – I should've *done* more –"

"You had no way of knowing what was going to happen," Cindy says. She reaches out, places a comforting hand on his shoulder. She squeezes. "You can't beat yourself up. You've already done enough of that. Right now is about being proactive. Just focus on that."

"I'm trying to," Chris says. "But it just feels like we've been wasting time – we've had to wait for Tom to get here, and now I'm having to fill him in on what's happened, and –"

"The most important and helpful thing you can do right now is continue to fill me in on what happened," Tom says. "Don't leave anything out."

Chris takes a deep breath, steeling himself, and he nods. "Okay," he says. He knows Tom is right. He knows Cindy's right, too. Tom can understand his frustrations. It's hard for him, knowing that his loved one is out there somewhere, and he has no idea where, and right now he feels like he's not doing anything to help. Tom doesn't hold his agitation against him.

"A few weeks ago, Louise and the agent had arranged to meet," Chris continues. "Louise said Lola described it as a vetting process. Getting to know her better. Making sure she was the right fit. They arranged to meet at a nightclub called The Lubbock Lounge. Louise said Lola had told her not to tell anyone about it – she said she shouldn't get her hopes up too high too early. She said if it didn't work out, she didn't want Louise to have to explain to people why nothing came of it.

"But, like I said, Louise told me everything. She knew if it didn't work out then she didn't need to be embarrassed telling me what went wrong. So, the night it was happening, I stayed home. I made sure I was close to my phone. I told myself it was so I could either celebrate or commiserate with her, but I knew that most of all I just wanted to hear from her and know that everything had gone okay. That she made it home and she was unharmed. Every part of me, all that day, had wanted to drive down here to Lubbock, to accompany her, but I knew that wouldn't be a good look for her. A twenty-four-year-old having to be accompanied by her older brother wouldn't have exactly screamed professionalism. I forced myself to stay away, and now I wish I'd forced myself to come."

"Did anything happen that night?" Tom says.

Chris nods solemnly. "Louise called me. I couldn't hear what she was saying. She must have been inside the club, and the music was too loud. I could hear her voice, trying to be heard, but I couldn't make out even snatches of words. She must have realised I couldn't hear, because she hung up and started messaging me."

"What did she say?"

"She said that the agent hadn't shown. She'd waited for

an hour, and the whole time she felt like there were people watching her. She said she'd caught a guy in the crowd staring at her, but when she looked his way he pretended like he wasn't. I asked her if she felt okay, if she thought maybe her drink had been spiked. She said she felt fine. She said she was going to leave the club – she didn't feel safe. She didn't like feeling like she was being watched. That was the last I heard from her."

"You came straight to Lubbock after that?" Tom says.

"Yes. I tried calling her, I messaged, and there was nothing. She wouldn't leave me hanging like that. I knew something was wrong. I got straight in my car and I drove here. I've been here since."

"I assume you contacted the police."

"First thing I did," Chris says. "They made me wait twenty-four hours before they'd talk to me, despite what I told them. When they'd eventually listen, I ended up feeling like I might as well have been talking to myself. They didn't find anything. If I'm honest, I picked up a vibe of indifference from them. Like they couldn't care less. One of them outright said to me, people go missing all the time. They said sometimes people couldn't be found because they didn't *want* to be found. They wouldn't listen when I told them I knew my sister, and I knew she wouldn't do that. Even reading the messages, it was like they just thought she'd decided to move on and start over somewhere else. They wanted to move on from her case. They didn't expect to ever find her, so they just wanted to forget about it.

"It was clear that if I was going to find her at all, then I'd have to do it myself. For two weeks, I hung around Lubbock. I showed her picture to everyone who'd look. No one knew anything. I talked to her friends. I talked to her neighbours. I wasn't getting anywhere. No one had seen anything, no one knew anything, no one knew who had taken her." He pauses to run his hands down his face. "That was when I found out about Cindy. I spoke to a friend back in Amarillo, and he gave me her number."

"I'd helped him get his money back after he'd been robbed online," Cindy says.

"He told me that she would be able to help," Chris says. "That she'd been more use to him than the cops, and maybe she'd be the same for me. Almost straight away, she found what had happened to Louise."

Tom looks at Cindy.

"I was able to find footage of the night she was taken," Cindy says. "It happened outside The Lubbock Lounge. Two men grabbed her from the street, bundled her into the back of a car. At the time, we thought we were maybe dealing with three men minimum, but it looks now that whatever is going on here is a bigger operation."

"Did you get IDs on the men? The vehicle?" Tom says.

"They were masked," Cindy says. "They kept their faces hidden. And the car they were driving didn't have any plates. I tried to track them through CCTV, trace their route, but wherever they went, they were careful. They took roads without cameras. They disappeared."

"It sounds like it wasn't a standard kidnapping," Tom says. "An organisation like this, with a lot of bodies – there must be something more at play. A trafficking ring, perhaps."

"That's what I've been thinking," Cindy says. "And if that's the case, she could be anywhere right now. The only thing that gives me hope that she's still nearby is the fact that they've been actively coming after us."

"How did that start?" Tom says.

"Right after I found the footage," Cindy says. "But listen to this first, regarding the footage. I found it via outside security systems. Cameras that just happened to be pointing in the direction of The Lubbock Lounge. The Lounge itself has cameras, and they were pointing right at the spot where Louise was taken from, but when I got into their system there was nothing."

"How do you mean?"

"I mean they'd wiped that night. The night before, the night after – all present. The night Louise was taken – nothing."

"You think they might be in on it?"

"It's a huge coincidence if they're not."

Tom nods, agreeing. That's how it sounds to him, too.

"So, I find the footage, and all of a sudden there's people following us," Cindy says. "Chris and I, that is. At the time, Chris was staying at a motel."

"I noticed there always seemed to be a car outside with men sitting in it," Chris says. "And I always felt like they were watching me. They weren't subtle about it. I walked past, their heads followed me. Then, whenever I went anywhere, I'd spot the car following behind, keeping its distance. One night, in my room, I wake up and I hear someone at the door. Testing the handle. Then, I could hear scraping. Like they're picking the lock. I got out of bed, and I'm panicking, because what am I gonna do? I didn't have any weapons, I didn't know how many men there were... Anyway, I started calling through the door, saying I could hear them and I'd called the cops. The scraping stopped. A waited a couple of minutes and it didn't start back up. I eventually looked outside and there was no one there."

"Is that how it was for you?" Tom says to Cindy.

"Well, from my apartment it was harder to notice if anyone was outside watching," Cindy says. "No one tried to pick my door. But if I went outside, I noticed I was being followed. They kept their distance at first, but like Chris said, they weren't exactly subtle about it. It was like they didn't care if I knew they were there. Like they *wanted* me to know. To spook me. When you were busy in San Francisco, I was being followed, trying to give them the slip. Soon after, I picked up on someone trying to hack into my laptop. I managed to keep them out, but they were careful. I wasn't able to trace it back to them."

"How do you think they became aware of you?" Tom says.

Cindy shrugs. "I don't know. I'd guess they were aware of Chris looking around, asking questions. After that, maybe they saw the two of us together. Could be they found out who I am. I'm careful about my identity, and what I do, but not everything can be foolproof."

"And that brings us up to date?" Tom says.

"Pretty much," Cindy says. "Except for the searches I've been running."

"How've they been going?"

"I've gone through police reports about missing people," Cindy says, "starting with those who looked similar to Louise, and then branching the search criteria out. I've sent messages to some of the people, trying to find further details about the disappearances, see if they have any further information." She lowers her voices, and adds, "I can't deny it, I've noticed that a lot of people who disappear around here never turn back up – either living or dead." She shoots a look to Chris. He understands. His jaw clenches. "But this isn't uncommon across the country. It doesn't mean they're never going to show back up, eventually."

"We all know what it means," Chris says.

"Have you heard back from anyone?" Tom says.

Cindy shakes her head. "Not yet, but it's only been a couple of days. I'm holding out hope that someone will be in touch soon."

They stand in silence for a moment. Tom looks out through the gap in the window. It remains quiet outside. Tom turns back to them. "We seem secure," he says. "And I'm up to date. So I think it's time we call this a day. We stay low tonight, rest, and then tomorrow we go to The Lubbock Lounge."

"You think they're in on it?" Chris says.

"They deleted their footage," Tom says. "We're going to ask them why, and then we're going to ask them what else they might know."

Cindy slides off the top of the washer. "I'm taking first watch," she says.

"No, I –" Tom begins, but she cuts him off.

"It's not up for discussion," she says. "You're going to sleep for a few hours, minimum, and *then* you can take watch. You're beat. We can all see it. You're no good to anyone if you're out on your feet, Tom."

He looks out the window again, but he knows that Cindy is right. He can trust her to keep watch. She's one of the few people he would trust with his life. "All right," he says. "But I take over after you. Don't swap out with Chris. No offence to you, Chris, but we've only just met. If you're going to be on watch, it's going to be by my standards."

Chris doesn't seem offended.

"Get to sleep," Cindy says. "Both of you. I've got this."

11

When Cindy wakes Tom, Chris is still sleeping. Tom is glad to see this.

"I gave you five hours," she whispers.

Tom looks around the old launderette. It's still dark. Cindy's laptop is open, balanced atop an old desk in the corner of the room, emitting a dim glow. She's turned its light down so as not to wake them, or draw any attention. Tom pushes himself and stretches out, twisting his head left and right and hearing pops in his neck.

"You want longer?" Cindy says.

"No, I'm good," Tom says. He goes to the window and looks out. It's deathly silent outside. No signs of any life, save for the insects that hover around the streetlamps.

"It's been quiet," Cindy says. "I've seen a couple of cars, but they went by and never came back. No signs of anyone searching."

Tom nods. This is good. "You should get some sleep now."

Cindy doesn't turn straight away. She hesitates, like she has something to say.

Tom looks at her, and waits.

She glances back at Chris, makes sure he's out, then turns her attention back to Tom. "We couldn't talk as much as I'd have liked when Chris was still awake," she says. "But what do you make of this situation so far?"

"I think you know what I make of it," Tom says. They both keep their voices low. They don't want to disturb him. "That's why we couldn't discuss it in front of him. But three weeks is a very long time."

Cindy chews the side of her thumb and nods. "There's still *some* hope though, right?"

"Always," Tom says. "The fact her body hasn't shown up is in our favour. Of course, you mentioned that there's a lot of people who've gone missing and their bodies have never been found. It could mean anything. But wherever she is, whoever has taken her, if she's still alive she's probably gone through hell these last few weeks. The highest chance she has of still being alive is if she's being trafficked. We touched upon that earlier. If that's the case, she could be anywhere. She could be in another country by now."

Cindy motions toward her open laptop. "I've been running searches in between looking out, and I've found something that could be of interest," she says. "Or I should say, some*one*."

"Who?" Tom says.

"Mandy Bliss," Cindy says. "I don't expect that name to mean anything to you. It didn't mean anything to me. But around seven years ago she was briefly reported missing for a few weeks, but she turned back up claiming to have been kidnapped and tortured. Cops gave her a drug test, which she failed. After that, they dismissed her as a hoax, a junkie looking for the wrong kind of attention. It could be worth talking to her, if we can find her."

"She's missing again?"

"There haven't been any further reports, but she's gone off-grid. I *have*, however, found the contact info for the person who initially filed the missing person report – her son, Freddy."

"He's in Lubbock?"

Cindy nods. "I've already messaged him, though I don't expect to hear anything back tonight. I know it's a longshot, but it's worth exhausting all avenues, right?"

"Right," Tom says. "Did the report say much else about Mandy Bliss?"

"Not really – the cops brushed her off as a junkie, so they didn't take as many details as they should have. They said all the injuries she had were concurrent with things she could have done to herself while in a psychotic state." Cindy shrugs. "Hopefully we'll find her, and we can ask her ourselves. If it's nothing, it's nothing, but if it's something, it could be a *big* something."

Tom agrees.

"By the way," Cindy says. "You never told me it was over between you and Hayley."

"It didn't seem relevant," Tom says. "How'd you find out?"

"When I was finally able to call you back, and you weren't answering, I called her." Cindy raises her eyebrows. "She did *not* sound happy to hear from me."

Tom frowns. "What did she say?"

"It's not what she said. Just her tone. Very cold. It was a

surprise, honestly. I liked Hayley, y'know? I thought we got along when we met."

"I spoke to her on my way here. She never mentioned that you'd called." Tom supposes he shouldn't be surprised. Hayley wasn't a big fan of Cindy, or of the amount of time they spent together.

"What happened?" Cindy says. "It just didn't work out, or...?"

"It didn't work out." Tom doesn't see any need to mention the jealousy to Cindy. "It is what it is."

"Truth be told, I was more surprised when it looked like you were gonna settle down."

"I guess I'm just not the settling type."

"Maybe not yet," Cindy says. "Maybe you just haven't found the right place. Or the right person."

Neither of them speaks while they look at each other. A moment passes. Tom breaks the silence. "Get some sleep," he says. "A few short hours and we're going to have a busy day ahead of us."

Cindy doesn't move instantly. She looks back at Chris. Tom studies her face in profile. She gnaws her bottom lip. "I hope for his sake that Louise is still alive," she says.

"We'll do the best we can for them both." Tom squeezes her shoulder. "He's got one more hour, and then I'm waking him up and showing him how to keep watch."

12

It's early, but when Tobin contacts his employers they're awake.

"How are things going out there?" It's Guy who answers his call. Guy Kennedy. No doubt his wife, Shannon Kennedy, is nearby, listening in. Tobin isn't surprised they're awake. They probably haven't been to bed yet. They're night creatures. Vampires. Sometimes he wonders if they ever sleep.

"The pause doesn't exactly fill me with confidence," Guy says, prompting.

Tobin gives him a rundown of the situation. Tells him of the mystery man who has seemingly arrived out of nowhere to help their targets.

Guy clucks his tongue, making disappointed sounds. "This isn't good, Tobin. This isn't good at all. Shannon wants to speak to you."

Shannon comes on the line. She has a sultry voice, like an old screen siren. It's a voice that did her well in her former profession. "I thought you'd trained these men yourself, Tobin," she says. Her voice sends a shiver down his spine. Even when she's admonishing him, Tobin feels like he's being seduced.

He clears his throat, ignores the feeling, and forces himself to be professional. "I've done the best I can with them, Mrs. Kennedy."

"But one of them has been killed, and another badly burnt," Shannon says. "I'd expect a couple of your men to be able to handle themselves against a little girl like that. Haven't you been teaching them any of your fancy MMA moves?"

"It doesn't quite work like that, Mrs. Kennedy," Tobin says. "I learnt MMA from thirteen years old. We can't expect these men to pick it up in just a couple of years. They're brutes – they're heavies. They're punchers. They're shooters. They couldn't perform a high kick to save their lives."

"Then why didn't they shoot?"

"Because I told them to keep things quiet. And because I wasn't expecting Cindy to put up so much of a fight. I don't think any of us were. She's a hacker, for Christ's sake. I thought she'd crumble and surrender at the sight of my guys. They weren't small guys."

"Uh-huh – and now one is dead."

Tobin sighs. "It's my mistake," he says. "My fault. I accept full responsibility. I promise it won't happen again."

"You need to tighten the leash, Tobin," Shannon says, and when she speaks his name he can't suppress a shiver. "We're going to need regular updates on how things are going there. We're not going to lose everything we've built just because of some punky hacker."

"No, of course not."

Guy comes back on the line. He's chuckling. "Y'know,

with how spunky she's been, I'm actually quite looking forward to meeting her in person. She could be quite a star for us."

"I'll keep that in mind," Tobin says.

"See that you do. Talk soon."

Tobin is glad they didn't summon him out to the compound, wanting to talk to him face to face. It would have been a waste of his time. He needs to be here, in the city, where he can make a move at a moment's notice.

Ordinarily, he doesn't mind going out to the compound. He spends a lot of time there. The Kennedys have a room in their house made up for him for the nights he stays over. They have a big house, ranch-style. Tobin prefers his own apartment, but he likes the house, too. His main problem with it is the proximity it puts him in to Shannon. He stays professional. This is his job, but he's had a crush on Shannon Kennedy – formerly Campbell – for more years than he's worked for her and her husband. He can still remember the first time he saw her on screen. A low-budget neo-noir called *The Last Take*. She played the femme fatale – what else, with that voice, that body, and that face? She stole the whole damn movie. She reminded him of Virginia Madsen in *The Hot Spot*, and she spent almost as much time in the nude as Madsen did in that role, too.

When Tobin retired from fighting, he got into the bodyguard business. Attending Hollywood parties and galas with his clients, he'd cross paths with Shannon Kennedy. The first time he saw her, he gritted his teeth and looked the other way and pretended he hadn't noticed the woman whose poster he'd had above his bed for the previous four years. But it wasn't always easy to pretend, and sometimes he'd snatch glances. Sometimes, she'd notice. She didn't seem annoyed. She was probably used to people looking and pretending they weren't. She'd flash him a smile – that famous little half-smirk, just like on his poster. There was a flirtatiousness about her, even then, before they had ever been introduced. It's never gone away. Tobin has often wondered if that's how she is with everyone, or if it's just for him. There's no one he could talk about it with. No one he would dare.

Tobin has read critiques of Shannon's acting ability – Guy's, too – and how she's been accused of being lazy, and unbelievable. Of being stiff and wooden. Guy came in for similar criticism. He's read how Shannon could be difficult on set, too, and having known her for a long time now, he can believe that. It doesn't bother him. She's never been difficult with him – nothing he can't handle, anyway, like the phone call they've just had.

Tobin expected his crush to fade over time, but it hasn't. He's spent his life as a fighter – MMA, and then bodyguard, and now head of security for the Kennedys – and yet when he's near to her, when he talks to her, she makes him feel like a schoolboy. There's nothing schoolboy about the things he wants to do to her, however. That's the difficulty with staying over at their home. When he can hear her and Guy fucking down the hall, or when he passes the bathroom and he knows she's in the shower, and she hasn't closed the door all the way. He has to take deep breaths, steel himself, and force himself to walk straight on by.

He takes a seat on the edge of his bed and pushes Shannon from his thoughts. Forces himself to concentrate. To focus. He turns his attention back to his phone and calls Brad. This time, when Brad answers, he is wide awake. He sounds overly caffeinated.

"It's been a few hours," Tobin says. "Do you have anything for me?"

"I wish I did," Brad says. In the background, Tobin can hear his fingers still clicking over the keys. "I've got footage of the guy, but he's careful."

"How do you mean?"

"What I mean is, we're struggling to find a clear shot of his face. I'm in touch with my guys, and we're all having the same issue. We can see him on security footage, but even then it's rare. It's like he's avoiding cameras. When we *do* get a shot of him, it's the back of his head. Never his face. He's careful."

"It sounds like he's doing it on purpose."

"Has to be," Brad says. "We should have found a clear shot of him by now otherwise. We should know who he is. But we'll keep at it. He can't be careful all the time, right?"

Tobin hopes so. "Right," he says. "Keep me updated."

13

It's morning. For the last few hours, Tom has shown Chris how to be on lookout. They haven't spoken much. Chris is still tired. Tom could see that he was pouring all of his concentration into staying awake and being alert.

Tom checks his Beretta and notices how Chris watches him out the corner of his eye. "You think you'll need that at the nightclub?" he says.

Tom tucks the gun down the back of his jeans. "We shouldn't, but I'll be keeping it close. We've had enough trouble already. We don't wanna get caught short."

Cindy is still sleeping. Tom goes to her and places a hand on her shoulder, gently shaking her awake. He flashes back to his time in the Army. The only time he'd be gently shaken awake was if there was a threat incoming and everyone needed to stay quiet. Otherwise, the shake was rough, or else it was a kick to the boots, or in the ribs.

Cindy looks up at him through one half-closed eye. "That time already?" she says.

"It's time to wake up," Tom says. "We'll head out soon." He goes into his backpack and pulls out a spare toothbrush, still in its packaging. He's taken to always travelling with a few at a time. He hands it to Cindy, along with a small tube of travel toothpaste. Cindy accepts both gratefully and then forces herself to her feet with a groan, stretching her body left and right, working out kinks and knots.

"It's not the most comfortable floor I've ever slept on," Cindy says.

Tom hands another packaged toothbrush to Chris. Tom has already brushed. He goes to the window and looks out while the two get ready. The road remains quiet, but there is more traffic on it now. Everyone seems to be going somewhere. No one is hanging around. No one is searching. They're still secure here. They haven't been tracked.

Tom turns to Chris and Cindy. "We go to The Lubbock Lounge," he says. "I know it's early and it won't be open, but I want to get a good look at the building and the area. When the manager turns up, we talk to him."

"He'll probably turn up before opening," Chris says. "So how do we get in to talk with him? Or do we wait until opening?"

"If we see him arrive, we grab him on the way in," Tom says. "And if he's compliant, we'll have a polite conversation in the back of my car. If he's not so compliant, then it won't be such a polite conversation. Otherwise, we'll work something else out. While we're there, Cindy can look up who the manager is and what he looks like. We'll know who we're looking out for."

"Before we set off," Cindy says, "let me take a look at my laptop. Make sure no one has tried to get in touch."

Tom nods, then turns back to the window. A moment later, Cindy says, "Oh," which gets his attention.

"What is it?"

She looks at him over the top of the laptop balanced on the washing machine. "Freddy Bliss has responded."

Chris frowns. "Who's Freddy Bliss?"

Tom leaves the window and joins her at the laptop. Cindy is already replying. Tom reads Freddy's response. He says the cops say his mom's story was a hoax, and he's been inclined to believe them.

"I'm asking him if we can talk," Cindy says, as she finishes typing. She hits send. "I've told him that any information could potentially help us, no matter how far-fetched it might seem. I've said we're willing to entertain any notion at this point. I've asked him for his number, and if I can call him."

"*Who* is Freddy Bliss?" Chris says again.

Cindy tells him what she read about Mandy Bliss while Tom watches the screen, waiting to see if a response from Freddy comes through. He knows it could take a while. The initial response from Freddy is from an hour ago. He could be at work by now, away from his laptop and his phone, away from any way of responding.

"We'll give him a half-hour to get back to us," Tom says. "We don't hear anything, we'll stick to the original plan and go to The Lubbock Lounge, see if he contacts us while we're out there."

They wait. The minutes crawl by. Tom returns to the window and watches the road. He doesn't think about the time. Thinking about the time is what makes it last. He busies himself. Tom has always been good at busying himself. There's always something to do. Right now, that something is keeping watch.

Cindy stays at her laptop. While she waits, she does other things on her computer. Tom isn't sure what. He assumes she's performing searches pertaining to Louise Parton. She could be looking up the manager of The Lubbock Lounge.

Chris fidgets. He's always fidgeting. Always antsy. Impatient. Thinking about his missing sister. Always desperate to be on the move. To be doing something active. He needs to learn patience. Nothing is accomplished by rushing around blind.

They're closing in on the thirty-minute mark when Cindy speaks up. "He's responded," she says. "It's just come through."

Tom joins her at the laptop and reads the message from Freddy Bliss. He says he's not sure that anything to do with his mother can actually help them, but if they're that desperate then he'll talk to them. He provides his cell phone number.

"I'm gonna call him," Cindy says, pulling out her own phone. "I'm going to put him on speaker phone so you can both hear, but *I'll* do the talking, okay? We don't wanna be talking over each other while we're trying to get information from him." She's looking at Chris when she says this. She knows Tom will leave her to do her thing.

Cindy dials the number. Chris answers on the second ring. "This Cindy?" he says. His voice is deep and slurred. It's early, but it doesn't sound like they've just woke him. He sounds stoned.

"This is Cindy," she says. "Freddy?"

"You wanted to talk about my mother?"

"That's right. Anything at all. You never know what could help."

"It was bullshit, though – you get that, right? The cops all said so."

"Why don't you tell me what happened? From the start. All the way through."

Freddy takes a deep breath, casting his mind back. "This isn't something I think about a lot, y'know? I try not to think about it at all."

"I get that," Cindy says. "And I appreciate you taking the time to talk to me."

There's a pause, and then finally Freddy begins. "So, it was about seven years ago. I'd just finished high school and I'd got my first job. I hadn't moved out yet. Was still saving up a deposit so I could rent a place of my own. Ever since I was ten it was just me and my mom. After she and my dad split, he moved to Arizona and I ain't see him since."

Freddy pauses, thinking where to go with his story next. "So, a couple of years after her divorce, my mom started going to acting lessons. I think it was a way for her to get herself back out there. Meet new people. My mom was still young after her divorce. She had me when she was seventeen. This whole thing, her disappearance, it happened when she was thirty-eight. I was twenty-one. I went to work on a Friday night, I came home, and she wasn't there."

"Where'd you work?" Cindy says.

"Drive-thru," Freddy says. "Same place I work now, but these days I'm the manager."

"You said your mom was attending acting classes?" Cindy says, looking at Chris. Tom knows what she's thinking. The agent approaching Louise, telling her she could be a model.

"Yeah," Freddy says. "She got a few parts. Theatre stuff, mostly, and she was in a commercial for moisturiser. She did small parts at first, but she did okay for herself as the years went by. She got to play Blanche in *A Streetcar Named Desire*. I mean, it wasn't Broadway or nothing, it was a small theatre, but that's pretty good, right?" Freddy sounds almost proud, but then his tone soon returns to its stoned indifference. "Anyway, it wasn't uncommon for her to go off and rehearse and stay over at people's houses. When she wasn't there, I didn't think anything of it at first. I went to sleep, and when I woke up she still wasn't back. Again, I wasn't concerned. I got dressed and went to work. It went on like that for a few days, and that was when I started to worry. Because even when she stayed over and was working and stuff, she'd still usually at least send me a message, just to check in. That was when I tried to call her. No answer. Her phone wasn't even on. That was when I went to the cops." He pauses. "Listen, you wanna talk to her yourself, right?"

"Yes," Cindy says.

"Then maybe you can just ask her about what happened yourself, because I won't wanna be the one telling her bullshit, you get me? When she finally came back, like a few weeks later or whatever it was, she was talking these *wild* stories. Said she'd been kidnapped. Wouldn't shut up telling these crazy stories about a kidnapping ring operating in Lubbock and the surrounding areas. If you talk to her, you probably ain't gonna like what she has to say. I know I didn't."

"Why was that? Why didn't you believe her?"

"She was on *drugs*, Cindy," Freddy says. "*Hard* drugs. *That's* why I didn't believe her. While I was worrying, she was out who knows where getting high. And when she came back, she was telling all these wild fucking stories?" Freddy stops. He breathes deeply. "I'm sorry," he says. "I guess... I ain't spoke about my mom in a long time, and I didn't realise some of these wounds are still as fresh as they are. Seven years feels like a long time, until you talk about it, then it feels like it was just yesterday."

"I'm sorry for what you've been through, Freddy," Cindy says. "It was her home you were living in at the time, right? What happened next?"

"I left," Freddy says. "Took the money I had and got what I could. It was a cheap, shitty little place, but it was all I could afford right then, and I couldn't be around her anymore."

"And that was the end of it?"

"Pretty much. For me, anyway. She's tried to reach out, but I'm not interested. She's still on the drugs, and she still tells those crazy-ass stories. She won't accept responsibility, and that's what really sticks in my craw, you get me? I think more than anything else, that's what I can't forgive – the goddamn *lies*. After I left, she sold the house. Up and left it. She's not even in Lubbock anymore."

"You're not in touch with her?"

Freddy pauses. "Not really."

"But you know where she is?"

"Yeah, I know. Every year, I hear from her twice. Christmas, and my birthday. She sends me cards. She reaches out, pleading for me to get in touch. I tried once, a few years back, but she wouldn't admit the lies. I walked away, soon as it was clear she was still clinging on to her fantasy. She lives out there, a total recluse. No friends. Doesn't let anyone know who she is, or where she is – other than me, that is."

"And you said she's still on drugs?"

"Yeah."

"Does she work?"

"No. She's off the grid. Doesn't want any record of herself anywhere."

"How does she survive? Is she living off the sale of the house?"

They hear a sharp intake of breath on Freddy's end. "I send her money," he says after a moment. "Post it to her, once a month. A PO box. Like I said, she's paranoid and she doesn't take chances."

"Why do you send her money?" Cindy says.

"To keep her off my back. So she'll leave me alone."

Tom thinks there's probably more to it than Freddy is willing to admit. He wants to present a front of bravado, of indifference, but Mandy Bliss is still his mother. He'll still love her. Still care for her. Despite everything he's said, he still wants her to be okay.

Cindy picks up on this, too. She doesn't push it. "But *you* know where she lives?"

"One Christmas – the Christmas I finally made the mistake of reaching out – the card she sent, she'd included an address. Far as I'm aware, that's where she still is."

"Where?"

"Do you know Roosevelt?"

"Yeah, I know it. It's not all that far from Lubbock."

"She's outside there. Away from everyone else. Like I said, a recluse. If you're planning on going out there to see her, you're gonna have to be careful. She's armed, and she doesn't like strangers. If you mention my name, say I sent you, I figure she should calm down and talk."

"Thank you, Freddy," Cindy says. "Can you send me the address?"

"Sure, I guess. It's your time." He hesitates, then adds,

"Listen, I doubt my mom can help, but…good luck with your sister, okay? I hope you…I hope you find her. I hope she's all right."

Chris doesn't say anything. He clenches his jaw and stares at the phone.

Cindy hangs up.

"New plan," Tom says. "We go to Roosevelt and we talk with Mandy Bliss. See what she can tell us. But we need to be careful."

"We heard what he said," Chris says.

"I don't mean about his mother," Tom says. "I mean this whole thing is suspicious. This could be a set-up, regardless of who contacted whom first. We go out there, and we do everything as I say. If it doesn't look or feel right, we walk away."

Cindy's cell phone buzzes. Freddy has sent the address.

14

It's a four-and-a-half-hour drive to Roosevelt. They've set off early. They should arrive before midday.

Tom has the wheel. He watches the mirrors while he drives. The roads are busy, but they're approaching morning rush hour and this isn't a surprise. No one appears to be following them, not that he can see. No one acting suspiciously.

They're outside of Lubbock now. Chris sits in the back, staring silently out of the window. Cindy is in the front, her laptop open, though she's not doing anything on it. She's telling them about Roosevelt. "It's a small place," she says. "And I mean *small*. Its population is showing as nine."

"Nine?" Tom says.

"That's what it says."

"I thought Freddy said she went there to hide out."

"Well, it also says there are ranching families outside the community limits. They're not included in the Roosevelt census. Presumably Mandy Bliss is out there somewhere."

Chris has turned his attention away from the window

and is watching them, listening. He leans forward. "If the place is that small, does it really sound like she's hiding?" he says. "What if Freddy is right, and she's a nutcase, and this is a huge waste of time?"

"We don't have anything else to go on," Cindy says. "Nothing is a waste of time for us right now."

"We have the nightclub."

"No one's going to be there for hours. We'll be back in time."

Tom glances at the rear-view mirror. Chris is chewing his bottom lip. "What if Tom's right," he says. "What if it's a trap? Does Roosevelt really sound like the kind of place someone goes to hide? It's not like it's even that far from Lubbock."

"That's why we're going to be careful," Tom says.

Chris takes a deep breath. He runs his hands back through his hair, opens his mouth, stops himself from speaking, and then sits back and resumes staring out of the window.

Cindy glances at Tom and then looks at her laptop.

"Have you heard back from anyone else?" Tom says.

"No," Cindy says. "Freddy is the only person who's responded."

They drive the rest of the way in silence. It's hot. The A/C blows through the car. Despite the monotony, none of them sleeps. They're all too wired. Tom stops for gas and they grab food from the station. They eat while on the move.

Cindy has the details for Mandy Bliss's home on her phone. It's not a straightforward address. They're directions, mostly. When they finally reach Roosevelt, Cindy directs Tom through the small community, and off the main road and into the scrubland. The road is not well maintained and the car bounces and creaks. Tom slows it down. Dust is thrown up behind them.

"Is she far from here?" Tom says, thinking of the dust, and how if anyone is looking out they'll see them coming.

"About a mile," Cindy says.

Tom pulls the car over and waits until the dust settles. "The two of you stay here," he says. "I'm going to continue on foot, check it out. If it's quiet, I'll come back and we'll drive the rest of the way. If I don't like what we see, we turn around and leave."

"Shouldn't we just come with you?" Chris says.

"I'm faster alone," Tom says. "And if something happens to me, you need to be ready to turn the car around and get out of here."

Tom gets out of the car. Almost instantly, sweat bursts on his forehead and back. He takes a long drink of water from the bottle he got at the gas station, tucks his Beretta and KA-BAR down his jeans, then sets off.

The land here is flat, and there are few places for anyone to conceal themselves. It doesn't take long before Tom spots the house in the distance. Mandy Bliss's home. It's set far from the main road. Tom wonders if the track that leads to it is left purposefully damaged, to slow people down and to make them loud so Mandy knows they're coming.

Tom lies flat and crawls forward from the scrub. He watches the house. Watches the windows that he's able to see. They're barred. The sun gleams off them between the steel. The roof is covered in barbed wire. It's like a fortress. The house is surrounded by trees, providing it with further camouflage. When he gets closer, he notices there are security cameras in the yard and on the house. Tom freezes, and checks the direction of them all. At least one is pointing his way, but he's hidden behind the long grass. Tom turns east and keeps moving, circling the house.

The flatlands are in his favour. There's nowhere for anyone to hide. He can see that no one is lying in wait. So far, this doesn't look like any trap.

Tom makes a loop around the house. There are no signs of life in the untended yard. On the porch there is an unoccupied rocking chair, a couple of propane tanks nearby. Behind the trees that surround the property, there is a chain-link fence, the height of a man. This, like the roof, is topped with barbed wire. The track leads up to a gate. Atop the gate there is a camera, and at car level there is an intercom.

Tom continues to crawl until he's out of view of the house, then he rises and runs back to the car. Cindy and Chris have the engine running, and the A/C still on, and Tom is glad to slip into its cool. He feels the sweat chill upon him. "It's clear," he says.

"We're good to go?" Cindy says.

Tom drinks more water. "It's like Freddy said, though – she doesn't like strangers." He tells them about the house, and the surrounding, desolate area. "I couldn't see anyone inside, so we need to remain aware. We're not completely convinced yet."

"All that barbed wire – it sounds like she doesn't want anyone to come in," Chris says. "How can we be sure she'll talk to us?"

"Because I can be very charming," Cindy says. "And because Freddy told us to mention him. Let me drive. If there's a camera and an intercom, it's best if I speak to her. She might not be so threatened by me."

Cindy takes the wheel and they make their way down the uneven track. Tom watches the windows of the house as they approach. He can't see anyone watching them, but he's sure whoever is inside is observing their approach through the cameras. No doubt armed to the teeth, too. A person doesn't live in a house like this without a strong supply of deadly weaponry.

Cindy stops the car at the gate. She winds the window down and reaches out to the intercom, pushing the button. They don't hear anything for a while. Tom watches the area. No one approaches. It's as clear as when he did his sweep.

A woman's voice comes over the intercom. It's deep, and sharp, and doesn't sound at all happy to have someone outside her home. "I don't know any of y'all," she says.

"Ms. Bliss, my name is Cindy Vaughan," Cindy says. "With me, I have Chris Parton and Tom Rollins. We –"

"I can see y'all through the camera," Mandy says. "So don't try anything stupid. I can see every move you all make."

"Ms. Bliss," Cindy says, "we were hoping we could talk to you. About when you were kidnapped." Cindy pauses, waiting.

There's silence on the intercom. She's no doubt still watching them.

"Freddy sent us," Cindy says. "That's how we got your address."

"Freddy?" Mandy says. "You've talked to my Freddy?"

"Just this morning," Cindy says. "We spoke to him on the phone. He told us some of what happened to you. Not everything. We were hoping you could fill in the rest."

"Why would Freddy tell you about me? I don't want anyone knowing about me."

"It's not like that, Ms. Bliss –"

"Just call me Mandy, damn it," Mandy says. "You already

know where I live. It ain't like you gotta keep up with the politeness, so cut the shit."

"I promise you it's not shit, Mandy," Cindy says. "Chris Parton – he's the one sitting behind me. His sister has gone missing. She's been missing three weeks now. We're trying everything we can to find her. I read your case – how I got hold of it wasn't legal, but I read it. From there, I contacted Freddy. Freddy told us about you. He said you wouldn't want to talk, but if we mentioned that we'd spoke to him you might be more open to it."

There's a pause, and then Mandy says, "Three weeks?"

"Yeah."

"Three weeks is a long time for someone to be missing."

"We know. But that's how long you were gone, too, isn't it?"

Mandy doesn't respond.

"And we've got to hold out hope, don't we? If there's anything you could tell us that might help, we'd appreciate that."

There's a pause. It's a long one this time. "I'm gonna let y'all in," Mandy says. "Don't get out of the car until I say so. And I'll tell you my story, but if what happened to me is the same as what's happened to your sister, you ain't gonna like it." Another pause, briefer this time, then, "And don't try anything stupid. I got a shotgun right here beside me, and I ain't afraid to use it."

"We don't doubt that, Mandy."

The gate begins to open.

15

Tobin waits in his apartment. He wants to be out with the others, pounding the streets, but he knows that the best place for him is waiting right here. If anyone finds anything, if they need to contact him, this is where he needs to be.

There's little for him to do. He's slept for a few hours early this morning, after he last spoke to Brad. It was a difficult, broken sleep. They have a major situation on their hands, one that Tobin is expected to resolve. His thoughts are consumed by it.

He dropped out of bed and did push-ups. He went to his bag in the spare room and worked it over with punches and kicks in an effort to exert some of his remaining wild energy. It didn't help. The shower didn't, either. Deep, meditative breaths did nothing for him. Instead, he paces the living room of his apartment, and waits for phone calls that feel like they might never come.

He forces himself to stop at the window and stare out. The sun cuts through his half-closed blinds and puts spots in his vision until he has to turn away. He takes a seat and stares at the blank screen of the television. It's a struggle for him to sit still. His right knee bounces. His fists open and close.

Then his phone rings.

Tobin grabs it from his pocket and checks the ID. It's Brad. "You got something good for me?"

"Maybe," Brad says. "Nothing about our mystery man, not yet. But something of interest."

Tobin frowns. "I'm not sure if something of interest is enough for me right now."

"Wait until you hear what I got to say," Brad says. "One of my boys got onto me, and he thought you'd wanna hear about it."

Tobin looks around his empty living room. "I've got nothing else going on."

"You remember Mandy Bliss?"

Tobin sits up, instantly alert. "Of course I do." Mandy Bliss. The only person to ever escape them. They've been looking for her ever since. Seven years, if he remembers correctly.

"Then you remember her son, right? Freddy Bliss?"

"We have his house bugged – did you get something?"

"Potentially. He had a long and interesting conversation this morning – we think there's some potential he was talking to Cindy Vaughan."

"What makes you think that?" Brad has his full attention now.

"Well, it's guesswork, but just from what he was saying, what they were talking about. The bugs can only pick up so much. We've never been able to get one into his cell. We have one half of the conversation, and a lot of it's garbled, but there's enough there that we think it's Cindy, and we think it ties into his mother."

"He knows where she is? Seven years, he's never said a goddamn thing in that house. Did you get the address?"

"No. But you could hear what we got for yourself. I've isolated the various audio files we caught from the different bugs, mixed the best of them together into one streamlined recording."

"Good," Tobin says. Finally, something that could prove useful. "Send it to me."

16

Mandy Bliss stands on the porch and watches the car as it slowly approaches. Cindy drives carefully over the pot-holed ground. True to her word, Mandy carries a Mossberg 590A1 shotgun with an eight-shot magazine, and she makes sure they can all see it. Her staring eyes are narrowed and unblinking. She points at the ground, directing them to drive in a straight line. Cindy stops the car close to the porch, and Mandy watches until they've all got out.

Tom glances around the yard. He spots a beat-up old truck parked down the side of the house. On the ground, he spots areas that look like they've been dug up, the earth slightly higher than in other places. There could be mines. Judging from the rest of the house's fortifications, he wouldn't be surprised. "Watch your step," he says.

"That's right," Mandy says, overhearing him. "Walk straight on up to the house from where you are and you'll be all right. Any of you armed?"

"I'm carrying a Beretta and a KA-BAR," Tom says.

They're here to talk to this woman, to see if she can help them. There's no point in lying to her, and if they get inside and she spots either of them it could go badly for them.

"Leave them in the car," Mandy says. "Both of them."

Slowly, Tom does as she says.

"Nothing else?" she says.

"Nothing else," Tom says.

Mandy watches them make their way to her porch. As they come up the steps, she turns and heads inside the house. Tom notices she has a Sig Sauer P365 tucked down the back of her jeans. She's not just relying on the shotgun.

Tom takes point and steps into the house first. He follows Mandy through into the living room.

The house is sparse. The wallpaper is old and peeling in places. In the kitchen, there are pots and pans piled up in the sink, and plates stacked on the counter. The floorboards throughout the property are exposed. The varnish is dull and fading away in places. There is little in the way of decoration, save for on top of the mantelpiece where there are framed pictures of a young boy, growing up into a young man. Tom assumes this is Freddy Bliss. He can put a face to the voice now.

Next to the mantelpiece, there is a gun cabinet. There's no lock on it. Inside, there are rifles. A Browning, a Remington, another Mossberg, and a Winchester. Tom imagines they're all loaded and ready for immediate action. Mandy won't want to waste time reloading.

"Take a seat, right there," Mandy says, motioning with the shotgun to a beaten old leather sofa draped with a threadbare throw.

As the three sit, Mandy lowers herself into a recliner chair in the corner. She doesn't recline it. Before she sits,

Tom sees her move something to the ground, tucking it behind the chair and out of view. She's careful about it. She doesn't want them to see what she's doing. Tom saw what it was. A syringe and a rubber tube. Her works.

Next to the chair there is a radio. In the corner directly opposite, there is a television. It's an old model. Behind the television is a bank of screens, and these look more up to date. They show the live feed outside the house, everywhere the cameras point.

Tom gets a good look at Mandy as she sits, the shotgun resting across her lap. Freddy said his mother is forty-five, but she looks older. She's skinny, skeletal gaunt. Her features are pinched and drawn. The lines around her eyes are deep from her perpetual squint. Her long hair hangs loose. She's a brunette, with streaks of grey. On her wrists she wears jewellery. The sleeves of her shirt are long. Tom spots why. There are scars there. Scars all over her. There's a particularly bad one on her left wrist that the bangles and bracelets can only do so much for. It's shiny and pink, and still gnarled around the edges. She's trying to cover the scars up. She's probably covering the track marks, too.

She eyes Tom. "Which one are you?" she says.

"Tom," he says. "Tom Rollins."

She's staring at him hard, like she might know him. Cindy sits in the middle of the sofa, between the two men. Tom is closest to Mandy.

"It ain't your sister that's gone missing?" Mandy says.

"No," Tom says.

"Louise is Chris's sister," Cindy says.

Mandy's eyes are still on Tom. "You look familiar. Why is that? We met before?" Tom notices how her hands are tightening on the shotgun.

"I've been in the news lately," Tom says.

Mandy's head tilts. She continues to stare, then says, "San Francisco?"

Tom nods.

"Shit, that was only a few days ago, feels like. How'd you get here so fast?" Mandy's grip is loose on the shotgun now.

"I called him," Cindy says. "You're not the first person we contacted to help us."

Mandy looks at Chris now. "Your sister, huh? And you think there's a chance the same people who took me could have taken her?"

"We're not ruling anything out," Cindy says.

"Is your sister pretty like you are?" Mandy says, still looking at Chris.

"Uh," Chris says, back-footed. "I, uh, I guess –"

Cindy holds out the picture of Louise. Mandy leans closer to inspect her further. "Oh yeah, she's a beauty all right." She sits back. "From what I saw, they like them pretty. That's how they get them. They play on their vanity. There needs to be some believability first, though, doesn't there? You can't just walk up to anyone in the street and tell them this could be their big break. Believe it or not, I used to be a looker myself. I know how I look now. I have a mirror. Before time and everything else got its claws into me, I could still turn heads. But maybe that just depends on what these folks are looking for at any given time – pretty faces, I mean. I don't have all the answers. I only have my story."

"A big break?" Tom says.

"What did you mean by that?" Cindy says. They're thinking the same thing. The agent.

Mandy glances toward the bank of security screens. "Any of y'all want a drink? I ain't offered you anything yet."

"We're fine," Cindy says. "Please, what did you mean by that?"

Mandy pauses. She sighs. "How much did Freddy tell you?"

"He said you were an actress," Cindy says. "He said he went to work one weekend and you weren't home and didn't come straight back. Beyond that, he said we'd have to talk to you."

"For Freddy to send you all out here, all the way from Lubbock, you must've sounded real desperate for him to humour you like this."

"We *are* desperate," Chris says, leaning forward.

Mandy watches him in silence. Thinking about Louise, perhaps. The picture of her she was just shown.

Mandy sits back. Her hands are merely resting on the shotgun now. She may not trust them entirely, but she trusts that they're not here to hurt her. She believes they're here looking for help. "I only started the acting so I wouldn't be so goddamn lonely. Freddy tell you that? It was after my husband split. I just wanted friends." She stares off into the distance. "Seven years now. Ain't that a pisser? Where's the damn time go, huh?"

"Freddy told us you were doing well," Cindy says. "That you got some big parts."

Mandy nods. "I suppose so. Big parts for where we were playing them. I was doing okay. People kept telling me I had a future. A big, bright future, away from Texas, under the bright lights of the west coast. A woman came to see me. She said she was an agent."

Tom feels Cindy and Chris leaning forward beside him.

Mandy notices, too. "That excites you, huh? Sounds familiar?"

"What was the agent's name?" Chris says. "Lola Knox?"

"No, not Lola. She was calling herself Libby Shell." Mandy thinks back, remembering this woman. "She was just a few years older than me. Probably be in her fifties now. Someone approach your sister?"

"Told her she could be a model," Chris says.

Mandy snorts. "Sounds like their way of doing things. Could be the same woman. The same 'agent'. It would make sense, after I got away, if she started using a different name. Lola Knox, huh? Sounds like a porn star or something. Anyway, this Libby – and I doubt that was her real name, either – she came to me one night after we did a show of *Cat On A Hot Tin Roof*. We did a lot of Tennessee Williams. She said she was impressed. Said she'd seen me in *A Streetcar Named Desire*, too. *Then* she said I'd be perfect for this little indie movie they were casting right here in Texas. Of course, I agreed to go along to the audition. You can probably guess what happened next, right? You all look like smart kids. There was no audition. It was a trap." She trails off, staring at the ground, her gaze dark while she remembers this turning point in her life, whereafter everything went wrong.

No one says anything. The three wait for Mandy to continue. The minutes tick by.

Mandy breathes in. A deep, shuddering, shivering intake. "When I came to, I didn't know where they'd taken me. I was kept in a dark room, shackled to a bed frame. And there was a camera pointing at me."

"A camera?" Cindy says.

"In the wall at the foot of the bed," Mandy says. "They filmed everything. I don't know how long I was in that room. I didn't know whether it was day or night. The windows were boarded over. They didn't let in any light. It felt like…it felt like it would never end. Like it went on forever. I was tortured. I was raped. They pumped me full of drugs so they could hurt me for longer. They'd leave me lying in my own blood before they came back and did it all over again. It just went on and on and on, until I was ready for them to kill me."

"And they filmed the whole thing?" Cindy says.

"Everything. What happened to the footage, I don't know. I never got to ask, and they didn't provide many answers. I never saw the agent again, but I know she was part of it. She found me for them. Why, I don't know. But there was never any indie movie. They were making snuff films."

The three absorb this.

"Did you ever see anyone else?" Tom says, first to speak. "Any other captives, I mean."

"A couple of times," Mandy says. "When the bedsheets got too filthy. They'd take me from the room and hose me down, and throw me in a cell with others. We were beat up, half-dead. Drugged out of our minds. We could barely talk, but what little we did say, we were all telling the same stories. We were lured with promises of something more. Lured and lied to, and taken out to our deaths. I was never in that cell for long. A few hours, tops, and then straight back to the room, with its nice fresh sheets, and that same camera, always pointing at me." She swallows, but her face is hard. Her eyes are steely. It's a painful memory, but one that she has girded herself against.

"Did you see any of your attackers?" Tom says.

Mandy shakes her head. "They wore masks. I never saw anyone's face, other than the agent."

"How did you escape?" Cindy says.

"I wonder that myself sometimes," Mandy says. "It all

feels like a fever dream. Sometimes, even now, I wake up screaming, pieces of dislodged memory coming back to me. I wake up in my room and I think I'm back there. I have to – I have to dull it. If I don't dull it, I can't sleep." She looks at Tom. "I know you saw."

She's talking about the works. The heroin. Tom doesn't say anything. He doesn't judge. He just nods.

"Another curse from that place," Mandy says. "They hooked me on the damn stuff, and now it's all that can get me through." She shakes her head, resuming her story. "It was after one of those changeovers, when I was brought back, hosed down and dried off and there were fresh sheets on the bed, that I was able to get away. Normally, they shackled both my wrists. This time, it was just my left. The other shackle wasn't there. Of course, they didn't tell me why. I've wondered about that. I've figured maybe there was a problem with it. Maybe, in all my thrashing while they were torturing me, I'd damaged it somehow. Or maybe, the next time someone was coming to see me, it was going to be the end. The next person through the door would have been my killer, and he wanted me to have an arm free. He wanted me to put up a fight." She bites her lip. "I don't know.

"But I lay there, just my left wrist shackled, and I knew it was now or never. I didn't believe anyone was manning the camera that was pointing at me. It was there in the wall, running non-stop. I'd never seen anyone at it, no one working it in person, or working *on* it, nothing like that. While I was alone, I knew I had to take my chance. I clawed at that goddamn shackle. I tried to tear it from the frame, but it was no good. So I did the only other option left to me." She holds up her left wrist, the one with the worst scarring that Tom earlier noticed. "I pulled my hand out. The shackle was tight, but if I stayed where I was, I was as good as dead. I knew that no matter how painful it was, the alternative was worse. In that moment, while I degloved myself and bit my lip bloody to keep from screaming, I thought about my son. About how I couldn't give up for him. How I needed to stay alive for *him*."

She trails off. They know how things went with Freddy. She looks down at the scar on her left wrist, poking at it with the tip of her right finger. "You should have seen how this looked when it was fresh. I thought I would lose my hand. It still doesn't feel right sometimes. But, after I tore it free, I made my way out. The door wasn't locked. They were careless – they didn't' ever expect me to get free, especially not the way I did it. I was dazed from the drugs and the pain, and all I remember is walking down a hallway. It was so dark. Eventually, I got outside. It was night. It was pitch black. I started to get my bearings. I was out at some ranch in the middle of nowhere. There were guards outside, a couple of them, but they were standing off to the side, smoking. They didn't see me. I slipped right by them. I escaped.

"I walked all night, back to Lubbock, careful because I knew they'd be looking for me. When I reached the main road I stayed close to it, but I didn't go near it. If they were coming, it was the first place they'd look. When I finally got to Lubbock, I went straight to the police while the route was fresh in my mind, but they wouldn't head straight out there with me, no matter what I told them. They checked me over. They took my bloods. They found the drugs they'd put in me, and that was that. They thought I was a junkie telling tales – and it was a *hell* of a tale, but *they* were the ones who put me on the drugs. I'd never touched them before then.

"Eventually, the cops agreed to take a look at the place.

Two days had passed. You believe that? Two fucking days. We went out there – the place was empty. No one there. No sign anyone had ever been there. They'd cleared out."

"You said it was an old ranch?" Tom says.

"Yes."

"Where was it?"

"On the way to Idalou," Mandy says. "But don't waste your time out there. Nothing to see. Apparently it hasn't been occupied in years – officially. So the cops said, anyway. And so that just added further credence to their belief that I was some whacko. And Freddy believed it, too. The son I escaped for. Mutilated myself for.

"I had trauma from what I went through. PTSD. I started drinking. It wasn't strong enough. There was an itch I couldn't scratch. The drugs they'd put me on when I was out there. I couldn't kick them. As well as the fear, I escaped that place with an addiction. When I wasn't high, I couldn't sleep. If I was straight, I was constantly terrified they would come for me to finish what they started. Freddy blamed it on the drugs. He said my junkie mind had concocted it all. But I was sure I was being followed. Freddy believed I used the story as an excuse for the drugs. No matter what I said, he wouldn't believe me. Even when I saw cars outside, when I pointed strange men out to him, he wouldn't believe me. And then he moved out. Up and left. I begged him to stay, but he wouldn't hear.

"So I left. I had to, really. Whether he believed the story or not, it was for his safety – and for mine, too. That was when I ended up here. It's quiet here. It was the first time I felt remotely safe."

"Why do you stay in the area, Mandy?" Cindy says.

"You're not too far from Lubbock, and you don't know where those people went. They could still be close."

"I won't leave because Freddy won't leave," Mandy says. "One day, the truth will come out. Somehow, some way, I'll be vindicated. I stay for him, regardless of what he thinks of me." She pauses, just a moment, then adds, "And I stay for the people who took me, too. Who hurt me. If they ever raise their heads, I want to be right here to see them. I want to be the one who shoots them right between the eyes."

"Do you know who they are?" Tom says. "Do you know who's behind the operation?"

Mandy shakes her head. "I never saw any faces. I never heard any names."

Cindy turns to Tom. "I could look into anyone who purchased new property in the area seven years ago," she says. "Or, if they continued to squat like they did when they had Mandy, I'll see if anyone knows anything about that."

"If the same people took your sister as took me," Mandy says, looking at Chris, "she's probably dead already. And if she's not, she probably wishes she was."

Chris's face is pale. He already knows this.

"But listen to me, kid – hope ain't all lost. When I was there, those people liked to take their time. Three weeks is a long time, but she could still be alive. If she's resourceful, if she's willing to make sacrifices," she taps her left wrist, "then you all still have a chance, and so does she. Before they took me, I never thought of myself as a survivor. It's amazing what you can do when you've got no other choice."

The three say their thanks and their goodbyes, getting to their feet. Tom pauses on the way out. He turns to Mandy. "Sounds like we could be stirring up a hornet's nest here," he says.

"Sure sounds that way." She looks Tom up and down. "It seems to me it's a good thing they have you with them. I saw what they were saying about you on the news. You can take care of yourself. You can take care of others, too. You saved that senator and his family."

"I did what I had to," Tom says. "Listen, I want you to take my number."

"I can take care of myself, Rollins."

"I know you can. Do it for my peace of mind. We're potentially all outnumbered here. We need to be able to look out for each other. Take my number, and if anything comes up, don't hesitate to call me."

Mandy pulls out her cell phone. It's old. She gives it to Tom to input his number. Tom hands it back when he's done.

"Good luck with your search," Mandy says. She nods toward Chris, getting into the back of the car. "If you've got bad news coming your way, I'm not so sure that boy can handle it."

Tom grunts. "Then let's hope it's not bad."

17

Chris sits in the front passenger seat. Tom drives them back to Lubbock. Cindy chose to sit in the back. She has her laptop open. She wanted the space.

Chris doesn't want to believe that his sister could already be dead. He doesn't want to believe that she could be getting tortured right now. "That's too wild, right? Like, it's like Freddy said – she's a junkie. She's coming up with all these – these *stories*. Those scars she has, especially that one on her wrist, she probably just did it to herself and she doesn't even remember how it happened."

Tom says nothing. He drives. He understands Chris's concerns. He understands that he doesn't want to believe any of what they just heard, and that it could be happening to his sister.

"True or not, we have to take it into account," Cindy says from the back. She puts her laptop aside so she can lean forward and better see Chris. "We can't just dismiss what

Mandy told us. What if someone like that *does* have Louise? What if the same people who took Mandy have taken her?"

Chris runs his hands down his face. "Did you believe her?" he says, turning to look into Cindy's face.

"I believe something happened to her," Cindy says. "And that she's doing the best she can to cope with it."

"But do you believe the story she told *specifically*? That she was kidnapped because people wanted to film her being tortured and killed?"

"Yes," Cindy says. "I've heard of far worse things happening."

"Well, maybe she's heard about those things, too," Chris says. "And maybe that's how she justifies what she's done with her life."

"Then why did she have all the guns? All the defences?"

"I don't doubt that she's seeing *something*," Chris says. "If she's on drugs, hard drugs, she could be seeing any number of things."

"Chris," Tom says, his voice low but firm, getting everyone's attention.

"What?" Chris says, exasperated. Tom doesn't hold his tone against him.

"Do you want to find your sister?" he says.

Chris hesitates, not sure he's understood the question. "What? Of course I do. What kind of a –"

"Then you need to accept that bad people could be doing bad things to her right now," Tom says. He takes his eyes from the road long enough to lock on to Chris's, to impress on him what he's telling him. Tom turns back to the road. "We're all doing everything we can to find her. I understand that you don't want to think of her being hurt, but after three weeks, if she isn't dead already, then you have to accept that things have happened to her. That she *has* been hurt. That when we find her, she's not going to be the same person you remember. Three weeks is a long time. It's an eternity when you don't know if you'll ever see the sun again."

The car is silent. The hum of the engine and the blow of the A/C are the only sounds.

"Do you understand why I'm telling you this?" Tom says.

Chris doesn't answer straight away. He breathes deeply. He opens his mouth but no words come out.

"We have to be realistic," Tom says. "*You* have to be realistic. Mandy's story may have sounded wild and unbelievable to you, but it could be happening to Louise right now. Not wanting to believe something won't make it false. We're going to explore every avenue until we know what has happened. You have to let us help. All of this huffing and puffing, all of these doubts, all it's doing is hindering us. Are we clear?"

Chris clears his throat. When he speaks, the exasperation has faded from his tone. Everything has faded from him. He sounds numb. "Okay," he says. "You're right. We're clear." He turns away from Tom, away from the windshield. He looks out of the window on his side.

Tom knows he shouldn't be so harsh with the kid. He's worried. He's scared. He's desperately afraid for the well-being of his younger sister. This is all acceptable. What is *not* acceptable, however, is his argumentative tone. Is his doubt. Is his interference and interruptions. Tom and Cindy have worked together plenty of times before. They know what they're doing. This is all new to Chris. He's a civilian in all of this. He has to let them work. He has to trust their process.

Cindy squeezes Tom's shoulder like she can read his

thoughts, then settles back and puts the computer on her lap.

As per usual, Tom watches his mirrors while he drives, making sure no one is following. He was particularly cautious after they left Mandy's home, making sure no one was lurking once they emerged from her dirt road. He hasn't seen anyone. It's currently clear behind them. "Have you looked into land purchases like we discussed?" Tom says to Cindy.

"I'm running searches as we speak," she says. "So far I've got nothing – nothing obvious, that is. There was, of course, plenty of property and land bought up seven years ago. There was no reason to think there wouldn't have been. The issue is knowing who to think is suspicious. Plus, with these people Mandy told us about, we have no idea what size their operation is, nor how much funding they have behind them. If they're buying up land and property, they're probably doing so through a third party or a shell corporation, something to keep their own names out of any legal documentation. I think it goes without saying, for that to matter to us right now I'd need to *know* their names."

Tom nods.

Cindy leans forward again. She speaks to Tom in a lowered voice. "I've got other searches running, too," she says. "I'm on the dark web, trying to find info on the snuff movies."

If Chris hears what she's saying, he doesn't react.

"I'm trying to find anyone who might have had a similar experience to Mandy. It's worth looking into, but I doubt I'm going to find anything, to be honest. I just have to check."

"I assume you're not having much luck on any front," Tom says.

"None," Cindy says. "I've been looking into the snuff movies, into a group kidnapping people off the streets to make them, but you can imagine how that's going. It's very easy to find videos of people being killed online. There's a lot of cartel stuff. But if these people are making this footage in order to sell it, they're gonna be more secretive. They probably don't want it leaked online for anyone to see. It's gonna make finding their videos more difficult."

"It's still worth looking into what's available, just in case," Tom says.

"Oh, for sure," Cindy says. "I have facial recognition software running for Louise. So far, I haven't had a hit."

Tom drives in silence for a moment, thinking. They still have a long way to go until they get back to Lubbock. "What about the men who came to your apartment?" Tom says. "Have you looked into them?"

"I have," Cindy says. "Each of them is currently listed as either unemployed, or claiming disability. They're not even listed as living in Lubbock."

"Where does it say they live?"

"All over – Miami, Utah – anywhere other than here."

"Sounds like an effort has been made to keep these men under the radar."

"Third parties, shell companies – it could be extending to the goons, too."

Tom doesn't like it. Too many questions, thus far no solid answers.

Chris turns away from the window. It's hard to tell if he's been listening to them. "What do we do next?" he says.

"We go back to our original plan," Tom says. "We go to The Lubbock Lounge, and we see if they have any answers for us."

18

Tobin has his men watching Freddy Bliss.

Two are at his home, though he's not there. He's at work. Tobin has two men on him there, too, at the fast-food drive-thru. He's told them to keep a close eye on him.

"When he leaves," Tobin said, "when he gets home, that's when we'll take him. He lives alone. It'll be quieter. There's no witnesses."

Tobin is in his apartment still, waiting for the call to tell him Freddy Bliss is on the move. He's itching to go. He paces the floors while he places a call to the Kennedys. Guy answers.

"I could have good news," Tobin says. "Just not the good news you're expecting."

"I'm listening," Guy says, sounding intrigued.

"I'm sure you remember Mandy Bliss."

Guy chuckles, though it's without mirth. "The one who got away? I'll never forget."

"You know that we've been keeping tabs on her son."

"Yes."

"We may have hit pay dirt."

"He's talked to her?" Guy says, and Tobin can hear his excitement rising.

"Not her directly, no," Tobin says, and he explains the audio footage that Brad pieced together and sent to him. They're convinced that Freddy was talking to Cindy Vaughan. If Freddy ever said her name it was lost in the signal, but their conversation was too tied to recent events to be a coincidence. "All these years, Freddy has never mentioned his mother," Tobin says. "We couldn't be sure he knew where she was, and we didn't want to show our hand too quickly by going and talking to him. Observation has been our best option, and it's finally paid off."

"Sharon is going to be very pleased to hear this," Guy says.

"I'm sure she will," Tobin says, imagining the smile it will bring to her face. The thought makes him smile, too. "I'm taking point on this. I don't want any more mistakes after what's happened recently."

"Good man."

"I'll talk to Freddy Bliss directly. I'll *make* him talk. If he knows where his mother is, then by the end of today so will we."

Guy sounds almost giddy. "And Tobin," he says, "when you find her – you know what to do, right? You need to film it."

19

Tom and the others are stiff and tired by the time they get to Lubbock, but there are no complaints. They don't have time to waste. They go straight to The Lubbock Lounge.

The nightclub is in a converted warehouse. Tom parks the car on the opposite side of the road. They have a clear view of the front of the building. Its loading bay is down the side, and they can see activity there. The club doesn't open for a few more hours.

"Keep an eye on it," Tom says to Cindy and Chris. "I'm going to take a walk around the block."

He leaves the car and heads off on foot, watching the building out the corner of his eye. He wants to see the back of it. Wants to check the area, too, see if there's anyone lying in wait nearby that they need to be concerned about.

The block is clear. Nearby, there are other businesses – small shops and restaurants. This isn't a bad neighbourhood. A perfect place to lure unsuspecting victims to. Why would they expect anything bad to happen here?

The only sign of life at the nightclub is the activity at the loading bay. Big burly men who drive the truck unload kegs and crates of alcohol, and big burly men who wear polo shirts with The Lubbock Lounge logo embroidered above their hearts stand and watch them. There are three employees. They look like they're the doormen. Tom wonders if there are more inside, or if these are the only people present. The bartenders and all the rest probably don't turn up until later.

Tom spots an opportunity. He's around the back of the building. He goes to the activity, gets the attention of one of the three men standing around. The big man looks him up and down, unimpressed and agitated at being approached. The man is built like one of the kegs currently being rolled inside. His neck is so thick it's as if he doesn't have one.

"I was just wondering," Tom says, "if the manager is in? I'm looking for a job."

The other two doormen look in Tom's direction, too. Tom shifts his weight from foot to foot and pretends he's intimidated by the three. He avoids eye contact. He looks past them, into the building. All he can see is the storage room, but there's no one else in there.

"The manager's in," the first man with the thick neck says. "But he won't see you. What kind of job you looking for?"

"Bartending," Tom says.

"Come back when we're open," the man says. "Ain't no guarantee he'll speak to you then, but that's when he's more likely to. Depends on his mood."

"Okay, sure, thanks," Tom says, then turns and hurries away like he's desperate to get away from them. He doesn't look back as he goes. He's sure they're watching him.

He makes his way back around the block, not wanting the men to see him return to the car. He stands on a corner at the end and waits until the delivery truck drives away. He waits a further beat, hearing the loading bay shutter shrieking down, and then makes his way back to Cindy and Chris.

"We saw you talking to them," Chris says as he gets back into the car.

"The manager is in," Tom says. "Along with those three big guys. I didn't see anyone else."

Cindy is in the back, laptop open, fingers clicking at the keys. "The manager's name is Ricky Buxton," she says, and pauses her typing to turn the laptop around and show Tom a picture. It's a posed picture from the nightclub's social media page. Ricky wears slacks and a loose lilac shirt with the top few buttons undone. His hands are held out to his side in a 'You Got Me' kind of pose. His head is shaved down to stubble, and he's showing off all of his teeth with his grin. He has veneers. His teeth are so white they look like they could glow in the dark.

"Okay," Tom says. "Have you found anything else?"

"From pictures they've posted on social media, and been tagged in, I'm putting together a layout of the nightclub," Cindy says. "A rough floorplan so that when we go in we know exactly where we need to be. I'm plotting the best route direct to the manager's office. It won't take me much longer."

"That's good," Tom says. "We'll memorise the floorplan and then go straight in. We know he's there. No time like the present." He looks at Chris. "You wait here."

Chris bites his lip. He hesitates. "I'm not trying to be difficult," he says, speaking slowly, "but I really want to come inside. I can help."

"How can you help?" Tom says.

Chris stays calm. He doesn't get worked up. "Please," he says. "She's my sister. I acknowledge that you're right – I've been questioning you both and second-guessing you. That ends now. Just let me help. Let me find my sister. I'll hold back. I won't get in the way. Just let me come."

Tom watches him. Chris doesn't falter. He's sincere. "All right," Tom says. "You come in, but you hold back and you do exactly as we say. That understood?"

Chris's face is solemn. He nods, once. "Understood."

20

Tom crosses the road to the nightclub. Cindy and Chris follow close behind.

Tom doesn't knock on the main door. He tests the handle. It's unlocked. He walks straight in.

The three men from earlier are sitting at a table in the middle of the nightclub floor. They're playing cards. The other tables have their chairs turned upside down on top of them. It looks like the cleaners have been in not so long ago. The nightclub is clean and ready for the night ahead. Behind the bar, the bottles on display are stocked up and prepared for business. The club's colours are red and black. Beneath them, the floor is tiled in an alternating pattern of the two colours. The walls are panelled with mahogany, buffed to a bright red shine. Towards the rear of the club, in the VIP area, the ground is carpeted, and the pattern is a deep red and black, the two colours swirling and mixing.

The man with the thick neck looks up first, his head swivelling slowly toward the people entering the club. He does a double-take and frowns. He sees the three of them, but his eyes settle on Tom.

"I thought I told you to come back later," he says. The other two look up when he speaks.

"Later didn't work for me," Tom says. "Any of you three recognise this girl?" He motions to Cindy. She's ready with the picture of Louise. She steps forward and holds it up.

"We ain't open," Thick-Neck says, refusing to look at the picture. "You're gonna have to leave – and your friends, too. And don't bother coming back later. There's nothing for you here."

While Thick-Neck refuses to look, one of the other men at the table glances at the picture, at Louise, and Tom can see recognition flicker across his eyes. He turns to the other man and speaks to him in a low voice. The other man sneaks a glimpse at the picture and responds to the first, the two of them whispering between each other.

Tom is convinced. They at least recognise her.

"Take a look at the picture," Tom says to Thick-Neck.

Thick-Neck won't. "Get out," he says. "I ain't gonna ask you again." He has a look on his face, and across his whole stance. He wants Tom to make trouble. Thick-Neck has bunched up his shoulders, and his fists are balled. He's lowered his weight. He's ready to get physical. He *wants* to.

"Take a look at the picture," Tom says again, speaking slowly. "Or I'll make you look at it."

Thick-Neck shows his teeth. "That's enough," he says. He motions to the other two to follow him. Tom places an arm in front of Cindy and manoeuvres her behind him. She steps back, keeping out of his way. She motions for Chris to do the same.

Tom looks the three men over. One of the other men, one

who has a neck, rolls it on his shoulder and pops it in preparation. The other opens and closes his fists, warming them up.

Tom holds up a finger. "I'm going to give you all one more chance," he says. "There's no reason this has to get messy. No one needs to get hurt. Take a look at the picture of the girl and tell me how you know her. Then, step aside while we go and talk to Ricky."

The three men exchange brief glances at the mention of Ricky's name. They know they haven't mentioned it. It's clear to them that Tom is not as dumb, nor as intimidated, as he presented himself to them outside.

"No?" Tom says when none of them speak. "All right, then." He shrugs out of his jacket, but he doesn't slip it off all the way. He pulls his right hand free and he starts to move.

There are three of them, and they are bigger than him, and heavier than him. He can't afford to give them a chance to hit him first. If they do, if they put him down, it's game over. They'll promptly lay into him with boots and fists. They'll pound his skull into the hard ground. Cindy and Chris will be on their own. Neither of them is a match for the doormen.

But Tom is faster. He feints left and dodges right. As Thick-Neck grabs for where he used to be, Tom slips out from under him and slams the sole of his boot into the side of Thick-Neck's left knee, blowing it out. Thick-Neck doesn't scream, to his credit. He grunts and goes down, and makes a choked cry when he lands with all of his weight on the busted knee.

Tom keeps moving. He whips the jacket out, holding onto one of the sleeves, and grabs the other sleeve as it whips across the front of one of the other men's chest. Tom pulls it up and tight so it's around the man's neck, then uses him as a shield against the remaining man. Tom chokes the man in front of him with the jacket, keeping him under control. The man claws at the jacket with his fingertips. He throws elbows back toward Tom, but Tom stays out of range.

The other man tries to throw a punch around his colleague, trying to get at Tom, but Tom shifts his weight and puts the shield in front of him. The punch connects with his temple. The shield goes limp. Tom lets go of the jacket and shoves him forward, into the other man. While they stumble together, Tom steps forward and slams a forearm across the fresh man's jaw. He stumbles back and falls over the table where they were playing cards, sending their game flying. The table falls and he hits the ground. He's out cold.

The man Tom was using as a shield works to push himself up, trying to shake off the blow to his temple, and gulping in breaths to replace the oxygen that was choked out of him. Tom kicks him hard in the ribs, knocking the wind out of him further.

Only Thick-Neck remains, and he's on his ass now, nursing his blown knee. He looks at his two fallen colleagues, and he looks up at Tom with concern. He tries to scoot back across the floor, but he's too heavy and he quickly gives up.

Tom slides his arms back into his jacket, then holds a hand out to Cindy for the picture of Louise. She gives it to him. Tom crouches in front of Thick-Neck and bunches up the front of his shirt in his left fist. With his right, he holds the picture in front of Thick-Neck's face. "Take a good look," Tom says.

Thick-Neck swallows. His face has blanched with the

pain in his knee. "Look, I – I recognise her, okay? But that's all. I don't know who she is. I just know she was in here something like, what, three, four weeks back? I can't remember. We were just told to keep an eye on her, and make sure no one tried to pick her up."

"By whom? Who told you to do that?"

Thick-Neck hesitates, but Tom changes his stance and presses his weight down on the wounded knee with his own knee. Thick-Neck cries out, then grits his teeth, choking it off. "By Ricky, goddamnit," he says, spittle flying from his pursed lips.

"And he's in his office now?"

"Maybe not anymore," Thick-Neck says. "He would've seen this whole thing happen through the security. He could've split already."

"Shit," Tom says.

"I'm on it," Chris says, already running. He's memorised the layout of the nightclub, same as Tom and Cindy. He knows the way to the office.

"Please," Thick-Neck says. "*Please*, get off my knee."

Tom lets go of Thick-Neck's shirt and places his hand flat on his forehead. He pushes him back and slams the rear of his skull into the ground. There's a dull thud, and Thick-Neck's eyes close.

Tom starts running. Cindy is ahead of him. They go straight to Ricky's office. It's clear. The door is wide open.

"This way," Cindy says, pointing.

They run down the corridor toward the back of the building. Tom soon sees why Cindy chose this direction. The fire door at the end of the corridor is open, light from outside shining in. They burst out and see Chris chasing after Ricky Buxton. He's gaining on him. Tom and Cindy follow.

Just when it seems like Ricky will stay out of Chris's reach, Chris dives. He propels himself forward and wraps his arms around Ricky's legs on his way down. Ricky's legs lock abruptly and he topples forward, landing flat on his face, barely getting his arms up in time to protect himself.

Tom and Cindy reach them. Tom grabs Ricky by the back of his shirt and hauls him up to his feet. His nose is bloody and his lips have mashed against his teeth.

"I'll – I'll scream," Ricky says, breathless. "Let me go, or I'll scream."

Tom places two fingers and a thumb either side of Ricky's windpipe. He squeezes, choking him. Ricky gags. He can't make a sound above a choke. "No," Tom says. "I don't think you will."

21

Ricky's office is the same red-and-black colour scheme as the nightclub. It has the same mahogany-panelled walls, and there is a mahogany table in the centre of the room, facing toward the door. The floor is wall-to-wall carpet, the same as what's down in the VIP area. It's soft to stand on.

Ricky is pinned to his leather office chair. They've bound him with masking tape that Tom found in the cleaner's closet. Blood drips from Ricky's nose and mouth down onto his chest where he has the top four buttons of his shirt undone. It mingles with his greasy-looking chest hair. It stains his white shirt.

"I'll talk," Ricky says, quickly. "Whatever it is you want, you got it. You wanna know where the safe is? There ain't much in it right now, but I'll give you the code. You don't gotta hurt me, okay? I'll cooperate. Anything you wanna know, I'll tell you."

On the desk, Cindy moves the computer to the side and pulls up a chair. "What's the password?" she says.

At this, Ricky hesitates.

Cindy shrugs. "I'll be able to get in. It's just faster if you tell me. You said we didn't need to hurt you, right?"

Ricky swallows. "Onetwothreefour," he says. "All lower case – words, not numbers. Then the numbers seven, six, two, ten, and a hashtag."

Cindy types. She gives Tom a thumbs-up to show she's in.

Tom clears some space on Ricky's desk, pushing aside a stack of paperwork, a holepunch and a stapler, as well as a couple of pens. He stands close to Ricky and leans back against his desk where he's cleared the space, arms folded. Ricky looks up at him, terror in his eyes and face. "Why do you think we're here, Ricky?"

"I – I don't know," Ricky says.

Tom tilts his head back toward the TV showing the security feed from inside the nightclub. The three men Tom beat down are still lying on the ground, unmoving. "You saw what happened there, right? That's why you ran."

Ricky nods. "I can't hear anything, though."

"But why did you run? My problem could've just been with them. Or did you see the picture we were showing?"

Ricky grits his teeth. "I couldn't see the picture," he says. "It wasn't clear."

"Gave you enough of an idea though, didn't it?"

Ricky tries to exhale through his nose, but it's broken and blood and mucus sputters out. He has to breathe through his mouth.

Chris stands to the side, out of Tom and Cindy's way. He bounces on the balls of his feet, staring at Ricky. Tom can see he wants answers. He wants to lay into Ricky with his fists and force him to speak, but he's keeping his promise to Tom. He's behaving himself.

Tom holds up the picture of Louise. Ricky recognises her. He doesn't try to hide or deny it. "Oh, God," he says.

Chris freezes.

"Your men out there on the floor said they'd seen her three or four weeks back," Tom says. "They said you told them to keep an eye on her. Make sure no one hassled her. They claim they don't know why. Say they don't know who she was."

Ricky swallows. "I tell them as little as they need to know," he says. "It's for the best that way."

"Why did you tell them to watch her?"

"Because I was told to." Ricky is talking easily, Tom notices. He's not a man used to being in violent situations, and he doesn't like where he currently finds himself. He's already shed more blood than he'd like to.

Tom straightens, looming over him.

Ricky winces. "A few weeks ago, but that wasn't the first time she'd been in," he says.

"What do you mean?" Tom says.

Ricky's eyes flicker toward Cindy at his computer. Tom has noticed this happen a few times. When Ricky speaks, however, he speaks directly to Tom. "She'd been in here as a customer. A night out. She was with a group of friends. I saw her. I saw her on the security."

"What does that have to do with anything?"

"I get paid a bonus," Ricky says. "I get paid to keep an eye out for people who fit a certain description. It changes every time, and sometimes it's men, sometimes it's women, sometimes it's androgynous, but it's usually always fairly generic – like with the girl. I was told to keep an eye out for a tall, attractive blonde. In this place, they're a dime a dozen. I knew it wouldn't take long. She was the first one I saw."

Chris almost steps forward, but he stops himself.

"And you get paid a bonus if you find someone matching the description?" Tom says.

Ricky nods.

"By whom?"

Ricky hesitates. He's scared of what he could reveal. He looks up at Tom, and his more immediate fears win out. "Jilly Beck," he says.

Tom looks at Cindy. "I heard," she says, pulling out her phone and making a note.

"Is Jilly Beck in Lubbock?" Tom says.

"I – I don't know where she lives," Ricky says. "We don't have that kind of relationship, y'know? We're strictly professional. I don't know where she lives."

"Does she also go by the names Lola Knox and Libby Shell?"

Ricky blows air. "I haven't heard Libby Shell in a long time."

"Is it her?"

"Yeah – both of them."

Cindy holds up her phone, flashing a picture of a middle-aged woman with short, greying hair. "Is this her?" she says to Ricky.

"That's Jilly," he says.

"She's got an address in Lubbock," Cindy says. "She's not hiding herself the same way the others are."

Tom nods. "And Jilly runs things?" he says to Ricky.

"Jilly is the middle person," Ricky says. "I don't know who she answers to."

"And do you know what these people are doing?"

Ricky shakes his head. "I don't know, and I don't want to know. This is just money to me, you understand? I get paid to do something, and I do it. We've all gotta make a living, right?"

Tom stares at him. Ricky can't look back at any of them. He stares at the ground, chewing on his mangled, bloody bottom lip.

"Let me get this straight," Tom says. "Jilly Beck is a broker – from someone else, someone you don't know, she passes on to you descriptions of men and women that they need for reasons you're unaware of. You, in turn, keep an eye out for anyone who fits the criteria, you pass that on to Jilly Beck, and then the person you've found is taken, and you don't know where they go or what happens to them. And sometimes they're taken from right here either in or just outside of your club."

"I never said they were taken from here," Ricky says.

"Louise was," Tom says. "She was snatched from right outside, on the street there. You told your doormen to keep an eye on her. She was taken from here, and you know damn well she was."

Ricky still can't meet their eyes. Tom and Chris stare at him. Cindy is working at his laptop again. Head lowered, Ricky's eyes flicker her way once again. He swallows.

"How does that all sound to you, Ricky?" Tom says. "If you were in my position, and I spun that story, and claimed I didn't know what happened next – how would that sound to you? Does it pass the smell test?"

"I swear," Ricky says. "I promise, I've told you all I know."

"Why did you erase the footage from the night Louise was taken?"

Ricky sighs. "You already know the answer to that, right?"

"Of course I do," Tom says. "There won't be any reward for lying to us. What else do you know, Ricky? Don't make me pull teeth – I mean that literally."

Ricky swallows. He thinks, eyes flickering left and right. He glances Cindy's way again, and Tom sees a bead of sweat roll down the side of his face. "Uh, I have a tech guy come here every couple of weeks. He's called Brad. I don't know his last name. Jilly set me up with him. He's the one that erased the footage of Louise. Last time he was here, he said that he could tell someone had been trying to get into the system, scrubbing through the footage. That was you all, right?"

Tom doesn't answer.

"I, uh, I passed that information on to Jilly."

"That'll be around the time you were looking into them," Tom says to Cindy. He turns back to Ricky. "Do they know anything about us?"

"I – I don't know. We don't keep in touch. I told you, it's just quick money for me. I pass the info on and I don't give it another thought."

Tom is blunt. "Are they making snuff films, Ricky?"

He blinks. "Look, I've – I've heard rumours, okay? Wild fucking rumours. But that's all they are. It's gotta be. That's crazy, right?"

"What do you *think* happens to the people you give up to them?"

Ricky doesn't answer this. He knows there isn't a good answer for it. "I'm sorry," he says. "I'm so sorry..."

"You're only sorry because we're here," Chris says. His eyes glare. He stares at Ricky. He looks like he wants to tear his head off. He glances at Tom and tries to calm himself down.

"He's right," Tom says. "Would you be thinking about Louise, or any of the others, at all if we weren't here? Do you ever see them again?"

Ricky doesn't answer.

"You have to have a pretty good idea of what happens next, right? You're holding out on us, Ricky." Tom reaches back and picks up the stapler from the desk. He opens it and squeezes it, firing a couple of staples at Ricky's chest. "What am I going to have to do for you to just open up and share?"

"He knows exactly what happens next," Cindy says. They look at her. She's stopped typing on Ricky's computer. She's paler than usual. She's staring straight at him, hate in her eyes.

Ricky swallows. Tom hears a dry click in the back of his throat.

Cindy turns the computer around. The screen is paused. It's muted. It's hard to tell what they're looking at. The footage looks grainy and unclear.

"Chris," Cindy says, "you might want to look away."

"Is it Louise?" he says, his voice cracking.

"No," Cindy says. "But you still might want to look away."

Chris doesn't.

"Please," Ricky says, his voice weak. "Please... I'm sorry..."

Cindy hits play.

The image, in motion, comes into focus. There's a woman strapped to a medical bed. The room is dingy and undecorated. There are stains upon the walls. The woman is naked, and fighting against her binds. There are already cuts across her body, and bruises upon her face. Her hair is matted and wild. She's staring at something off-screen, terrified. If the volume were not muted, they'd be able to hear her scared screams.

A man steps into view from off-screen. He wears a butcher's apron, and a mouse-face mask. He's carrying a chainsaw. Tom can see that it's running. He gets closer and closer to the woman. She's frantic. She can't get free. The man raises the chainsaw. He lowers it slowly, taking his time, enjoying himself, and presses it into the woman's left thigh.

As her blood begins to spray, Cindy hits pause. She turns the computer back around. She's staring at Ricky. Her voice shakes when she speaks. "Did you think I wouldn't find them?" she says, rising to her feet. "Did you think they were tucked far enough away that you'd be able to hurry us out before I could find them?" She steps closer to him and jabs a finger toward the computer. "There are *dozens* of video files on there."

"Is – is Louise in them?" Chris says.

"I didn't see her, but I've transferred the files to my own computer," Cindy says. "I'll look properly later."

"She's not," Ricky says. He's crying. "I promise. If they've killed her already, I haven't seen it."

"Your promises aren't worth *shit*," Cindy says. She spits on him. She looks at Tom, and at the stapler, and holds out her hand. Tom gives it to her. "What haven't you told us?"

Ricky swallows. "You know everything now," he says. "You know everything I know."

"Who does Jilly answer to?" Cindy says.

"I swear, I don't know," Ricky says. "I asked. She wouldn't say. Just tapped the side of her nose."

"They send you the videos."

"I pay, same as everyone else. I get a discount, sure, but I pay. And you saw the dude in that video, right? He's masked. Every video you watch, they'll all be masked. It's anonymous."

Cindy squeezes the stapler. "How many people?" she says.

Ricky waits, as if she's going to add more. "What?"

"How many people did you give to them?"

Ricky doesn't answer.

"There are twenty-seven files on your computer," Cindy says. "Did you give them twenty-seven? Did you give them *more*?"

Ricky doesn't answer.

Cindy slams the stapler down into the back of his right hand, embedding a staple there. Ricky cries out. "One for each of them," Cindy says. She slams the stapler into his chest. She slams it into his left cheek. Ricky screams. Cindy embeds him with metal pins.

The stapler runs out. She throws it aside and it smashes against the wood panelling. Cindy is breathing hard.

Ricky shudders and sobs.

"Why do you have those videos, Ricky?" Tom says. "Why did you *pay* for them? Is that the kind of thing you like? Does that get you off?"

"I – I –" Ricky hiccups. He can't finish. There's nothing to say.

"Look at me, Ricky," Tom says.

Reluctantly, Ricky raises his head.

"Do you know if Louise is still alive?"

He shakes his head.

"Do you know where they took her?"

Again, he shakes his head.

Tom believes him. He slams the heel of his hand upward

at the base of Ricky's nose, driving the bone back into his brain.

Ricky convulses in his chair, then slumps, eyes open.

Chris watches the scene before him, eyes wide. His hands shake. He stares at Ricky's corpse.

Tom steps out from behind the desk. "You need to decide right now if you can handle this," he says to Chris. "If you can't, that's fine. Go back to the launderette and lie low. Me and Cindy can do the rest. But there's going to be more of this. A lot more. We've found a monster, and now we need to cut off its head."

Chris takes a deep breath. His body shudders. "I'm with you," he says, tearing his eyes away from Ricky's body and looking at Tom. "All the way. No matter what."

22

Tobin finally gets the call from his team. Freddy Bliss has left work. He's on his way home.

"Are you following him?" Tobin says.

"At a safe distance. Doesn't look like he has any detours in mind."

"Good. Make sure he doesn't see you. I'll make my way straight to his home. You'll get there before me. Don't do anything until I arrive. And I *mean* that. Not a movement. Just watch the place."

"Got it."

Tobin leaves his apartment, his tension finally having somewhere to go. He grips the steering wheel tight as he drives across the city to Freddy Bliss's home. Tobin is confident his men won't do anything stupid. Not this time. He's pressed upon them the importance of his taking point. He's told them to make sure they have a camera, too, at the behest of the Kennedys.

Tobin reaches Freddy's neighbourhood and drives around the block. He can see Freddy's car parked in the driveway. There's no sign of his men. They've parked around the corner. Tobin goes to them. He parks in front and goes to their car, climbing into the back. Jagger, Donkin, and Davies are in the car. It's the first time Tobin has seen Donkin since Cindy burnt his face. Donkin is in the back next to him, and his left cheek is toward the window.

"Let me see," Tobin says.

"Not much to see right now," Donkin says, turning his head and showing the dressing that covers his cheek. It clings to him. Part of the bandaging looks yellow in the centre, like pus is leaking through.

"How's it feel?" Tobin says.

"Tight," Donkin says. He pauses for a moment, then adds, "And hot."

Jagger and Davies are in the front. Davies is behind the steering wheel. They're both looking back at Tobin. Tobin can see the severe, dark bruising on Jagger's neck. "And how are you?"

"Hard to speak," Jagger says, sounding like he has laryngitis, forcing the words out in a whisper. "We got a name for that motherfucker yet?"

"Not yet," Tobin says. "But we're working on it."

"Brad?"

"And his team. They'll have something soon, I'm sure."

"Could be we'll find something tonight," Davies says. "If it *was* Cindy that Freddy was talking to, then he should have some answers for us."

"Who's on his house?"

"Carter and Daniels," Davies says. "You didn't spot them on your way past?"

"No," Tobin says. This is good. He's pleased that they've been so secretive. "Where are they?"

"Bush of a house opposite. We've been checking in regularly. Freddy is home, and he's alone. No company, and it doesn't look like he's heading out."

Tobin checks the time. "It'll be dark in an hour," he says. "We wait until then. Tell Carter and Daniels that. Tell them to get in touch immediately if anyone goes to the house or if Freddy heads out."

Davies nods and sends the message.

"I'm gonna take a walk around the block," Tobin says. He gets out of the car. He heads down the road and around the corner, taking his time, hands in his pockets, as he walks toward Freddy's house.

On foot, drawing closer, he's finally able to see Carter and Daniels. They see him approach but they don't wave or try to speak to him. Tobin nods subtly, then keeps moving, walking parallel to Freddy Bliss's home. It's a peaceful neighbourhood. A quiet suburb. Affordable homes for the lower middle class. People who can afford the rent, and take pride in their street. The houses are kept presentable. They all look identical – single-storey homes with shingled roofs. Some of them are different colours, though. Most of them are cream and white, but some have been painted blue or green. The two front windows on each house have an A/C unit in them. Trees line the street, planted haphazardly with no real pattern. Most of the lawns are dried out and dying, patches of dirt showing through, but there are no weeds, and there is no trash.

Tobin watches Freddy's house out the corner of his eye. The blinds are drawn. There's no sign of Freddy peering out. He's inside, going about his business, probably making dinner. There's no sign to suggest he thinks he's being watched.

In the other direction, Tobin looks at the house where Carter and Daniels lie in wait, watching. The house is in darkness. No cars on the drive. There are no blinds or curtains on the windows. He can see straight inside, and it looks empty. Could be the property is in between tenants. Carter and Daniels may have chosen it for this reason.

Tobin keeps walking. There's no rush. Dusk is settling. Tobin wants to wait for full dark. Make it difficult for anyone to see when they make their move on Freddy. He checks the rest of the houses as he goes, too, all the way around the block. They're quiet. No one's nosily twitching their curtains.

Tobin gets back to the cars. He doesn't sit with the others. He gets into his own, and he waits.

The remainder of the hour passes fast. The darkness settles in. The streetlamps come on. The evening air has chilled, the temperature continuing to drop. Very few cars have passed by on the road while Tobin and the others have been waiting. This is good. Tobin wants it to be quiet.

He gets out of his car and goes to the others. He leans down next to the window with Davies. "I'm going in with Carter and Daniels," he says. "The rest of you move the car around to the back of his house. Park in front of the house that his backs onto. If he starts running and gets out that way, run him down."

"Keep him alive?" Davies says.

"Absolutely," Tobin says. "We need to talk to him." Tobin straightens and the car's engine starts. He watches it as it rolls down the road, past the first junction and onto the next. Tobin glances around, then heads to Carter and Daniels.

"What's the plan?" Carter says.

"I'm gonna knock," Tobin says. "He's not expecting us. There's no reason for him to be suspicious. Carter, you're with me – Daniels, you hold back at the end of his driveway. If he gets by us, it's up to you to grab him. Chances of that happening are slim, but I'm not taking any risks."

They both nod.

They cross the road and Tobin and Carter continue straight up to the house. Daniels holds back, as instructed. Tobin looks up and down the street, makes sure once again that it's clear, and then he knocks on the door. He knocks lightly, with regular pressure. Doesn't pound on it. Doesn't want to alarm Freddy and freak him out.

After a moment, he hears someone approaching. The door unlocks from the other side. Freddy Bliss pokes his face through the gap. He's kept the chain on the door. "Yeah?" he says, looking both men over.

Tobin smiles at him. Freddy looks just like his mother. Tobin remembers her well. He's been looking for her for seven years. He's well acquainted with her face. "Freddy, right?" he says, pointing a finger at him like they've met before.

"Uh, yeah?" Freddy says. "Who are you?"

The question, the finger point, it was all a distraction. While Freddy stared into Tobin's grinning face, trying to work out who he was and how they might know each other, Tobin was subtly shifting his weight. He planted his left leg. He draws his right back. He makes like he's about to say something further, to keep Freddy's focus on his face, but instead of speaking he lashes out, kicking hard into the door with the flat of his boot.

The chain snaps with ease. Tobin's legs are muscular, powerful, and well-trained. The door flies back into Freddy, connecting hard with his shoulder and chest. He stumbles back and Tobin follows him in. Carter motions for Daniels to join them.

Freddy hits the wall, but Tobin is already upon him. He side-kicks him, his shin lashing across Freddy's midsection, driving the air out of him. While he's winded, Tobin grabs him and throws him into his living room. Carter and Daniels follow him through while Tobin closes the front door. Carter and Daniels pin Freddy to the ground. Daniels pulls out a Glock and waves it in front of Freddy's face so he knows to keep quiet, then presses the barrel into his temple.

Tobin crouches in front of Freddy. The room stinks of marijuana. If Freddy has been smoking tonight, the sight of the gun, of his door being kicked in, has promptly straightened him out. "I'm gonna get straight to the point," he says. Freddy looks back at him, startled and confused. "Have you spoken to Cindy Vaughan?"

"What – what – what is this about? Who are you?" Freddy says.

"That's not what I asked," Tobin says. "And you're not in any position to ask any questions at all. Now, are you gonna make me repeat myself?"

Daniels presses the Glock harder into Freddy's temple. Freddy winces. "I've spoken to her," he says. "How do you know that?"

Tobin raises a finger and waves it side to side like a metronome. "I ask the questions," he says. "Cindy was talking to you about your mother, right? Sweet Mandy Bliss. She was asking about her? Maybe wanted to know about what happened to her seven years ago?"

Freddy's eyes are wide. He looks around at the three men, and Tobin can see it all falling into place for him. The stories his mother told – they were true. He didn't believe her. Tobin knows he didn't. It's one of the reasons they haven't come to see him before now. That and the fact he's never talked about her, to her, or given any indication that he knows where she's gone.

"I'm waiting for an answer, Freddy," Tobin says.

"Y-y-yes," he manages to stammer out. "She – she wanted to talk to my mom. She said maybe she'd be able to help them find her friend's sister."

Tobin smiles. "Do you know where your mother is, Freddy?"

Freddy purses his lips. He swallows. He nods, once.

"I'm very happy to hear that," Tobin says. "We've been dying to see her again for a very long time." He looks at Carter and Daniels. "Lift him up. He can show us the way. I'll call the others and tell them to bring your car around."

While they stand, Tobin strolls around the home and makes the call to Davies, telling him what he wants. In the living room, the television is on. In front of the sofa, on the ground, Freddy's laptop is open. Tobin goes to it, closes it, and picks it up. There could be something of use for them. He'll pass it on to Brad and his team.

"They're outside," Carter says, peering through the blinds.

Tobin gets close to them by the front door. He pats Freddy on the shoulder. "Let's go see Mom, huh? And don't try and mess us around. All those horror stories your mom used to tell you, the ones you dismissed? We got all the time and inclination to inflict some of that on you."

Freddy is pale. He's scared. He should be.

They take him out to the waiting car.

23

The plan is to talk to Jilly Beck next. Tom drives toward her listed address. She has a luxury apartment at Tuscany Place. When they arrive, they don't head straight for the building. Tom drives around the rear and parks up. They stay in the car for now.

Cindy is in the back, on her laptop. She's looking further into Jilly Beck. Now that they have her real name, it's been easier to find out more about her. She really was an agent, once upon a time, out in LA. She had a roster of clients, some of whom they'd heard of. She represented some movie actors, but mostly she worked with television stars. Then, abruptly, about ten years ago she retired and left California. There's not much more about her professional life after that. She's lived in a few different places in and around Lubbock since, but has been at Tuscany Place for the last four years.

"I just want to make sure this is where she lives for sure," Cindy says, still typing, eyes glued to the screen. "Everyone else that seems connected to this has been using fake addresses. It could be the same again."

"She's been using fake names, though," Tom says. "Maybe she thinks that covers for her enough. She's more brazen because of it."

Cindy nods, still looking. "I'm accessing security cameras close to here," she says, "and running facial recognition software. If it picks up on her coming and going, we'll know this is where she is."

Tom looks at the back of the apartment building. They drove by the front on the way here. It's gated there. At the rear, there's a fence. It'll be easy enough to scale. There are balconies at the back of the building. It's late, dark out, and the balconies are all currently unoccupied. Some of the apartments are in darkness, but most of them are lit up from within. The road they're parked on is quiet. They're in front of a pair of buildings, signed as the West Texas Builders Association and, next to it, City Bank Event Centre. Both buildings are in darkness, illuminated only by the streetlamp in the centre of the empty parking lot.

Tom glances across at Chris. He's staring straight ahead. He hasn't spoken since they left The Lubbock Lounge. He's barely spoken since Ricky was killed. Just sits and stares straight ahead, thinking. There was already a lot on his mind, and now there's more.

"How you feeling?" Tom says to him.

Chris snaps out of his thoughts. He clears his throat. "I'm fine," he says, forcing himself to look at Tom.

"You sure?"

Chris nods. "I'm sure."

"If this is too much for you –"

"It's not," Chris says. "I'm not...I'm not thinking about *that*. About Ricky. I'm thinking about the video we saw in his office. The girl…the chainsaw… I'm thinking about her, and I'm thinking about Louise."

Cindy has been listening in. "I've still got the facial recognition software running on the videos we took from Ricky – there's only a few left to search and they haven't brought anything up yet. I think he was telling the truth when he said Louise isn't in them."

"I think he was telling the truth about a lot of things," Tom says. "He was too much of a coward not to. He thought he could tell us what we wanted to hear, fast, and then we'd leave before Cindy could find anything incriminating."

"He had those videos hidden deep in his files," Cindy says. "I had to brute-force my way in – but I *did* get in."

"Could you trace where the videos were coming from?"

"It would take too long," Cindy says. "These people aren't stupid. They filter the videos through server after server so it's not clear where it's originated. I had a quick look and the first place it brought up was Iraq, then Canada, and then the UK. It was just going to keep going on and on like that."

Tom nods. He looks at the building again where Jilly Beck potentially lives. "I'm going around the block," he says.

"When you get back, we should know one way or the other," Cindy says.

Tom makes his way around the Tuscany Place complex. He takes his time. He completes one lap, and then does another. He hasn't seen anything that alarms him. If Jilly Beck is connected to the people they're going after – and at this point it seems very likely that she is – Tom wants to be sure that none of them are nearby, on lookout. He doesn't see anyone. No one on patrol. No other parked cars watching the building. All the while he walks, he doesn't pass another person. There's no on-site security, either. This is good for them. When they go in, they want things to be quiet.

Tom returns to the car.

"This is where she lives," Cindy says as Tom sits down. "I'm sure of it. I can find footage of her coming and going for the last two weeks." She leans over him and points to an apartment on the top floor. The lights are on. "And she's right in there."

24

Tom scales the back fence first, then waits on the other side while Chris boosts Cindy over. Tom catches her on the way down. Chris follows them, then they continue on to the building. Tom watches the windows as they go, crouching low as they run around the outside of the grass at the rear, sticking to the shadows. He doesn't see anyone at the windows looking out. No one watching them.

The apartment building is three floors. They go to the ground floor porch beneath Jilly's apartment. Tom takes the lead, then Cindy, then Chris. Tom steps up onto the bottom railing, reaches up to the floor of the balcony above, then pulls himself up and over the railing there. The lights in the ground floor apartment were off, but on the second floor they're on. He's quiet and he's careful. They all are.

Tom pauses and listens to the apartment behind him, making sure that no one has heard anything and come to investigate. He can hear the television playing. The volume is turned up loud, and it does not get lowered for someone to better listen to something they think they might have heard outside. He leans over the railing and signals for Cindy to come up. She does the same as Tom. When she reaches out for the ground of the balcony, Tom reaches down and hauls her up the rest of the way. Chris comes last. Tom and Cindy pull him over the railing.

Cindy and Chris remain on the second floor, silent as statues while Tom makes his way up to the next apartment. Jilly Beck's apartment. Again, he pauses and he listens. He can hear sounds coming from inside, but they're fainter than the television below. He holds his ear close to the glass door, and picks out the faint strains of classical music.

Cindy follows him up, and she drops to her knees and gets to work picking the lock on the door. Chris comes up last. His grip slips as he reaches for the floor of Jilly's balcony. Tom manages to grab him, catching him by the wrist and holding on tight, but Chris's leg kicks out and connects with the railing. The whole thing vibrates. They all freeze. From above, Tom can hear the television's volume abruptly mute.

Straining, bracing himself against the railing with his left hand, Tom hauls on Chris with all of his strength, and pulls him up onto the railing of Jilly's balcony. Below, he sees the light change as the curtains on the door below are pushed aside, the occupant exploring the noise. They stay that way for a moment, while Tom, Chris, and Cindy remain frozen, holding their breaths like this could make a difference.

Then, the light returns to how it was below, the curtain dropped back into place. The occupant does not explore further, does not open their door, likely content to believe it was nothing more than a bird.

Inside Jilly's apartment, the classical music has not

changed in volume. She hasn't heard anything at all. Cindy resumes work at the lock. A moment later, Tom hears the low click of it unlocking. Tom pulls out his Beretta and leads the way inside. He steps into the bedroom. The bed is neatly made. The air smells faintly of perfume.

He's careful, but he moves fast. Wherever Jilly is in her apartment, there's a chance she could sense the change in the air after her balcony door opened. Tom glances toward the en-suite. The door is closed, but he can see through the gaps around the frame that the light is not on there. He passes by the vanity table close to the bedroom door. On top of it, centred, there is a small black-plastic box. Next to that is a tester for blood sugars. Jilly must be diabetic. The plastic box presumably holds needles and insulin. Tom makes his way through to the living room, where the classical music is slightly louder. Tom hears movement in the kitchen. The living area is open-plan. Only a breakfast counter separates the kitchen from the living room.

Tom scans the area before he confronts Jilly. It's clear. There's no one else here. He steps into view, pointing the Beretta toward her. She's in the kitchen, unloading the dishwasher, putting plates and cups back into their respective cupboards.

"Jilly Beck," Tom says, getting her attention.

She gives a start at the sound of his voice, then freezes. Her shoulders bunch up. Slowly, she turns. She spots the gun and raises her hands in surrender. Her eyes flick to the right, toward Cindy and Chris. She looks the three intruders over.

"Come out of the kitchen," Tom says. "And take your time."

Jilly does as she's told, keeping her hands raised. Her

eyes quickly take in the countertops on her way, like she's looking for something that could be useful. The knife-rack isn't on her route. It's out of reach. She hesitates as her eyes settle upon it.

"That would be a big mistake," Tom says.

Jilly knows he's right. She steps into the living room. Tom directs her to the nearest chair. It's padded, but she doesn't look very comfortable when she sits down on it.

"Find something to bind her wrists and ankles," Tom says.

Chris goes to the kitchen. He returns with a roll of tape. He wraps it around Jilly's wrists first, over and over, binding them tight together. Then, he does her ankles. No one says a word until he's finished. All the while, Jilly stares straight at Tom and his gun. Chris steps back, tossing the tape onto the sofa.

"Do you know who we are?" Tom says.

"Should I?" Jilly says.

Tom tilts his head toward Chris. "He doesn't look familiar to you?"

Jilly doesn't look at him. "Should he?"

Tom smirks. "That's cute."

"What's cute is you've broken into my home, and you've pointed a gun at me, and now you're asking me redundant questions." Jilly is stern, like a school teacher. She stares at the gun, but there's no fear in her eyes. Despite her predicament, she's surprisingly calm and collected.

Tom puts the gun away. He doesn't need it. It doesn't intimidate her, and thus it won't make her talk. Tom will need to take a different approach. "Should I call you Jilly?" Tom says. "Or how about Lola? Maybe Libby?"

Her face doesn't change.

"Let's stick with Jilly," Tom says. "I noticed you're a diabetic, Jilly."

At this, he spots the first flicker of concern cross her eyes. She clenches her jaw to keep her face impassive.

"Are you Type One, or Type Two? I'm curious."

"Do I look like I'm Type Two?" Jilly says, disdain in her tone.

"It's not always weight gain," Tom says.

Jilly sneers. Since Tom brought up her diabetes, she's showing more emotion. Her mask is slipping. Tom has pushed the right button.

"Type One it is," Tom says. "A whole lifelong thing, huh? That must be tough." Tom turns slightly toward Cindy and Chris. "How does she look to the two of you? She look like she's on the verge of going either hyper- or hypoglycaemic?"

"She looks fine to me," Cindy says.

"Uh-huh," Tom says. "Same. You know what happens to a diabetic if you pump them full of insulin when they don't need it? I'm sure Jilly does."

Jilly grinds her jaw. Her spine has stiffened slightly. She's battling to remain composed, but it's a losing fight.

"Why don't you tell us what happens?" Cindy says. "Just so we know."

"The last thing you wanna do to a diabetic is give them insulin they don't need," Tom says. "It'll strip all the sugar from their blood. That'll lead them to a severe hypo. When that happens, they go into diabetic shock. Seizures. Unconsciousness. Eventually, death. I hear it's a real painful way to go."

"Are you trying to frighten me?" Jilly says.

Tom starts to turn. "I'll get the insulin, and we'll see how scared you are."

Tom takes a step back toward the bedroom. Jilly holds out for two paces before she calls out. "What do you want?" she says.

Tom turns back to her. He points at Chris. "You know who he is, don't you?"

Jilly's breath is shaky. "I can guess. He looks just like her."

Chris takes a step forward, but Tom holds up a hand to keep him back.

"Tell us what's happening here, Jilly," Tom says.

She sighs. "You're going to have to be more specific."

"Who do you work for?"

Jilly hesitates. She's thinking. "I'll tell you," she says. "But not because of your threats. I'll tell you because you can't stop it. I'll tell you because the fact you're here right now shows me you're stupid enough to try and resolve this yourself."

"We could always call the cops if that's what you'd prefer," Tom says. It's a bluff. He wants her to keep talking.

"I'm sure the brother there has already tried. Right? How'd that go for you? They can't find us. We have friends. We have influence." She snorts. She grins, showing her teeth. "There's three of you. That's not enough. Tobin will tear you apart."

"Tobin?" Tom says.

Jilly smirks. "You'll find out soon enough."

"Does Tobin make the snuff movies?" Tom says. "Is he running the operation?"

"Tobin is the man who's going to tear your head from your shoulders," Jilly says. "Tobin runs the team who are going to shoot you down before you ever get close enough to the Kennedys."

"Who are the Kennedys?" Tom says.

"You've probably already heard of them," Jilly says. "You just don't realise it. Guy and Shannon. Ring any bells?"

Cindy frowns. "The *actors*?" she says. "I haven't heard those names in a long time. I can't even remember the last thing I would've seen either of them in."

"There you go," Jilly says. "You have the info you wanted. Feel free to run off and do whatever you want with it. I look forward to seeing how that plays out for you."

"We're not done here," Tom says.

Jilly laughs. "No?" she says. "Oh, boy, you don't have any idea what you're getting yourself into. Do you understand who we are yet, what we can do? No one can touch us. We cater to sheiks, oligarchs, businessmen, politicians, police, princes, and actors. And who are you? Who are any of you?"

"Ricky Buxton is dead," Tom says. He can see from Jilly's reaction that she didn't know this. He can also see that she doesn't particularly care. "We'll take this whole operation down, one person at a time if we have to. There's only three of us, and you might think that's funny, but I know that's more than enough."

Jilly chuckles. "Do you think killing Ricky accomplishes anything? I have connections throughout Lubbock – throughout the *state*. Ricky was a tiny cog in an overwhelming machine."

"That's impressive," Tom says, though his tone is flat. "I didn't realise so many people got off on torture and murder."

"They don't have to," Jilly says. "It's all about money. That's how I know your misguided crusade will fail. You're doing this for personal reasons – well, *he* is, anyway." She nods at Chris. "I'm not sure what's in it for the two of you.

But *money* – people will do anything if you pay them enough."

"Where is Louise?" Tom says.

Jilly grins. "You know, I've dealt with so many people over the years, their faces and their names get all muddled up in my head. If you didn't have him with you," again she nods at Chris, "I wouldn't have a clue who you were talking about. For our clients, I find the objects of their desires, I'm paid handsomely for it, and then I move on with my life. I don't spare them a second thought."

"You're sick," Chris says. "That's my *sister*."

"They're all somebody's sister, or brother, or mother, father, son, daughter, cousin, nephew – should I go on? They're just cattle who, for one brief, glorious moment in their drab little lives get to be movie stars."

Tom is about to press on, to ask where Louise is, where the Kennedys are, when he feels his phone vibrating. He glances down at the screen. It's Mandy Bliss.

Tom leaves the room to answer the call, stepping through into the bedroom. "Mandy?"

"I don't suppose you're outside right now," she says.

"No. We're in Lubbock."

"Figured as much," Mandy says. "I don't see your car, and there's more here than when you came last time."

Tom grits his teeth. "What's happening? What are they doing?"

"Nothing, yet. I can see them on the cameras, though. Probably don't realise I can see them. They're all just sitting out there in their cars, getting ready to come and knock."

"How many?"

"I don't see any bodies, but there's three vehicles."

"I'm on my way," Tom says.

"You'll never get here in time." There's no emotion in Mandy's voice. It's just a statement of fact.

"Then you'll have to hold them until I arrive." Tom hangs up. He puts his head through to the living room and talks to Cindy. "The two of you stay here, watch her," he says.

"What's happening?" Cindy says.

"Mandy," Tom says. "No time to explain. Call me if anything comes up."

In the background, Jilly is laughing. "Mandy?" she says. "Mandy *Bliss*? Oh, you are further along than I realised. How exciting. I'd heard a rumour she could be back on the scene."

Tom doesn't respond. He doesn't have time to engage with her. He hurries through to the bedroom and out onto the balcony. He scales his way back down to the ground, fast and silent, and then runs to the car.

25

Tobin has called in extra men. He's told them to come armed.

They met in Roosevelt and they've made their way out into the middle of nowhere where Mandy Bliss has been hiding herself all of these years. It's frustrating to know that, all this time, she was so close. Freddy sits in the back of Tobin's car, sandwiched between two of Tobin's men. His wrists are bound and since he's directed them to his mother they've taped his mouth shut. Tears roll down his cheeks. His eyes are red.

Tobin observes the house and the area through binoculars. They're parked way down the dirt road, close to some trees and bushes that provide them with cover. It's late, and it's dark, and Mandy Bliss is probably sleeping. Freddy said she's become a junkie in the last seven years. If they're lucky she's probably nodded out in her bedroom and this should be nice and fast and easy. In and out, no issues.

But Tobin isn't taking anything for granted. He speaks into the radio, communicating with his men. "We move in careful and quiet, understood? When we get into the house we don't have to worry so much about noise, but don't expect a cakewalk. That house is fortified. Freddy here says he wouldn't be surprised if his mom has laid some traps. Everyone needs to be alert."

Responses come back from his men that they understand.

"All right, move in," Tobin says.

He remains in his car. He watches as two groups leave the vehicles next to his own. Daniels leads the way, Glock out, held two-handed. Three men follow him, heading left, toward the front of the house. Kent leads another team of three, guns similarly out and ready, and they head right, toward the rear.

Tobin watches them as they separate and cross the scrubland, gradually drawing closer. He watches the house through the binoculars. It's in darkness. He watches the windows. He doesn't see any movement.

"Looks like your mom is sleeping," he says to Freddy in the back without turning. "Do you think it's a natural sleep, or do you think a needle helped her on her way?" Tobin grins to himself. Freddy can't answer through the tape. He doesn't make any sound.

Suddenly, as the men get close, security lights come on from the front of the house, from all around it, and Tobin is blinded through the binoculars. He curses and blinks his eyes to clear them of sunspots. When he looks again, without the binoculars now, he sees that his two teams of men have frozen in the lights, like rabbits in the middle of a road. They're waiting to see if they've been spotted, or if this is just a security feature and they've gotten too close.

Tobin hears the crack of a rifle. Kent's head snaps back and he falls to the ground.

"Shit!" Tobin says. "Get down!"

Tobin and the passenger beside him lower themselves. Tobin watches over the top of the steering wheel. He can't see which window Mandy is shooting from. The security lights are too bright. Another rifle crack, and a member of Daniels' team falls this time.

Daniels fires back, shooting blindly toward the house. The other men follow his lead. He starts running toward the house and they do the same, charging en masse, the original plan forgotten in the chaos. Mandy picks them off as they come. She drops two more as they run.

"Goddammit," Tobin says. He gets back on the radio, to the drivers who have remained with the vehicles. "Get out there after them!"

He sees them emerge from their cars, pulling their Glocks. They run after the others, though they don't charge blindly. They head around the side, trying to stay in the darkness.

"Should – should we go with them?" one of the men in the back says.

"We should've brought heavier weapons," the passenger says.

Tobin doesn't answer, watching the battle before him. "Just – just wait for now," he says, flustered, waving his hand blindly toward the other occupants of the car. Daniels has reached the main gate. Two men with him are firing at the windows, laying down covering fire while Daniels shoots off the lock and kicks the gate open. He gets inside, charging for the front door.

And then he explodes.

"Holy shit," the passenger beside Tobin says. "*Mines?* What else has this crazy bitch got?"

She appears at the front door. She's armed with a shotgun. She blasts one of the men behind Daniels, stunned by the explosion, full in the chest.

Tobin watches in horror as his men get killed. It's a slaughter. This is not how things were supposed to go. Tobin is not a strategist. This isn't his strong suit. He's a fighter. He's a bodyguard. He's muscle. What he's not, however, is a commander for field missions.

"Get him out of the car," he says, pointing to Freddy. Tobin gets out himself and then grabs Freddy from the others. He pulls his own Glock and marches Freddy forward, the gun pressed to the base of his skull. He can hear the shotgun blasting still. He can hear his men screaming.

When they enter the circle of light cast by the security lamps, Tobin starts calling Mandy's name. He wants her to see Freddy. Wants her to see him bound, gagged, with a gun to his head.

She can't hear him at first, not over the sound of the screaming and her own gunfire. Tobin can see that the remaining men, including the two drivers he sent late, are hesitant and holding back, sheltering behind the trees that line the property, afraid to set off another landmine like the one that killed Daniels.

The men from Tobin's car follow him, huddling close together, knowing that Freddy is their shield.

Eventually, Mandy hears Tobin's calls. She keeps the shotgun up, nestled into her shoulder, but she pauses, looking toward the sound. She freezes when she sees her son.

"That's right!" Tobin says. "We've got Freddy!" He pushes

him forward, holding him tight, moving to the edge of the property. "You drop that shotgun right now or you'll see his fucking brains!"

Mandy hesitates, but she does as he says. She puts the shotgun to the side and raises her hands to show they're empty.

"You got anything else on you? Throw it down now!"

Slowly, she reaches back into her waistband and brings out a handgun. It's too far, and the lights are still too blinding, for Tobin to see what kind it is. She tosses it into the front yard.

"That's good," Tobin says. "Now unless you want something real bad to happen to Freddy here, you're gonna behave yourself. Clear?"

She doesn't respond.

"I said, is that *fucking clear?*"

"Just let him go," Mandy says. "It's me you've been looking for. Freddy doesn't have to be part of this."

"I'm the one who'll make that decision," Tobin says. He pushes Freddy forward, onto the property. "You better tell us the safe route, or else Freddy's gonna go sky high."

"To the left," Mandy says, her voice trembling. "Your left. Walk in a straight line to the porch."

Tobin motions for his remaining men to follow. They fall into line behind him. Tobin mounts the porch, keeping Freddy in front of him, keeping him close. "Turn around and step into the house," he says to Mandy. "Do it slowly. No sudden movements."

She does as he says. They step through into the living room. Tobin whistles through his teeth. "Jesus, I thought this place looked like a shithole from *outside.*" He motions to one of his men to secure the gun cabinet in the corner.

Mandy turns. Tobin pushes Freddy aside and slams the handle of his Glock into the centre of her face. She goes down, holding her bloodied nose. Another of the men grabs Freddy and holds him up. They press a knife to his throat.

"Please," Mandy says, looking up from the ground. "Take me back, do whatever you want to me, just let my son go. Don't hurt him – I'm begging you."

"Hold him right there," Tobin says to the man with the knife. "He's not going anywhere," Tobin says to Mandy. "I want him right where you can see him, because I'm gonna ask you some questions, Mandy, and if you don't answer me in a timely manner, if you obfuscate or try to give me the run around in any way, we're gonna start cutting parts off your boy and you're gonna watch."

She swallows.

"We know you had a recent visit from Cindy Vaughan," Tobin says. "We know who they're looking for. We know you don't know anything about Louise Parton, other than what they've told you. So, what did *you* tell them?"

Mandy's eyes flicker toward her son. Her tongue wets her lips, tasting her blood.

"Don't keep me waiting," Tobin says, "or else we start cutting."

"I told them what happened to me," Mandy says. "I told them – I told them what you did to me."

"Well, no harm in that. It *is* your story to tell, after all. It's not like anyone's believed you for seven years, isn't that right, Freddy?"

Freddy can't respond with the tape across his mouth. He stares at his mother, a thousand apologies in his eyes.

"Y'know, we had to up and move the whole operation because of you, Mandy," Tobin says, chuckling like it's a humorous memory. "The night you got away, we cleared straight out. We weren't gonna take any chances. Scrubbed every room down and we were *gone*. Upped security since then, too. Hired more men. We've never had a runaway since."

Mandy grinds her teeth, staring back at him.

"Now, here's what I *really* need to know from you, Mandy," Tobin says. "We know about Cindy Vaughan. We know about Chris Parton. Who's the third? Who's the guy helping them out?"

Mandy doesn't answer.

Tobin points to the man holding Freddy. He takes the knife from Freddy's neck and presses it to the top of his right ear, where it connects to his skull. He starts sawing the knife back and forth. Freddy screams into the tape, the sound muffled but unmistakable. Blood runs down the side of his face.

"Stop it, stop!" Mandy says. She tries to push herself up, to go to her son, but Tobin presses his Glock into her forehead and pushes her back down.

"Keep going until she tells me what I want to know," Tobin says. "And if you get through that ear and she hasn't given me a name, cut off his other ear. And if she *still* wants to test us, cut off his fucking dick."

The knife is a centimetre through the ear, separating cartilage from flesh.

"Tom Rollins!" Mandy cries out. "His name is Tom Rollins! Now stop! *Stop!*"

Tobin holds up a hand for the man to stop cutting. "Tom Rollins?" he says, testing the name out. "Why does that sound familiar? Does that sound familiar to anyone else?"

There're a few mumbles from his men, a few agreements, but no one has an answer.

"I'll get Brad on it," he says. He reaches into his pocket and pulls out a balaclava. He holds it out for his men to see. "Mask up," he says.

They do so. The man with the camera steps forward, taking in the scene.

"Smile," Tobin says to Mandy. "You're back on camera. It's your big return."

"You son of a bitch," she says. "You lousy piece of shit."

The man holding Freddy cuts his throat. The man with the camera captures it all. Freddy falls to the ground, convulsing, his sounds muffled behind the tape on his mouth. His blood pools outward from his opened neck, spreading across the ground and sinking into it.

Mandy lets out an anguished scream. She sounds like a wailing banshee. The sound hurts Tobin's ears. She crawls to her son, reaching for him. Tobin holds his hand out for the bloodied knife. It's placed into his palm, handle first. He reaches down and catches Mandy before she can reach Freddy. He grabs a handful of her hair roughly, almost tearing it from her scalp, and he pulls her head back, exposing her neck. Mandy looks at him, her eyes blazing. Tobin has never seen such hate. He doesn't care. He cuts her throat. She doesn't cry out. Her blood gargles from her slit throat, but she doesn't make any other sound. Her eyes don't leave his. The hatred continues to burn as her blood sprays upon her dying son.

Tobin pushes her away. She lands flat close to Freddy, but they don't touch. She can't reach him. They die separate, and alone.

The cameraman films them until they're still. Until there's no more blood to leak. Until they're dead.

26

Cindy and Chris guard Jilly Beck. Tom has already been gone a few hours. They know he's going to be gone a while longer.

They're in silence. They've gagged Jilly to keep her from crying out for help. Cindy has turned off the music, too. She's never been a fan of classical.

Jilly sits very still. She doesn't seem at all concerned about her predicament. She shifts her weight on the chair on occasion, but other than that she sits still, resting her head on the back, and stares up into the far corner of the ceiling.

Chris stands. He can't bring himself to sit. He leans against the breakfast counter, his arms folded, his eyes on the ground, not focussing on anything in particular.

Cindy is on the sofa close to Jilly. She's searched Jilly's apartment but hasn't found anything of interest. She's looked through her laptop, too, but Jilly isn't as careless as Ricky was. She doesn't store anything incriminating on it.

Before they gagged her, Cindy asked her where Louise is, and where the Kennedys are.

Jilly grinned. "Shouldn't we wait for your friend to return?" There was something mocking in her smile. "Or are you concerned that he *won't* make it back?"

Cindy stared at her, holding her sardonic gaze. "He'll come back," she said, with no doubts in her mind.

Jilly shrugged, like she couldn't care less. "If you insist."

Cindy was glad to gag her after that. She's been glad of her silence since then, too.

As if sensing the thought, Jilly sits forward and starts to make noise, trying to speak. Cindy and Chris both look at her, then exchange glances with each other. Cindy goes to her and pulls the gag loose.

"I'm not feeling good," Jilly says. There's a slight slurring to her speech. "I ate before you arrived, and I haven't had insulin since. I can feel it – it's time."

"I'm not letting you loose," Cindy says.

"I don't need you to," Mandy says. "You saw where my kit is, right? In the bedroom? Just bring it through."

"I'm still not going to cut you loose," Cindy says. "If you need insulin, I'll be the one giving it to you."

"Yes, fine, whatever," Jilly says, starting to sound exasperated. "Just bring it through and I can talk you through the rest, okay?"

Cindy stares at her a moment longer, then tears her eyes away to look at Chris. "Watch her closely," she says.

Chris nods and steps forward, pushing himself off the breakfast counter.

Cindy goes through to the bedroom, to the vanity table where the kit is with the blood sugar tester next to it. She opens it and finds the needles and insulin inside. She takes out a needle and the glass vial of insulin. She puts the needle into the clear liquid and draws out the insulin until the needle is full. It's probably too much, but under Jilly's instruction she can squeeze out whatever isn't needed. She picks up the blood sugar tester, too.

Then, she hears a loud thud from the living room.

Chris calls through. "Shit – Cindy, she's fallen!"

Cindy frowns. "Leave her where she is," she calls back, returning to them, but as she enters the living room she sees Chris leaning down over Jilly, reaching to help her back up onto the chair. Jilly is lying very still, her eyes closed.

As Chris gets closer, Jilly's eyes suddenly open. Her hands are free of her tape binds. She claws at his face, slashing at him with something concealed in her hand. Chris falls back, grabbing at his face, and Cindy sees a splash of blood close to his eyes.

Jilly jumps to her feet. She wheels on Cindy, grinning. In her hand she holds a nail file, wielding it like a small blade. She starts edging her way toward the kitchen.

Cindy charges her. She still has the needle full of insulin. She holds it low, not wanting to damage it. Jilly slashes at her with the file. Cindy ducks her arm and grabs at the front of Jilly's shirt, but Jilly throws herself forward with all of her weight and lands on top of Cindy, pinning her to the ground.

Cindy's right arm, the arm with the needle, is pinned under Jilly's knee. Her left arm is free, and she manages to grab Jilly's wrist holding the nail file and keep it at bay. With her other hand, Jilly grabs Cindy by the throat. She squeezes.

"Go to sleep," Jilly says through her teeth, squeezing harder. "And when we wake up, you'll know exactly where Louise Parton is. You'll be right there *with* her."

Cindy struggles, tensing the muscles in her neck, trying to retain consciousness. She shoots her eyes to the side, toward Chris. He's on his knees, pushing himself up, but he doesn't see what's happening. There's blood running through his hands.

Against her right thumb, Cindy can feel the exposed flesh of Jilly's left calf where her trouser leg has ridden up. Cindy spins the needle around in her hand, pointing it toward the calf. She plunges the needle in, and sinks the plunger, pumping all of the insulin into Jilly's leg.

Jilly feels the sting and her grip loosens. She looks back to see what Cindy has done. She sees the empty needle.

"Oh, you stupid *bitch*," she says. "How much was in that? How much insulin was in there?"

Cindy pushes her back while she's distracted. Jilly hits the chair. Cindy coughs, her throat raw, and quickly refills her lungs. Jilly pulls the empty needle from her leg. She stares at it, deliberating. She throws it to the side. She knows she doesn't have long to wrap things up here. She scurries to her right, pushing Chris aside and moving toward the kitchen.

Cindy jumps to her feet and follows. Jilly reaches the knife rack. She pulls out the biggest knife there, and jabs and slashes at Cindy. Cindy dodges her blows, ducking and weaving like she's been taught in her self-defence classes, and never taking her eyes from Jilly, watching to see where she might attack next.

The knife comes in a sweeping arc. Jilly has swung too wide, and Cindy sees an opportunity to land a blow of her own. She spins, raising her leg high, and connects with a back-heel kick to the side of Jilly's face. Jilly rotates with the force of the blow, going down, the knife dropped. Her head hits the counter. Cindy hears the crack as Jilly's neck snaps. She hits the ground with a hard thud.

Chris has pulled himself up from the ground. Blood runs down his face from a cut on his left cheek, across the bridge of his nose, and through his right eyebrow, the slash perilously close to both of his eyes. Blinding him was likely Jilly's intention. "Is she dead?" Chris says, leaning on the breakfast counter.

Cindy checks her pulse. "Yeah," she says. "She's dead."

27

Tom already knows he's too late before he reaches Mandy's home. As he speeds down the road beyond Roosevelt, in the distance he sees an orange glow lighting up the night sky, and flashing blue lights accompanying it.

Tom dumps his car by the side of the road and continues on foot toward the house, ducking low as he runs through the darkness. He doesn't want to meet cops or emergency services on the road and be questioned as to what he's doing here. It would take up too much time, and they don't have any to waste.

Drawing closer to the house, Tom can hear the flames crackling as they come into view. He ducks low by a tree, out of view, concealed in the shadows, and looks the scene over.

Mandy's house is burning. The fire service douse it with water, trying to put it out. A few cop cars cordon the area off, though it's not like anyone is trying to get closer. The cops stand around and look toward the flames.

Tom notices that the front yard is ablaze, too. What he can see of the ground looks like it's been dug up. He assumes the mines have been exploded. Briefly, he wonders why.

There's an ambulance nearby, too. Its back doors are open. On the ground, close by, he sees two bodies. They're bagged, ready to be loaded into the back of the ambulance. The two are clearly dead. Mandy must be one of them. Who's the other? Did she manage to take out one of her attackers? That doesn't feel right to Tom. If the attackers have killed Mandy, and burned down her home, and seemingly dealt with the mines in her yard, then it wouldn't make sense for them to leave behind the body of one of their own.

Tom feels a cold chill run through him. Freddy. The second body could be Freddy. How else would the attackers know to find Mandy here? The only person who knew where she was, other than he, Cindy, and Chris, was her son.

Tom feels sick. He turns his head and spits into the scrub. He puts together a hypothesis in his mind. It's brief and to the point, and the most likely scenario. The attackers – likely employees of the Kennedys – captured Freddy and forced him to reveal his mother's whereabouts. They came here, killed them both, and burned down the house to make it look like they died in an accidental fire. Presumably got rid of the landmines so the emergency services could get inside and to avoid them asking too many questions about the fortifications.

But – Tom wonders – how did they think to confront Freddy? Did his, Chris, and Cindy's search for Louise reveal something to the Kennedys' organisation? He's not so sure. They've been careful. They've watched their backs. They never met with Freddy face to face.

It's a mystery Tom may never know the answer to. For now, he pushes it from his mind. The mystery doesn't matter. What's happened here does. What has happened to Mandy, and presumably to Freddy, is what matters.

And what Tom is going to do to the Kennedys in turn. That's what matters most of all.

28

In the early hours of the morning, Tobin goes to the Kennedys.

Their compound is three hours outside of Lubbock. A converted farm. The farm itself had been inactive and fallow for almost fifteen years. The Kennedys purchased it for a pittance through their third-party buyer. No one else wanted the land. It was no good for farming anymore, and it was too far out for anyone to want to live there. Tobin remembers when they first bought it, shortly after Mandy Bliss's escape. It clearly had promise, but it was rundown. Most of the windows on each building were smashed. Some of the doors were hanging off their hinges. Everything was in need of a good dust, polish, and paint. Despite the prisoners they were holding, and the commitments they needed to keep, they had to put a pause on filming for a couple of months.

The compound is in the middle of nowhere, surrounded by scrubland. It looks like a completely different place from that farm Tobin first saw seven years ago. The biggest building, the farmhouse itself, is where the Kennedys live. It's in the centre of the compound, which itself is surrounded by a chain-link fence and security cameras. No one comes onto the compound who shouldn't.

Its middle-of-nowhere location proved beneficial in more ways than one. Serendipitous, almost. Not far from here, it turned out there was also an old airstrip, abandoned even longer than the farm. The Kennedys bought this, too.

To the east of the compound, there is a smaller building, commonly referred to as the shed, though it's far too large to ever be mistaken for a shed. Tobin doesn't go in there often. It isn't anything unpleasant – it's just too hot in there, even with the A/C cranked high and the desk fans running. This small building is where the sales team, editors, uploaders work – basically, everyone involved in the making of the movies who needs to be busy on a computer. And, thusly, computers run in that building almost twenty-four seven. It's too hot. Tobin avoids it. The people in there all answer to Brad, but Brad rarely comes out here. He hates the shed, too. He prefers to work from home.

Between these two buildings there is a concrete block. It's seven foot high, has a door in the front, and goes back, at a slant, for eight feet. Through the door is a stairway. It leads underground.

To the north of the compound, all the way at the back, away from the main buildings, there is what used to be the barn. The front door is open to let air circulate. To keep the people inside cool, as cool as they need to be, and to air out their stink. The barn is heavily guarded. It always is.

But Tobin isn't here for any of the other buildings. He's here for Guy and Shannon. He goes up to the main house, carrying the camera that was used this morning at the siege of Mandy's home. He pauses at the door and knocks hard enough to wake them if they're still sleeping. He'd be surprised if they are. It feels sometimes like they're always awake. He tried calling ahead but there was no answer. He sent a message to tell them he was on his way. They haven't responded yet.

Tobin doesn't have to wait long. Guy answers the door promptly. It's still early, but he's dressed in jeans and a white T-shirt. He's smiling in anticipation. "Do you have something for us?"

Tobin holds up the camera. "I do."

Guy throws the door wide and motions for him to come in. Tobin steps inside and follows Guy into the living room. Guy takes a seat on one of the leather sofas, opening up the camera so he can watch the footage captured. "Shannon!" he calls. "Come on through here – Tobin has brought us a gift!"

Tobin remains standing. He folds his arms. He acts casual, knowing that Shannon will be here soon. He glances around the room. He's been here plenty of times before. He's stayed over. The living room hasn't changed. The floors are thick carpeting. The walls are wood panelled. Above Guy, on the wall behind him, there is a wide mirror that Tobin can see himself in. Behind him, in the far corner, there is a widescreen television. On the walls around them, there are framed posters of Guy and Shannon's biggest movies and TV shows. Shannon's movie, *The Last Take*, is on the wall closest to Tobin. The same poster he used to have. She was still Shannon Campbell back then. Tobin makes sure not to stare, especially not in front of Guy.

Of course, Guy Kennedy does not intimidate him. Despite being forty-six, he's still presenting himself as the James Dean wannabe he's always been, his whole acting career – blue jeans, white T-shirt, the quiff. Had Dean reached his forties, or even his thirties, it's unlikely he'd still present himself as the rebel without a cause, yet Guy doesn't seem to have realised this. Guy has also grown much fatter than Dean ever got to be. He's no longer the svelte heartthrob he once, briefly, was.

Guy is no fighter, not like Tobin. While he has a taste for torture and violence, and has partaken in the films on occasion, his victims have been restrained. They haven't been able to fight back. Tobin knows if he wanted to, he could snap Guy across his knee. It wouldn't accomplish anything, though. Shannon, unfortunately, loves her husband. And, together, they pay Tobin's wages. They're good wages, too. A few more years of heading up their security and Tobin is looking at an early retirement.

The two wait in silence for Shannon to join them. Guy stares down at the camera in his hands, grinning to himself, desperate to see the footage.

Shannon appears. Unlike Guy, she hasn't dressed yet. Her hair is tied back. She wears men's boxer shorts and a white vest, a silk dressing gown over the top. Her long legs and her feet are bare. Again, Tobin does his best not to stare, even when Shannon comes up to him and kisses him on the cheek. "I've heard this is a happy visit," she says, smiling broadly as she joins her husband on the sofa.

Tobin stands silent as they watch the footage. He overhears it. It wasn't so long ago he lived it. There's still some of Mandy Bliss's blood under his fingernails. He watches Guy and Shannon's faces. They sit close together, watching, smiling the whole while. Shannon holds on to Guy's inner thigh. She squeezes it tight.

The film ends. Shannon laughs. "This is exciting," she

says. "We can get a good payout for this. None of our films have ever had a sequel before."

"And this is a sequel no one realised they were waiting for, or ever going to get," Guy says. "I'll get this to the sales team, start drumming up some interest." He looks at Tobin now, and his smile gradually fails. He holds up the camera. "This is good stuff, Tobin. But before we get too carried away, where do we stand with our other problems?"

"They're still in the air, as of now," Tobin says. "But I'm working on them. We have a name for the mystery man, at least."

"Who is he?"

"Tom Rollins. He was in the news recently, out in San Francisco. You may have seen it."

"We don't watch the news," Shannon says. "Was it recent?"

"Just a few days ago."

She frowns. "If he was in San Francisco, what's he doing here?"

"I'm not sure, but he must have some connection to either Cindy or Chris," Tobin says. "I have Brad and his team looking into it. What we know so far is he's ex-Army, and potentially some form of either special forces or government agent. A lot of his records have been redacted."

Guy stands. He puts the camera to one side and begins to pace. "This situation stresses me out, Tobin," he says. "A soldier and a specialist? This is concerning."

"I can deal with him," Tobin says. "He doesn't concern me. We just need to find him – to find all of them."

"You've been looking for long enough."

Tobin grits his teeth.

"I don't want to have to move our operation again," Guy says.

"It won't come to that," Tobin says. "I promise."

Shannon stands and leans on Tobin's arm, as if defending him. "You hear that, Guy?" she says. "He promises. He's always kept his promises to us before. He found Mandy Bliss, didn't he? Try and relax. These things are in his more-than-capable hands."

"It took seven years to find Mandy Bliss," Guy says. "I'll relax when this is resolved, and not before."

"I have a plan," Tobin says.

"See, Guy?" Shannon says. "He has a plan."

"They're looking for Louise Parton," Tobin says. "Is she still alive?"

Guy waves a dismissive hand. "I don't know. You'd have to check the cages."

It's a frustrating answer. It's exactly the kind of thing Guy *should* know. "Then I'll do that first," Tobin says, stepping to the side, away from Shannon's body pressing against him and the distraction she serves. "And once I know for sure, I'll tell you my plan."

"Does it hinge on her being alive?" Shannon says as Tobin heads for the door.

"Not necessarily," Tobin says. "I have a Plan B in mind, too."

29

Tom, Cindy, and Chris wipe down Jilly's apartment and remove any trace they were ever there. Tom arranges Jilly's corpse in the kitchen to make her death look like an accident. Whenever she's found, it'll look like she accidentally overdosed on her insulin, got dizzy in the kitchen, then fell and broke her neck on the counter.

Tom turns on Jilly's television and switches it to the local news. The television plays in the background while they clean. Tom keeps an ear out for anything reported on Mandy's house.

It's early in the morning, and they're all tired. But they don't stop. They can't rest. They don't have time to waste. They've gotten names. They're getting closer.

Cindy has tried to contact Freddy Bliss, calling his number, but there's no answer. As Tom suspected, it doesn't look good for Freddy.

"Just don't contact him on your laptop," Tom says. "If they took him from his home, they might have taken his computer, too."

"How did it look out there?" Cindy says, giving up on the calls.

"There wasn't much to see," Tom says. "Place was swallowed up in a fireball. Considering all the weapons we saw she had, and the defences, the traps, the folks that went there must've had the numbers on their side to overwhelm her." Tom falls silent.

"What're you thinking?" Cindy says.

"That we're going to need more guns," Tom says.

"I'll look into it," Cindy says.

"Have you looked into the Kennedys?"

"Just on my phone," Cindy says. "My laptop was in the car – you took it with you."

"What did you find?"

"I couldn't go as deep as I ordinarily would, so just surface-level stuff. Their acting careers, how they petered out – they only have about one good movie between them – and how they retired over ten years ago and have lived quiet lives ever since."

"Mm," Tom says.

"I *did* find out who Tobin is, though. The man that Jilly mentioned."

"Who is he?"

"Tobin Klinghoffer – ex-MMA turned bodyguard. He was working for the Kennedys back when they were still out in LA. Could be the same guy."

Tom considers this.

"When I have my laptop I'll go deeper. I'll find them." Cindy nods toward the television. Her lips are pursed into a thin, grim line. "It's Mandy," she says.

Tom turns to see. The news is reporting on the fire at Mandy's property. They show an old picture of her, when she was younger, and unscarred. She's smiling in it. She looks full of life, hope, and promise. The news refers to her as a recluse who'd been living off the grid for the last seven years.

The news also says the fire at her property was caused by a gas leak. It mentions the two bodies, burnt to a crisp. Both are unidentifiable, but preliminary dental reports indicate that the bodies belong to Mandy and her son, Freddy Bliss.

"Shit," Cindy says. "Like you suspected."

Chris emerges from the bathroom. "I found some butterfly bandages in the medicine cabinet," he says. Tom sees the long, deep gash that runs across his face, narrowly missing both eyes. Chris has cleaned the wound and sealed it with the small, translucent band-aids.

"How does it feel?" Cindy says.

"It stings," Chris says. "But I know it could've been a hell of a lot worse."

"Did you clean up the blood?" Tom says.

Chris nods. "I was thorough. I got it all." His attention is distracted by the report on the television. The footage of the burning house taken in the early morning light. The corners of his mouth turn down while he watches.

Tom gives him a moment to watch the report, then turns off the television, covering his thumb with his sleeve so as not to leave a print. "There's nothing left here for us," he says. "We leave out the front door. I'll take point, make sure it's clear, make sure there's no one to see us leave. Hoods up and eyes down. Everyone got that? Leaving this way isn't ideal, but it's light out now, and it's not like we can climb down the balconies again."

"Where do we go next?" Chris says.

"We get out of here," Tom says, "and then we get guns."

30

Tom leaves Tuscany Place, and Jilly Beck's body, behind and drives a few blocks away. They go through a drive-thru to get breakfast and while they eat egg sandwiches Cindy starts talking about gun dealers.

"Due to the nature of my work, I'm aware of nearly all the shady people in Lubbock," she says. "And most of them are pretty dangerous, too."

"Have you worked for them?" Chris says, probing tentatively at the bandages under his eye.

"That's not something I would do," Cindy says. "I'm not in the business of ripping people off, or any other kind of scam these people would be interested in. I keep tabs on them so I know what they're up to. Ignorance isn't bliss. I need to know where they are and what they're doing."

"How many gun dealers are you aware of?" Tom says.

"Pretty much all," Cindy says. "I don't know any of them personally, or professionally. But I know who they are. The kind of lives we lead, I figure it's best to know where you can get a gun if you need one."

"This is someone you need to be okay with pissing off," Tom says. "I'm not interested in buying – we don't have the money, nor the time to get it. This is a situation where we take what we need."

Cindy takes a bite of her sandwich and chews while she thinks. "There's one guy I can think of I wouldn't normally go near with a barge pole," she says. "Fitzek. There's stories he's not a pleasant guy. Most recent rumours I heard are that he sold a gun used to kill a whole family – husband, wife, eleven-year-old daughter and six-year-old son. No one's even sure who the actual target of the hit was."

Tom frowns. "How true is that?"

"Well, I know it happened. It was only a couple of months ago. I could bring the report up right now if I needed to."

"Was the shooter found?"

"Yeah – same night. Cops were nearby responding to a domestic disturbance when they heard the shots go off. They managed to run the perp down. He ended up committing suicide by cop. Probably saw no other way out of his situation, and after what he'd done even prison wasn't gonna be a safe place for him."

"But nothing was traced back to Fitzek," Tom says.

"Well, like I said, it was a rumour that he was the supplier."

Tom nods. "Fitzek will do."

Cindy finishes the last of her sandwich and reaches for her laptop. "I'll find a way to get in touch and I'll set up a meeting."

31

Cindy has reached out to Fitzek. It's taken an hour. She had to jump through a lot of hoops online trying to get his number. She doesn't have it yet. She's waiting to hear back from the man himself.

"Do we know what he looks like?" Tom says.

Cindy turns her laptop around for him to see. It's not a great picture. It's been taken from afar, likely by a cop or FBI on surveillance. Tom wonders how the picture made its way online.

Fitzek is crossing the road, flanked by two heavies. The picture looks like it was taken in winter. Fitzek wears a heavy coat, the collar popped to cover his neck and ears. His face is turned slightly. He's wearing sunglasses. His cheeks are gaunt. His thinning hair is swept back. The picture is black and white, but Tom can imagine him as a pale man who rarely ventures out into the sun.

"It's enough to go on," Cindy says. "We'll know him when we see him."

Tom has kept the car moving while they've waited. He

doesn't want to stop anywhere for too long. Right now, they've parked up in the lot of a strip mall. Five more minutes and Tom will start moving again, whether they've heard from Fitzek or not.

Tom turns to Chris. "Have you ever handled a gun before?"

"At the range," Chris says. "I've never owned one, though."

"What have you used?"

"Handguns mostly – Sig Sauer, Colt."

"Anything bigger?"

"An AR15 once, but I didn't like it."

"But you won't need to be taught?"

"No – I remember."

"Okay." Tom nods. He studies the gash across Chris's face. It's deep. It will scar. "Going forward, I'm not comfortable taking you in with us."

Chris bites his tongue. He doesn't say anything.

"You nearly lost your eyes," Tom says. "Both of them. I've agreed to take you along thus far because Louise is your sister, and because the situations we've gone into haven't been immediately dangerous. They've been manageable. But what good is getting Louise back if we lose you in the process?"

Chris swallows. "So where do I go?"

"You hide out at the launderette," Tom says. "And you'll wait for us there until this is done. Hopefully it won't take much longer. We'll leave you a gun, just in case, and you'll call us if you see anything you don't like the look of."

Chris bites his lip now. He wants to speak. Wants to protest. He's stopping himself.

Cindy leans into the front and puts a hand on Chris's

shoulder. "This isn't our first time," she says. "But this is all new to you. We just don't want you to get hurt. These people who have taken Louise, their operation is looking bigger and bigger all the time. We can't take risks."

Chris looks at Tom. He breathes deeply. "Okay," he says. His hands are balled into tight fists on his thighs. He knows that Tom and Cindy are right, but it's clear how hard it is for him to agree to this. "Just…just bring her back to me, okay?"

"We'll do our best," Cindy says.

"So when do I get dropped off?" Chris says, letting his fists open. He looks around. "I suppose I could walk from here."

"You're not roaming the streets on your own," Tom says. "We'll take you."

Before Tom can say more, Cindy speaks. "I've heard from Fitzek," she says. "He's sent a number to call. I assume it's a burner."

"I'll talk to him," Tom says. "Read it out."

Tom punches the number into his phone. He calls. It rings five times before Fitzek answers. "Who is this?" he says. His voice is thin and gruff. He sounds like a smoker. A heavy smoker. He turns his head away from the phone and coughs.

"We've been talking," Tom says. "You sent me this number."

"I know *that*," Fitzek says. "What's your fucking name and what do you fucking *want*?"

"My name's Tom," Tom says, no reason to lie. If a surname is demanded he'll provide a fake, just in case. Since San Francisco, a lot of people are aware of Tom's name and his face. "And I want some guns. I was told you could accommodate."

"Who told you that?"

"You know they wouldn't be happy if I told you."

Fitzek grunts. It sounds like a smirk. "We talk face to face. No business until I've looked you in the eye. How many are coming?"

"Three," Tom says. "But one of my guys stays with the car."

Fitzek grunts again. "Fine. You know Teddy's?"

"What is that, a bar?"

"Yeah."

"I can find it."

"Come here now. We'll be on lookout. I see something I don't like, we're gone."

"I'm in a Ford," Tom says. "Two guys, one girl."

"Keep it that way. Anyone else with you, I'm gone." He hangs up.

"Chris, take the wheel," Tom says, getting out of the car and moving around to the passenger side.

"I know where Teddy's is," Cindy says. "It's a dump. Exactly the kind of place I'd expect a guy like Fitzek to hang out in."

Chris starts driving, Cindy pointing the way.

"You stay with the car," Tom says to him. "If we come running, be ready to gun it."

Chris nods.

"They might come out and talk to you. Play it cool. If they ask for a name, just give it, but if they press don't give your real surname. We don't know who else he might know, who he might be connected to. I'm Davidson, Chris, you're O'Connell, Cindy is Travis. Everyone got that?"

They say they do. Tom fills them in on the rest of their backstory on the way.

It takes twenty minutes to drive to Teddy's. When it

comes into view, Chris slows the car. The bar is a small, flat-roofed building wedged between an out-of-business warehouse and a car repair shop. The sign above the door used to be green writing on a varnished wooden board, Irish pub style, but it's all faded now. Most of the green paint has flaked away. The apostrophe in Teddy's has fallen off. The backboard is chipped and weathered, bleached pale by the sun.

The windows have metal bars and a grating over them. One of the windows has a spiderweb crack in it, presumably from before the iron bar defences were erected. Next to the front door, a big guy stands with his knee bent, sole of his boot against the wall. He's smoking a cigarette, and he's not paying any attention to the approaching Ford. He's not the lookout. He's just a guy having a smoke.

Tom spots movement on the flat roof, someone lying low and backing away from the edge. "Pull up in front," Tom says. "Opposite side of the road."

Chris does so. He leaves the engine running. They watch to see if anything happens. The man smoking flicks what's left of his cigarette, spits, and heads inside. He's never once looked their way.

A moment later, a broad guy in jeans and a flannel shirt comes to the door. He looks up and down the road, then straight at the car. He waves for them to come inside.

"That must be our invite," Cindy says.

She and Tom get out of the car and cross the road. Chris kills the engine and stays behind.

The inside of Teddy's is just as dire as the outside. It's made up of shadows, the lights turned down low. The man they saw smoking is behind the bar now, serving. A few faces turn their way as they enter, but Tom and Cindy follow the big guy in flannel and attention soon diverts.

Fitzek has a corner booth in the back of the bar. He's flanked by two big guys, who make him look extra small and dwarfed between them. He chews gum with his mouth open and plays with an empty tumbler on the table. "Tom," he says, looking Tom up and down. The man in flannel stays close to Tom and Cindy. Tom notices how his right hand stays close to his waist. There's a concealed weapon there.

Tom nods and Fitzek turns his attention to Cindy, looking her up and down in much the same way, except this time his tongue flickers out over his lips and there's a hungry look in his eyes. "And you are?"

"Cindy," she says.

"Cindy," Fitzek repeats, trying the name out for himself, seeing how it feels in his mouth. "That's a beautiful name."

Cindy says nothing. She looks back at him.

Fitzek grins. He flicks his head to the big guy in flannel. "Go and speak to the third."

The man turns and heads back outside to Chris. The men either side of Fitzek slide out of the booth.

"They're gonna pat you down," Fitzek says. "And then I'm gonna ask you some questions."

The men pat down Tom and Cindy. Tom left his Beretta and KA-BAR in the car, tucked safely into his backpack. The man on Tom pays close attention to his chest. He's checking him for a wire. The two men step back. They don't slide back into the booth. They nod at each other, then the man who patted down Cindy says, "They're clear."

Fitzek smiles. "That's good. That's real good. You can never be too sure, you understand. Gotta be careful for cops and undercovers."

"We just want guns," Tom says.

"So I understand. And what do you need them for?"

"Why do you care?"

Fitzek shrugs and holds out a hand. "Professional curiosity. And *I'm* the one asking questions, Tommy-boy."

"We're going hunting," Tom says. "And we're not planning on getting a permit."

"I get a lot of that," Fitzek says. "You wouldn't believe how popular the hunting in Texas is, all year round. And what kind of hunting are *you* doing?"

"The kind that needs handguns and automatic rifles," Tom says.

Fitzek whistles low. "It'll cost you, but it's doable." He stares at Cindy. "And what's she to you? Sister?" He pauses. "Lover?"

"Friend," Cindy says, holding his eye.

Fitzek grins. "I feel like there's a story there, right? What happened to you, little girl? Someone hurt you? Women don't come to me often, and when they do it's usually because someone *hurt* them, you get my meaning?"

The man in flannel returns. "Driver's clear," he says. "Jumpy, but clear."

Fitzek chuckles.

"How clean are your guns?" Tom says. "If we're going to do business together, I need to know it isn't going to blow up in our faces."

Fitzek holds out his hands. "I'm still here, aren't I?"

"That's not enough."

"The numbers are filed off, if that's what you're asking," Fitzek says. "My guns are clean. If anyone using one of my guns has ever been caught, that's their own stupid fault. My shit is faultless. It's trustworthy."

Tom waits, like he's thinking this over, like he's still not convinced. "I need proof," he says.

"Proof?" Fitzek says. "What kinda fucking proof can I give you?"

"An example."

Fitzek looks to the man in flannel. Something unspoken passes between them. Fitzek smiles. "All right," he says. "Here's a recent one. You from around here? She's got the accent, but I notice you ain't."

"Close enough."

"You hear about that family that got wiped out, and the shooter had it out with the cops and ended up dead in the street? That was one of mine. Now, *that* was high profile. And, like I said, I'm still here. That gun ain't been traced, and it never will."

"But the shooter got killed," Tom says.

"And that was *his* fault. Nothing to do with my merchandise."

They watch each other across the table. A minute passes. Fitzek sniffs.

"So," he says. "I'm satisfied with what I've found. And yourself?"

Tom nods.

"Good." Fitzek gives them an address. "Find your way there in two hours. I'll bring the stuff you need, you bring cash. *Cash* – that clear? I don't carry around a card reader."

"Of course," Tom says.

"Two hours," Fitzek repeats. "I'll see you there."

Tom and Cindy leave the bar. Chris is watching the door. He sits up when he sees them. They're not running, so he waits until they're back in the car before he starts the engine.

"How'd it go?" Chris says.

"He's going to sell to us," Cindy says. "Start driving – we don't want him to see us hanging around in front."

Chris does as he's told.

"This time, you're coming inside with me," Tom says to Chris. "Cindy is the getaway driver. I'll need someone to carry the guns."

"You said we're going to take them," Chris says.

"That's right."

"But the guy who came out to see me – he was *big*. And they're going to be armed, right?"

"I expect so," Tom says.

"Then what are you going to do?"

Tom doesn't answer straight away. He thinks about what Fitzek told him. About how he told the story of the murdered family almost as a brag. "I'm going to kill him," Tom says.

32

The suburb is a half-hour away from Teddy's bar. Tom and the others go straight there. Chris parks the car around the corner at the end of the block. Tom gets out of the car to circle the area, check it over. Once he's out, Chris slides across to the passenger seat and Cindy gets behind the steering wheel.

The neighbourhood is rundown and nondescript. It looks like the kind of place a street-level arms deal would go down without any of the neighbours batting an eye. Tom checks the time while he beats the pavement. He wonders if the address Fitzek has given them is a stash house, or just a safe house. He wonders how many safe houses he could have throughout the city. Tom doubts this is the only one.

He slows as he reaches the house. The windows are clear, no curtains or blinds. It looks empty. There're no vehicles parked out front. Tom looks to the houses either side, and opposite. There's no one looking out, keeping guard. Tom slips down the side of the house and goes around to the back. He stays low and close to the building.

He peers in through the rear windows. He can see into a back room and, to the right, the kitchen. Through the kitchen's open door, he can see all the way through to the front. The home is mostly empty. He can see the arm of a sofa in the living room, and in the back room next to the kitchen there's a bed with no duvet or blanket. The kitchen counters are clear. There's no pots, no pans, no plates. No sign of mess. It's clear to Tom that no one lives here, at least not regularly.

Tom stays low, and he waits. He keeps an eye on the time. An hour and a half has passed since they left Teddy's. A few more minutes go by and Tom hears a car pulling up out front. The engine dies. Tom peers over the frame and watches through the kitchen window, all the way through to the front.

A moment passes, and then the front door opens. The three heavies from the bar come inside. The man in flannel is carrying a duffel bag. Fitzek follows them in. The man in flannel is coming through to the back. Tom ducks low, steps to his left, and peers into the back room. The man in flannel places the duffel bag on the mattress.

Tom ducks low again and slides down the side of the house. He walks briskly to the end of the block without looking back, and gets into the Ford with Chris and Cindy. They're out of view of the house. Cindy looks back at him.

"Are they there?"

Tom nods. "And they've brought the guns, as promised." He checks the time. "Twenty more minutes – five minutes late – and then we drive round."

"How many of them is there?" Chris says.

"Three of them, plus Fitzek," Tom says. "Same guys we

saw at the bar. You stay behind me. I'll deal with everything else."

"Where are the guns?"

"In a duffel bag in the back bedroom. You grab them and bring them back here to the car. Depending on how things go, I might be a while in the house."

33

Cindy pulls the car around to the front of the house. Tom and Chris get out and head up to the door. They knock and wait.

The man in flannel answers. Fitzek is waiting for them in the living room. He's sitting on the sofa, one leg crossed over the other. He's grinning at them as they enter. He looks Chris over. "The man from the car," he says. "I'm afraid you're both going to need patted down again. It's been a couple of hours, and we're not stupid. We're not taking risks."

Tom spreads his arms and legs while one of the men searches him. Again, Tom has come in unarmed. The heavies nod at Fitzek that they're clear.

Fitzek gets to his feet. He curls a finger for Tom and Chris to follow. They do. The heavies fall into line behind them. They go through to the back bedroom. Fitzek opens the duffel bag on the bed.

"They're all unloaded right now," Fitzek says. "But as you can see, the magazines are right there. While you're looking, we leave the bullets out."

Tom can see the magazines. They match up to the weapons available. A few Sig Sauers, an AR15, an M4, and a Winchester 70 with a scope.

"You mentioned hunting," Fitzek says, motioning to the Winchester. "It's not an automatic, but I wanted to cover all bases."

Tom takes each weapon from the bag and looks them over, checking them for defects.

"You look like you know your guns," Fitzek says. "What takes your liking?"

"All of them," Tom says. He puts back the Winchester and picks up the magazines, checking the bullets over, too. Fitzek strikes him as the kind of man who would try to get defective merchandise past someone who wouldn't know better.

Fitzek's face lights up at Tom's words. "All?" he says. "Well, hell yeah. But it's gonna cost you. You got the green for them?"

Tom straightens. The man in flannel is closest to him. The other two heavies are behind Chris, blocking the door. None of them have their guns out. "We won't be paying," Tom says.

Fitzek cocks his head. "What?"

Tom spins on the man in flannel, fist balled. He drives it into the man in flannel's throat. He falls instantly to his knees, clutching at his neck, coughing and gagging, his face turning beet-red.

The two men by the door are startled. Chris leaps to the side to clear the way for Tom. The man on the left stands with his legs parted. Tom kicks him easily between them, crushing his testicles under his shin. The man's eyes bulge and water. Tom drives a left hook across the jaw of the man on the right. He has a glass jaw. It knocks him out cold instantly. He hits the ground like a sack of dirt.

Tom turns. Fitzek has thrown open the back window and is climbing out. He shoots a look back, face twisted in terror. He sees Tom and he throws himself to the ground below. Tom can hear his footsteps racing down the side of the house, their sound growing fainter.

Tom grabs one of the Sig Sauers, a magazine to go with it, and zips the duffel bag closed before handing it to Chris. "He's getting away," Chris says.

"He's got a head-start, that's all," Tom says. "He won't get away."

They leave out the front door. Chris carries the duffel bag, slung over his shoulder. Tom looks left and right. Fitzek is in his car, driving east. He's on his phone.

"Take the guns to Cindy," Tom says. "Go to the launderette and wait. I'll be there soon."

"What are you going to do?" Chris says.

Tom doesn't answer. He's already turned away. He starts running.

34

Cindy drives Chris and the guns back to the launderette. Chris hasn't said a word on the drive. Cindy drives around the block to make sure it's clear, then parks around the back of the building and they go inside. They make sure it's clear inside, too. Cindy carries one of the Sig Sauers while she checks for an ambush. The building is empty.

Chris carries in the duffel bag. He sets it on top of one of the machines. Cindy goes back to the car for her laptop. When she returns, Chris is loading up the weapons.

Cindy puts her laptop down. She watches Chris. "Are you okay?"

"It's...it's nothing," he says.

"You're very quiet for *nothing*."

Chris puts down the M4. "I promised not to keep asking questions," he says. He holds up his hands. "I'm in the launderette, and this is where I'm staying going forward. I have to be fine with that. I don't have anything to say."

"If there's something on your mind, I'd rather you tell me," Cindy says. "I assume it's about Tom."

Chris sighs. "All it is, I just don't understand why he's going after this Fitzek guy. He doesn't have anything to do with this. He doesn't have anything to do with my sister."

Cindy suspected this was the issue. "You need to understand something about Tom," Cindy says. "And it's the whole reason I knew I could call him to help *us*."

Chris looks at her.

"If Tom sees something wrong, he's going to step in. That's just who he is. If he meets a man like Fitzek, someone who has caused death and suffering to dozens, if not hundreds, of people, then he can't let that stand. He can't let a man like Fitzek go unpunished. It was the same with Ricky Buxton. And now we *know* that Fitzek supplied the gun that killed that family. He might as well as killed them himself. We've seen how careful Fitzek is – he must have been able to tell that the man who bought from him wasn't psychologically sound. And he doesn't care. You saw it. We all did."

Chris says nothing. He understands, but he doesn't feel good about it. "Just...Louise..."

"I know," Cindy says. "But we haven't given up on her, and we haven't wasted any time here. We have the guns. Tom might be out dealing with something else, but the search hasn't stopped." Cindy pats her laptop. "While he's doing that, I'm going to find the Kennedys."

"All right," Chris says. "Okay." He walks to the window and looks out, checking the road. He speaks without turning. "There's something I didn't tell you..." He pauses. "About our dad."

"Oh?"

"I *did* see him again, after our mom died." Slowly, he

turns back around. He doesn't look at her. He leans against the window frame and stares hard at the ground, his brow knitted. "We were both still very young, Louise especially. I... I couldn't be her father as well as her brother. We weren't even that close at the time. There's six years between us. I had my own life. My own friends. I was still in school. I had a part-time job. I was thinking about myself, about my future." He breathes deeply. "I didn't have much money, but I saved enough to hire a private investigator. I got him to track down our father. He found him in Sweetwater. All that time, and he wasn't even that far away.

"So I went to see him. Turns out he was remarried, had two more kids. They were just small. Not much more than babies. I saw them through the window before I knocked on the door. Boy, he was *not* happy to see me." Chris grins bitterly. "Stepped outside with me and closed the door real quick. Didn't want me to be seen by his new family. You know what his first words to me were, after all those years apart?"

Cindy waits.

"He said, 'What are you doing here?' No 'Hello,' no 'How you doing?' No, 'I'm sorry I didn't keep in touch, I'm sorry it's been so long' – no apology of any kind. 'What are you doing here?'" Chris's face twists as he's remembering. "I told him what I was doing there. I told him how Mom had died. I told him how Louise needed a parent, and how I couldn't be that for her... That's...that's the story I told. The truth is, I needed – I needed someone to take her off my hands. But I couldn't say that. I had to try and play on his better nature, so she could go with him and his new family and she would be their problem.

"Except, he didn't *have* any better nature. He *knew* Mom

had died. He knew, and he never came to us. Never tried to get in touch. Didn't expect us to be able to find him. He said no, and he told me to leave. Didn't *ask*, he *told*. Said that if I ever came around again, he'd call the cops on me for trespassing and harassment."

Cindy watches. The memories still burn for him. He opens and closes his fists. He can't look at her. He stares at the ground still.

"I drove back to Louise, and I was just *burning* all the way. I was so angry – angry at *him*, angry at her, angry at our mom. And then I got home, and she looked at me as I walked through the door, and she smiled at me, and the only person I was angry at anymore was myself. It was me – *I* was the problem. Our dad wouldn't step up, so I needed to. Louise was innocent in it all. I was all she had left, and she saw that, even if I didn't, not at first. So I became her father. I did everything I thought I couldn't. I stepped up. At first it was out of guilt. Guilt that I'd betrayed her, that I'd let her down, that I'd tried to get rid of her, handing her off to someone else who didn't want her. And then it was out of love. It was because she was my family. My *only* family. I should never have gone to Sweetwater. I should never have tried to find our father."

He pauses. He raises his face, but he still doesn't look at Cindy. He looks at the ceiling. Cindy thinks he's trying not to cry. He touches the butterfly bandages on his eyebrow. "But now she's been taken, and I just feel like, after everything, I've still let her down. I feel like everyone in her life has let her down, and I swore I would never do that again."

He stops. The story is over. His eyes are locked on the ceiling. They're glassy. The whites are strained red.

Cindy goes to him. She wraps her arms around his waist and holds him tight. She doesn't say anything. She doesn't need to. She holds him until he lowers his head and wraps his own arms around her. Cindy feels the heat of his tears dripping onto her scalp. He trembles. Cindy doesn't let go.

35

Fitzek's car easily got away, but Tom expected it to. He wasn't trying to run it down. He wasn't chasing it at all, not directly. He committed the details of the vehicle to memory, and ran back to Teddy's.

There's no sign of the car at the bar, but Tom is patient. He slips down the side of the bar, between it and the old warehouse, and he waits in the shadows. It stinks of piss and trash here, but Tom ignores it. He compartmentalises. He's always been good at it. Since leaving San Francisco, with his various aches and pains, he's become a pro.

He feels like Teddy's must be a regular meeting point for Fitzek and his goons. A nerve centre. He was on the phone as he drove away, and chances are he's calling in reinforcements to track down Tom and the others and look for his stolen weaponry.

Tom could be wrong, of course. Teddy's could be one of many meeting points, just like the house in the suburb could be one of many. Teddy's is closest, and the one that Tom knows about. He'll wait, he'll give it a few hours, and if Fitzek or his men don't show, Tom will return to Cindy and Chris and they'll get on with tracking down Louise. Hopefully by then Cindy will have found where the Kennedys are. Fitzek can wait. Tom can track him down after. Louise is the priority right now, and if they already had a good idea of where she is Tom wouldn't be here.

The minutes pass. Cars go by but none of them stops. People come and go at the bar. Tom waits.

And then, forty-five minutes later, Fitzek arrives. His car screeches to a halt on the other side of the road and he gets out flanked by three men Tom has not seen before. Fitzek is antsy as they cross the road, looking left and right and all around. His hands fidget together, popping his knuckles. He's shaken by what happened out at the house.

They enter the bar and disappear from Tom's view. Tom has had time to recall the interior of Teddy's. If Fitzek and his heavies go to the same booth he earlier occupied, they'll be close to the rear of the building. There was a window at the back, barred and meshed like the ones at the front, but this one didn't have any cracks or boards up. Clear to see out, and clear to see in.

Tom turns, scales the fencing behind him, and goes to the back of the building. There's another building at the rear, and an alleyway between them both. There's no windows at the back of the other building. It smells like piss here, too. To the right, there's an open window at the back of Teddy's. Tom looks inside. It's the men's room. There's no one in there right now.

Ducking low, Tom peers into Teddy's. Fitzek and his new men have gone straight to the booth from earlier. Fitzek is gesticulating wildly. He's animated. He's so gaunt and so pale he looks like a lively skeleton.

Another ten minutes go by, and two more men arrive. A few minutes after that, two more walk in. Seven men all told. Fitzek talks to them all. Tom lipreads a little of what he's saying – he's giving their names. Tom, Cindy, Chris. He gives them the number they called him from, though he doubts it'll be much use. He speaks too rapidly for Tom to make out much else.

Then, when Fitzek is done, six of the men leave. Only one stays behind with him. The heavy goes to the bar and orders drinks. He returns with a shot and a beer for Fitzek. The shot is likely to calm his nerves. Fitzek carefully raises it with shaking hands. He's angry. He's *furious*. Right now he's running on hope that his guns will be found. He has to know the chances are slim.

Tom knows that the chances are non-existent. Those six men, and anyone else Fitzek may have been in touch with, will not be able to find the guns, or the thieves. They have no idea who they are, not really, and they have no idea where they could have gone.

Tom watches, and he waits. Fitzek has settled a little. He's sipping at the beer. He doesn't talk, and neither does the man with him. Fitzek stares at the door, as if hoping someone will walk through with good news. He has his cell phone out on the table in front of him, probably willing it to ring, though it never does.

Then, Tom's opportunity to strike arises. Fitzek gets to his feet and steps out of the booth. He jerks a thumb back toward the bathroom and motions for the heavy to stay where he is and keep an eye on the door and the phone. Fitzek crosses the bar. Tom watches him go, then slides along to the open window of the bathroom. He watches through the crack. Sees Fitzek make his way to the urinal.

He grumbles to himself on the way, working at his button and fly. Tom looks around the rest of the bathroom. It's empty. Fitzek is the only person present.

Tom eases the window wider. He climbs in through the opening. Fitzek doesn't hear him coming. He's nearly done pissing. He zips himself back up and he turns. He sees Tom and he starts, jumping back, eyes popping. Before he can cry out, make a sound, Tom grabs him by the throat with his right hand and covers his mouth with his left. He doesn't say a word. He doesn't need to.

He drives Fitzek back into the toilet stall and slams the back of his head into the tiled wall. Fitzek's eyes flicker back into his skull. There's a bloody print left on the tiles. Tom uncovers his mouth. Fitzek is dazed. He's not in any state to make noise. He mumbles, trying to cry out. Tom turns him around and forces him down onto his knees. He pushes his face deep into the toilet bowl, into the water.

Fitzek starts to struggle, but his movements are weak from the head injury. Tom sees bubbles rising in the yellow water. Tom holds him there until the bubbles stop, until Fitzek's arms drop flat and his body is limp. When he's sure he's dead, he lets go of him.

Tom leaves the stall and washes his hands. He doesn't leave through the window. He walks through the bar. The man at Fitzek's booth briefly glances up from his cell phone as Tom crosses the bar, then looks back down and doesn't spare him a second glance. The man either doesn't know who Tom is, or doesn't care. As Tom suspected, the men don't know what he, Cindy, or Chris look like. Tom walks straight past him and out the front door.

36

Jilly Beck and Ricky Buxton are dead.

Tobin is still at the compound. He's in the gym at the back of Guy and Shannon's house. He works over the heavy bag, punches and kicks, exerting his frustrations upon the leather.

Jilly's death looks like an accident. An accidental insulin overdose, and then a fall when she was dizzy. Ricky was tortured and killed. The doormen at The Lubbock Lounge have given descriptions, and they match up with Tom Rollins, Cindy Vaughan, and Chris Parton. There were no witnesses to Jilly's death, but it feels like too much of a coincidence.

Tobin's men found the bodies. Ricky first. Then, when they couldn't get in touch with Jilly, Tobin sent a couple of guys over to her place. They've covered up Ricky's death, but they left Jilly as she was. Tobin told his guys to make sure they didn't leave any trace that they'd been there.

Guy and Shannon, naturally, are not happy. Not so much

about Ricky – sleazy guys like him are a dime a dozen – but Jilly has been a part of this whole operation from the start. It's through her that they're able to find their stars. Going forward, they're going to have to find someone new. Either that, or take a more proactive approach with the victims themselves. Shannon could be good at that. She's always had a way with people.

But Tobin can't look too far ahead. They have plenty of people in the cages right now. That will see them through until they become desperate. What Tobin needs to do is focus on the present. Focus on the problems they're experiencing, and find a way to solve them.

He needs to capture Tom Rollins, Cindy Vaughan, and Chris Parton.

And if they can't be caught, he needs to kill them.

Tobin slams fists into the bag, feeling the sweat running down his face, his chest, his back. It drips from his nose. It gets into his eyes. He punches harder. Blinks the sweat away. Pictures Tom. Pictures his face split and bloodied under his onslaught. What is he – a fucking soldier? He hasn't had training the way Tobin has had training. Tobin has been doing this for nearly his whole life. There's no one can stand against him.

He switches to kicks, imagining Rollins's ribs collapsing under their impact, his chest crunching, compacting his heart and lungs until he's coughing blood. He may beg for mercy, but Tobin will have none. He will have zero mercy for any of these pains in his ass.

He realises someone is behind him and he slows, bouncing on the balls of his feet in his defensive stance. He takes quick breaths and glances back.

Shannon is in the doorway, leaning against the frame.

She watches him. Tobin isn't wearing much. Just shorts, with wrist and ankle tape.

"Impressive," Shannon says. "Does it make you feel any better?"

"It helps." He goes to his bottle of water and takes a long drink. Shannon wears high-waisted jeans, and a white vest tucked into them. Tobin tries not to stare. It doesn't matter what she wears, she always has his attention.

Guy and Shannon took their frustrations regarding Jilly out on him. They chewed him out. Blamed him for how long this is taking, how things have not yet been resolved. "The security of this operation is *your* responsibility," Guy said. "And how many of our people are now dead? And more importantly of all, *Jilly* is dead. Do you understand how vital Jilly was to us?"

Tobin stood and took it. The good graces he'd earned from tracking down Mandy Bliss and filming the murder of her and her son had seemingly instantly expired. Their happiness only went so far, and Rollins and co ensured that it didn't stretch very far at all.

"How are things progressing for your plan?" Shannon says.

"I'm going to take a shower and then find out," Tobin says.

Shannon is silent for a moment. She watches him sweat. "Jilly was the only agent I ever had," she says. "When I first got to LA, I went to every audition I could book, and nothing took. I was waitressing to make ends meet. I hated it, but I made good tips – I mean, is it a shock? With *this* winning personality?" She grins. "That was where Jilly found me. She was eating with another of her clients, but the whole while I waited on them she only had eyes for me. After, she ditched him and came straight to me, told me I could be a star. I told her I'd been trying. She said with her, I wouldn't have to *try* anymore. And she was right. Six months later, it was day one on the shoot for *The Last Take*. We went *back*. She was like family to me."

"I'm sorry for your loss," Tobin says.

"Guy rants and raves, but he's thinking about the *now*. He's not thinking about the *then*, about where we came from, what we went through together back when we were in the trenches in LA. His anger comes from a professional place, not the personal. Don't take what he says to heart. We can get past this. We can pull through. We can find a way to fix things. It won't bring Jilly back to us – back to me – but it doesn't destroy everything we've worked toward, either."

"Aren't *you* angry?" Tobin says.

"Yes," Shannon says. "Very. But not at you. That would be a waste of my energy. I'm angry at the people who are ruining this for us. And I assume, from the way you were hitting that bag, that they're the same people *you're* angry at, too."

Tobin nods. She's staring into his eyes. Her gaze makes him feel uncomfortable, but not necessarily in a bad way. She hasn't seen him post-workout before. She hasn't seen him sweating, glistening, pumped with blood. He shifts his weight, foot to foot. Shannon's tongue briefly flickers out.

Tobin clears his throat. "Do you know if Brad has arrived?" he says, needing to make an excuse, to extricate himself from this situation before something could happen that they'll both regret.

Shannon nods, her eyes never leaving his. "He's out in the shed, with the others." The shed. The hot building where the computers are always running.

"I'd better go see him."

"Looking like that?" Shannon grins.

"After I shower."

She smiles with the corner of her mouth. "Do you need someone to get your back?"

Tobin stands frozen on the spot. He has to clear his throat again. The sweat is dripping from his body still, pooling on the ground at his feet. "I'm not sure how Guy would feel about that."

"I could always invite him to join us."

Tobin says nothing. He's not sure what he can say.

Shannon steps closer to him. Tobin forces himself to stand still. She trails the back of a fingertip up his torso, starting in the middle of his abs, up between his pecs, along his throat and to the tip of his chin. "Maybe Guy *would* get jealous," she says, her voice soft and low. "It's been a long time since *he* kept things so tight."

"I should really shower," Tobin says. "I have work to do."

Shannon smiles. "Of course," she says. "Don't let me keep you."

Tobin steps around her. Shannon stays right where she is. She speaks up before he leaves. "I've seen how you look at me, Tobin," she says. "It hasn't gone unnoticed. Not by me, at least." Tobin doesn't look back as he leaves the gym. He can't. If he does, and she's still watching, he's not sure he'd be able to stop himself from going back to her, and that would be a fucking disaster right now, combined with everything else going on.

He runs the shower cold, dulling his inflamed passions. He tries not to think about Shannon. About her implications. About all that she said. It's difficult, of course. After years of admiring her from afar, and then having to force himself to walk away while she admired him up close.

It's not a long shower. The cold water helps. He dries himself, dresses, and heads out to the shed. Brad is outside when he reaches the door, and Tobin is glad he won't have to go inside. It's already a hot enough day.

Brad leans in the doorway, smoking a cigarette, wafting himself with his spare hand. He's a short man, thick around the middle, balding on top. He has a goatee that he trims so short it's barely an outline around his mouth. He sees Tobin approaching. "Jesus Christ, it's like a fucking sauna in there," he says, tilting his head back toward the building. "This is exactly why I work from home. Why've I gotta come all the way out here? I do my best work at my own place."

"Because we're all safer here, together," Tobin says. "We've already lost people. We can't afford to lose more. And you're valuable, Brad. You and your whole team."

"That serious, huh?" Brad says, sucking hard on his cigarette, the tip flaring.

"Unfortunately," Tobin says.

"But this guy, this Rollins, is he really gonna come after someone as low level as me?"

"We're not running that risk. We don't know what they know about us, or who's a part of this. They could go after anyone, and they could do anything. You heard about Ricky, right? And Jilly?"

"It's all anyone can talk about in there," Brad says.

"Yeah, well, make sure they're doing more working than they are talking, or else they could end up like that, too. Where you at with Freddy's laptop?"

"Oh, I'm in," Brad says. "Piece of cake. I haven't gotten into his emails yet. Looks like he logged out after use, but that doesn't concern me. He seemed to be using pretty basic passwords, so it shouldn't be too much trouble."

"Then what are you doing out here?"

"Trying to avoid heatstroke."

"I'd say you've avoided it by this point," Tobin says. "I'm gonna need you to get back inside, Brad, and get into those emails."

Brad finishes his cigarette. "You're a real slave driver, you know that?"

"I only push people as hard as I push myself."

Brad looks him over. He pops a double bicep pose. His arms are flabby. He laughs and says, "Heh, no, thank you." He turns to head back into the hot, hot building.

"Come and get me as soon as you're done," Tobin says. "I'll be around."

37

It's dark when Tom gets back to the launderette. He's careful on the way, of course. Makes sure he isn't followed.

It's quiet and the night is cool. He calls ahead to let Cindy know he's almost there. "I'll look out for you," Cindy says, her voice low.

When Tom gets inside, he sees why she was almost whispering. Chris is asleep, curled up in the corner, facing the wall.

"How'd it go?" Cindy says.

"It's done," Tom says. He goes to the window and looks out at the road.

Cindy is standing close by. She reaches out and puts her hand on his arm. "You good?"

Tom nods. "I'm good." He looks at her. "How about you? Things have been nonstop since I arrived. We haven't really had much time to check in."

"Ah, y'know," Cindy says. "Other than the current, can't

complain. Except, that's not true. Someone broke into my apartment. *Again*. So I guess I have a lot to complain about."

"Are you going to move again?"

"I don't know, maybe." She sighs. "Let's see how we get on here, first. Make sure I'm still alive come the end of it – cos if not, I won't have to worry about it. Or maybe I'll just come and join you on the road. It couldn't be any less dangerous, huh?"

"You'd be surprised," Tom says. He pauses a beat, then adds, "But you're always welcome to join me."

Cindy looks at him. "Are you getting lonely out there?"

"I'm never lonely," Tom says. "But sometimes I miss certain people. You're one of them."

"I hope I'm high on that list." She grins.

Tom doesn't. He nods. "Could be you're at the top."

"The top, huh? What an honour." She pauses. "What about Alejandra?"

"I'll always miss her," Tom says. "The difference is, I know I'll never see her again."

"Well, you've got that picture of us now," Cindy says. "So any time you're missing me too bad, you can always remind yourself of my face."

"A picture's a pale substitute."

They stare at each other. It's a long moment. Cindy looks down, as if realising her hand is still on his arm. She doesn't take it back. She locks eyes with him again.

Behind them, Chris snorts in his sleep, and rolls over onto his other side in an effort to get comfortable.

Cindy shakes her head as if snapping out of a spell. She takes her hand back. "I've been trying to find the Kennedys," she says.

Tom notices that her eyes are bloodshot, the skin around

them pinched, as if she's spent most of the evening and night staring at a screen. "Any luck?"

"They're listed as living in LA," Cindy says. "No record of them ever having lived in or around Lubbock, or of owning property in the area. And not just Lubbock – the whole of Texas. If they *are* around here, it's like I've suspected and they must've used a shell corporation to buy up their property. I'm going to keep looking, though. I want to know for sure that they're not in the area before we go traipsing off across the country to LA in search of them."

"You should get some rest first," Tom says. "Come at it with fresh eyes. I'll take first watch."

"You sure? You've travelled a long way on foot."

"And I'm still wired from it." He places a hand on her shoulder. "Go sleep," he says. "I'll wake you in a few hours."

Absently, looking at him, she strokes the back of his hand on her shoulder. Then, slowly, she nods. "Okay," she says. She steps forward, closer to him, a hand on his chest, then she stops and looks back at Chris, still sleeping. She stops herself from going any further, forces herself to smile at Tom, and then she goes and finds a spot to lie down.

Tom turns back to the boarded window, the feel of where her hand was upon his chest still warm through his shirt. Where she stroked the back of his hand tingles. Tom grits his teeth. He forces himself to stare through the gap in the board. It's quiet out there. He's certain no one knows where they are.

He turns to Cindy. She's already asleep.

38

It's the morning. Tom let Cindy sleep through. He woke Chris to take over on watch and Tom got a few hours. They're all awake now. Cindy has gotten straight onto her laptop.

Tom leaves the launderette and sweeps the block. He takes an early morning run, too, watching the vehicles and other buildings as he goes. He remains confident that they haven't been tracked.

The jog gives him time to think.

Tom is confident that Cindy will track down the Kennedys. All it will take is some time. If they're close to Lubbock, which is the most likely outcome, that's ideal. But even if they're all the way out in LA, then they'll go there. It won't be the first time Tom and Cindy have hit LA. And for what these sick bastards are doing, Tom will go anywhere to shut them down permanently.

They'll shut down what the Kennedys are doing no matter what. But the main concern is Louise. The main question is, is she still living? Are they doing all of this to rescue her, or at this point are they seeking revenge?

Tom runs, and ponders the possibility of her still being alive. He knows it's a slim chance. He's known since they started this whole endeavour. Three weeks is a long time, and since then it's only been longer.

Tom hopes, for Chris's sake, that Louise is still alive. Chris nearly lost his eyes for her. He's been a part of things he never expected to. There needs to be a light at the end of the tunnel for him.

39

Cindy is on her laptop, continuing her search. Chris stands by the window. He yawns and covers his mouth with the back of his hand.

Cindy rubs at her eyes. She's spent a long time staring at her screen. She watches Chris. He picks absently at the peeling edge of a butterfly bandage. Cindy wants to say something, to tell him that it'll all be over soon. To tell him that he'll be okay while he's here on his own, that it's the safest thing for him.

She doesn't say anything. Chris isn't concerned about his own safety. No matter how long he's going to have to wait here, it'll be *too* long.

Cindy gets a message. She looks at her laptop.

It's from Freddy Bliss.

Cindy frowns. She doesn't open it straight away. Freddy is dead. They know he's dead. What they don't know is if his laptop was taken. Or if his email account was hacked into. Whoever is messaging Cindy right now from Freddy's account, it can't be anything, or anyone, good.

Cindy glances at Chris. He's still looking out the window. He scratches his chest. Cindy reads the email preview. It says:

My name is Tobin Klinghoffer, but I suppose

It cuts out there.
At least he's not trying to lie about who he is.
Cindy runs a virus check on the message. She won't run the risk on opening the message and granting them access to her own account, to her own laptop. The email is clear. Cindy opens it.

My name is Tobin Klinghoffer, but I suppose you already know that. Freddy Bliss is dead – you probably know that, too. We need to talk.

A brief message. To the point. Cindy stares at it. Reads it over and over. She responds. She keeps her own reply brief and to the point.

So talk.

It doesn't take Tobin long to respond. He doesn't send a written message. Instead, he sends a phone number.
"Chris, I'm going to make a call," Cindy says.
Chris turns from the window. "Who to?"
"I need you to stay quiet," she says, dialling the number. "No matter what you might hear, don't say a word."
Chris steps closer to her. "What's happening?"
The phone rings only once. Tobin answers almost imme-

diately. "Cindy Vaughan," he says. "I've heard your name a lot. I'm glad we can finally speak."

"I can't say the same," Cindy says.

"Uh-huh. And is Tom Rollins there with you? And Chris Parton?"

"They're here," Cindy says. A half-truth. "What do you want?"

Chris stands close, listening in.

"Let's get straight to the point here, Cindy," Tobin says. "You're causing us problems. Noise. Now, we both know how this is going to go. Right now, you're a gnat. You understand that, right? You're a nuisance, nothing more. You're buzzing around our heads, but soon enough we're going to swat you down. There's too many of us. I know you're not stupid. What I'm saying makes sense. You probably already realise this yourselves. But we're willing to come to an arrangement. We can cut a deal."

"What kind of a deal?"

"Louise Parton," Tobin says.

Cindy sees how intense Chris's eyes become.

"She's still alive?" Cindy says.

"Of course," Tobin says. "You think I'd be calling you right now if she wasn't? We'd have nothing to talk about."

"What's your deal?"

"We give you Louise back, and we all go our separate ways. No more noise. You're a gnat that just flies away, never to be seen again, and in turn we won't crush you."

"Have you ever offered anyone this deal before?"

"We've never had anyone cause us these kinds of problems before."

Cindy waits a beat. Chris stares at her expectantly. "We'll

have to think about it," she says, holding up a finger to keep Chris from complaining.

"Don't take too long," Tobin says.

"And we'll need proof of life."

"Of course." Tobin hesitates. "Just be aware, Louise has incurred some...damage. You have this number. And to save you some time, this is a burner, and I'm calling away from any point of interest you may try to trace. I expect to hear back from you within an hour."

Cindy hangs up and starts dialling another number. She calls Tom. It doesn't take him long to answer. "I've heard from Tobin," Cindy says, and tells him what was discussed.

"I'm on my way," Tom says.

40

By the time Tom gets back to the launderette, there's an oppressive air in the room. Chris is pacing angrily, his jaw working, his eyes narrowed, and his fists balled furiously at his sides. Tom looks at Cindy. She chews her bottom lip in consternation, watching Chris. She looks up at Tom as he enters.

"We got proof of life," Cindy says.

"They've fucking *mutilated* her," Chris says, halting, spinning on them both.

Cindy holds up a hand, as much to hold him at bay as to calm him. "I know," she says. "I know. Just let me show Tom, and then we can decide what we do next."

Cindy's phone is already in her hand. She opens her messages and holds the picture out to Tom.

The image is dark. The subject of the picture – a blonde woman – is in a cage. She wears a tattered, stained white dress, or perhaps a hospital gown. It's hard to tell. She's holding up a newspaper. It has today's date and headline. An arm has reached through the bars and taken her jaw in its hand, turning her toward the camera. The right side of her face is badly burnt, almost beyond recognition. Tom inhales deeply through his nose, staring at the picture. He looks up at Chris. "This is her?" he says. He knows what Louise looks like, but with the burns and in the dark it makes it difficult to be sure.

Chris swallows. "It's her," he says. "They've tortured her, and they've disfigured her, but it's my sister." His breathing is ragged. He can't calm. He doesn't want to.

"Tobin wants me to call him back within an hour," Cindy says.

"How long is left?"

"Forty minutes," Cindy says. "You got back fast."

Tom stares at the picture. He sees the fear in Louise's one unscarred eye. It's a look that can't be faked. She knows her death is coming, and she isn't prepared for it.

"These wounds aren't fresh," Tom says. "These burns didn't happen recently. They've scarred over. The image is blurry, but you can see that they're not new."

"They're willing to give her back," Chris says. "We should call them."

"We're not rushing into anything," Tom says. "Can any of us really trust these people?"

"No, but –"

"You're thinking with your heart," Tom says. "You need to think with your head. We know she's alive now – she's hurt, but she's breathing. So that's a weight off all our minds. But next we need to consider the fact that they've reached out to us. That means they're scared. We're causing them problems."

"He said as much –" Chris says.

Again, Tom cuts him off. "They're going to give us Louise

back because we've created some noise for them and killed some of their people? And in return they expect us to back off and say nothing? They expect us to be okay with everything that they've done – and not just to your sister – *and* be okay with the fact they've burned her? Does that sound about right to you, Chris?"

"What are you saying?"

"I'm saying that this is a set-up," Tom says. "I'm saying that they're not interested in making any deal with us. They want us dead. They've figured out what we're coming for, and now they're trying to use that against us."

Chris grinds his teeth, exasperated, but he knows Tom is right. He paces again, doesn't speak for a couple of minutes. His brow furrows. Tom can see him thinking, trying to figure out what their best option is. Tom and Cindy exchange glances. Cindy reaches out and squeezes Tom's hand.

Finally, Chris stops. He rocks back and forth on his heels. He checks the time. Takes a deep breath and blows it back out. "So, *what*? What do we do? Do you have a plan?"

Tom has been thinking. He nods. "Let's say, on the slim chance, that they're true to their word and are going to give us Louise back and walk away, never bother us again in return for us never bothering *them* again. What about everyone else? Do we think Louise is the *only* person they're holding captive? Mandy didn't think so. But even if they were to follow through on what they promise, I'm not going to let them walk away unpunished."

Chris looks at Cindy. He doesn't say anything. Cindy nods. Something unspoken has passed between them. Tom doesn't know what it is, but it doesn't matter.

"We meet with them," Tom says. "We play along for now. I assume when I call Tobin back he's going to arrange a meeting point with us. I imagine it'll be a secluded area – they're not going to exchange a tortured woman in downtown Lubbock. I'll hold back, keep my distance. That Winchester from Fitzek will come in handy. I'll watch the area. The two of you go to the meeting point."

"You're taking me along?" Chris says.

"She's your sister. You'll know her best. We need to be sure they're not handing us a fake."

"But, the picture –"

"Just because she's alive doesn't mean they're going to bring her," Tom says.

"We'll need to get some ear pieces to keep in touch," Cindy says. "That won't take long. I know a place."

Tom nods. "If they attempt anything, I open up and you two get away – hopefully with Louise in tow. If not, if this is all nice and quiet and goes exactly as they say it will, then you keep driving and leave me behind. I'll follow them back where they came from. I'm not going to let them walk away."

"They'll ask about you," Chris says. "They know who we all are. If you're not there, they'll be suspicious."

"Then tell them the truth," Tom says. "I'm nearby. I'm watching. If they try anything stupid, they'll regret it."

"And what if they refuse to hand Louise over until you show yourself?"

"We don't budge on this," Tom says. "They hand her over and then we leave – that's your story, and you stick to that. They came to *us*. You remind them of that."

"All right," Chris says. "Okay." He's calmer now. His breathing has returned to normal. His brow is permanently knitted, but his pent-up frustrations have momentarily dissipated.

Tom checks the time.

"We're still early," Cindy says. "Do we want to keep him waiting, or do we want to get this over with?"

"I'll get it over with," Tom says, holding his hand out for the phone. He looks at Chris as Cindy gives it to him. "I need silence while I'm on the call."

"I know," Chris says. "I won't say a word." He's stepping closer so he can listen in.

Tom dials the number. It rings once and Tobin answers. "Nice and prompt," he says, "I like that. Didn't eat up the whole hour. Didn't waste my time. I assume you've had a chance to talk among yourselves? And I assume you've had a good chance to look at the proof of life we sent."

"We have," Tom says.

"Ah – let me guess," Tobin says. "Is this the famous Tom Rollins?"

"And this must be Tobin Klinghoffer," Tom says. "The failed cage fighter."

There's a pause at this, and Tom assumes he's wounded Tobin's vanity. "Failed?" he says. "I wouldn't say that. Sixteen wins, fourteen by knockout."

"And four losses," Tom says.

"That's an exemplary record," Tobin says, bristling.

"And yet you gave it all up," Tom says. "And you don't hear anyone talking about you anymore."

Tobin is silent.

"What was it you did after MMA again, Tobin?" Tom says, needling. "Bodyguard, is that right? What happened to all of your money?" He waits a beat. He already knows the answer. "Bad investments. It's a common story, right? There's nothing *exemplary* about you."

He hears Tobin breathing deeply, trying not to lose his cool. "Well," Tobin says. "This is quite an introduction, Tom

Rollins. And here I was thinking we were going to talk business."

"We are," Tom says. "We're not happy about the burns."

"I didn't expect you would be, but take her or leave her."

"And what if I choose to leave her?"

Tobin hesitates. He clearly wasn't expecting this response. "Then like I told your friend, you'll be crushed."

"We're not the ones looking for a compromise."

Another pause. Another hesitation. This isn't going how Tobin wanted or expected. Tom has backfooted him.

"How did she come to be burned?" Tom says.

"You spoke to Mandy, right?" Tobin says, trying to reclaim control of the situation.

Tom doesn't answer. He waits.

"She probably told you as much as she knew. So you have a fairly decent understanding of how things work here. A client wanted someone just like Louise. We procured her for them. They burned her. We realised we had a problem on our hands, and we talked them out of killing her. We had to refund a lot of money. They were satisfied, at least, with the damage that they got to do. You'd be amazed at how many people just want to destroy something beautiful." Tobin pauses, letting this sink in. "And how's Mandy now? I saw it made the news. You probably saw that, too. What a terrible, terrible accident." Tobin's tone is smirking. He's making it clear it was no accident. "We've both lost people in this little war, haven't we? And we both have so much more to lose. Except, in your case it's your friends and loved ones. For me, it's business associates – and believe me, Rollins, I have a *lot* of associates, and I don't mind throwing them at you."

"Uh-huh," Tom says. "I don't enjoy talking to you, Tobin,

so what do you say we wrap this up? We've already heard your terms and we're willing to accommodate them. All we need to know is where to meet."

"I'm glad you're seeing sense, Rollins," Tobin says. "When we terminate this call I'll send you coordinates. We meet there in ten hours."

"Ten hours?" Tom says. "Why so long?"

"Because we're not exchanging cakes, Rollins. It's still early in the day. An exchange like this, it doesn't happen under the midday sun."

"Then we have nothing left to discuss." Tom hangs up.

Tom glances at Cindy and Chris. They watch him. Tom looks at the phone. It buzzes. As promised, Tobin has sent through the coordinates.

"I'm going to go check it out," Tom says. "Get the ear pieces and then come straight back here. Make sure everything's ready. Ten hours and we move."

41

It's been a long ten hours for Tobin and his team. Their preparation didn't take too long. It made for a lot of waiting.

It's early evening. It's getting close to when they need to set off. Tobin waits outside by the all-terrain vehicles. There's two of them. He looks toward the shed. Brad is standing outside, smoking. He sees Tobin looking and raises a hand in a wave. Tobin returns it. He doesn't need to chase Brad back inside and back to work. Brad has done everything needed of him so far. He needs to remain on the compound for now. They all do. This should be resolved soon, and then people can start returning home.

Tobin's team approach, gathering around the vehicles in front of him. Tobin motions for them to come closer and listen up. The men are armed with FX5510 tactical rifles and Glocks. Tobin has a Glock. He won't be carrying a rifle. It'll be too cumbersome for what's going to happen. Besides, with eight of his men behind him, that's more than enough firepower.

"You all know what's happening here," Tobin says. "But we're going through it one more time. We need to be clear." He holds up a finger and raises his eyebrows. "No mistakes. So everyone listen up. I don't trust Rollins and the others. Despite what we discussed on the phone, this is not the end of things – for peace of mind, we need them captured, and we need them killed. But we can't expect them to be stupid. I doubt they think this handover is going to be straightforward, either.

"We split into two teams. Team A are with me. Team B hold back, stay out of view. When we arrive, if all three of our targets are present, Team B comes up and we take them. However, if they're being careful, if any of them are not present, Team B will hold back. We hand over the parcel and we pick them up later."

Tobin looks around at his men. They watch him intently, focussed on what they're soon going to do.

"We need to be careful," Tobin says. "Rollins is dangerous. Ideally, we want him captured, but don't take any unnecessary risks. If we have to put him down then and there, then so be it. Is everyone prepared?"

His men nod and voice that they are.

Tobin looks at his watch. "Five minutes," he says. "Everyone get ready to go."

42

Cindy gets to the coordinates early. Chris is with her in the Ford. They dropped Tom off a couple of miles back. He said he'd continue the rest of the way on foot, make sure that anyone approaching wouldn't see him coming.

The location is, as expected, in the middle of nowhere. Far outside the city, and just as far from any towns or farms. Nothing to see but scrubland in every direction, broken only by a boulder formation about a mile to the north. Cindy has a feeling this is where Tobin and his people will approach from. The boulders are why this location would have been chosen. It gives them cover. If they bring anyone else with them they can easily hide behind it.

Cindy and Chris are still in the car. Chris is squinting into the distance, looking for signs of approach. The sky is still blue above them, but it's dimming. The sun is slowly going down. "What do we do?" Chris says. "Stay in the car, or get out?"

"Inside, for now," Cindy says. "We're early. We'll get out when we see them coming."

Chris sits back. "Have you heard from Tom yet?"

Cindy shakes her head. She wears a flesh-coloured earpiece in her left ear, her hair hanging down to further hide it. Chris doesn't have one. He doesn't need one. Cindy and Tom have done this before, many times now. They trust each other implicitly. Neither of them needs to train the other.

They wait. Five minutes pass. It's still another twenty before they hit on ten hours exactly. Cindy remains calm, keeping her breathing level. Chris tries his best to do the same. She can see his jaw clenching, causing muscles to dance in his cheeks. He stares straight ahead, at the horizon and the boulder formation.

Tom contacts her through the earpiece. "I'm in position," he says.

She motions to Chris that Tom is in touch. "Where are you?" she says, looking back.

"Do you see the bushes about five hundred yards behind you, to the east?"

"I see them."

"I'm here."

"I don't see you."

"That's good."

"I thought you'd like to know." She can imagine Tom grinning at this. "Do you see anything with that scope of yours?"

"Not yet, but I'll let you know if that changes."

"Do you see those boulders?"

"I see them, and I don't like them."

"It looks like they're taking it all the way down to the wire, time-wise."

"Tobin strikes me as the kind of man who'll leave it until the last minute, despite this being his timeframe."

"Fashionably late. He's from Hollywood, after all."

"That, or just trying to be a prick."

They fall silent. They're all watching. All waiting.

"What if they don't turn up?" Chris says.

"They don't have anything to gain from standing us up," Cindy says. "It's not going to help them find us."

Chris nods, though he looks like he's still pondering this possibility.

The minutes pass. The twenty minutes go by. Another five. Tobin is now late. The sky is much darker. It's harder to see into the distance.

Chris checks the time repeatedly. He's very aware that Tobin is leaving them in the lurch.

"I have visual," Tom says.

"I don't see anything," Cindy says.

"Inbound from the north, still distant right now, kicking up dust that could potentially be concealing another vehicle. I'll know for sure when they get closer. They're on the way to you. Another few minutes, they'll be with you."

"Got it," Cindy says. She taps Chris on the thigh. They get out of the car.

43

Tom watches through the Winchester scope. He lies flat in the scrub, concealed by a bush. He's directly under it, poking the rifle through its branches. He has an M4 with him, too, in case things get dangerous. Cindy and Chris both have Sig Sauers, but hopefully they won't have to use them. Tom has them covered.

He sees the vehicles drawing closer, heading toward the boulder formation. Tom soon sees why they're heading that way. There are two of them. Modified SUVs with all-terrain tyres. One of them peels off toward the boulders. The other continues on straight, toward Cindy and Chris. It slows as it gets nearer to them.

Cindy and Chris are out of the car, standing in front of it, waiting. The SUV has slowed to a crawl. Its windows are blacked out. Tom can't see inside. He keeps both eyes open, his right looking through the scope. His finger is close to the trigger. He's ready if they try anything.

The front passenger door of the SUV opens. Tobin Klinghoffer steps out. Hearing he's six foot five is one thing, but seeing him in comparison to others is another. He could be taller. He looks around the area before his eyes finally settle on Cindy and Chris. Tom can see his lips moving. He hears Cindy's response in his ear.

"He's close," Cindy says. "He's making sure this goes down how it's supposed to."

Tobin smirks at this. There's some more back and forth. No one else gets out of the SUV. Tom looks toward the other, parked behind the boulders. He doesn't think it's trying to hide. It's just holding back. Its engine is still running. Tom can see the fumes rising from its exhaust. Its windows, too, are blacked out.

Tobin turns and slaps the flat of his hand against the rear door of the SUV. The handover is about to happen.

"Let's take this slowly," Cindy says as the rear door of the SUV opens. "I can see your guys in there, and I can see that they're packing." Tom knows that this is for his benefit. "None of us want this to turn ugly."

Tobin says something with a smile. Presumably reassuring.

One of his men gets out of the back. Tom sees he's armed with an FX5510. He keeps it pointed at the ground. He reaches into the back of the SUV and pulls someone out.

It's a woman. She's not in a dress or hospital gown like Louise was in the proof of life picture. Instead, she's wearing jeans and a top. Chris doesn't seem thrown by this outfit change – presumably he's seen these clothes before. They must belong to his sister. Perhaps what she was wearing the night she was taken. They're torn and there's bloodstains on them, which are especially easy to see on the jeans.

Her head, however, is covered by a towel. The woman steps forward tentatively, held up by the man who has pulled her out of the SUV. Tom watches. He doesn't like that he can't see her face.

"We need to see her face," Cindy says. "This could be anyone."

Tobin says something. Tom's able to read the last word from his lips – *burns*. Then, he turns to the man holding onto the woman's arm. The man hurries her forward. He pushes her toward Chris, who has to catch her to stop her from falling. The woman is shaking, traumatised. She buries her face into Chris's chest, shaking, her fists holding onto the front of his shirt.

Tobin points at the car and motions for them to get out of here.

"After you," Cindy says.

There's a lot going on. Almost too much for Tom to take in. Chris places his hands firmly on the woman's shoulders. He's frowning. Gently, he forces her off him, holds her away from himself. Keeping her at distance, he peels the towel from her face. His eyes instantly narrow.

Tom doesn't need to be told what's wrong. "It's not her," he says to Cindy. He opens fire, his first bullet catching the man who was manhandling the mystery woman. Tobin instantly throws himself to the ground. "Grab her and get out of there," Tom says.

He fires again, this time into the centre of the SUV's windshield. Cindy and Chris duck low and hurry back into the Ford, bringing the woman with them. Chris gets into the backseat with her. Cindy dives behind the steering wheel.

Men are getting out of the SUV. Tom gets the driver, catching him between the eyes. He lays down further fire to keep them ducking behind cover as Cindy peels away.

Tom spots Tobin on the ground still after the Ford

moves, still flat, crawling behind the cover of the SUV. Tom aims for the tyres, crippling the vehicle.

"I'm on my way to you," Cindy says.

The other SUV is speeding onto the scene. Tom drops the Winchester and grabs the M4 lying next to him. He pushes his way clear of the bush and opens up on the SUV as Cindy circles toward him. He hits the tyres and the front of the SUV. The driver loses control. The SUV tilts onto its side as the driver tries to bring it under control. It flips, rolling onto its roof. Tom puts a few more bullets into it.

The Ford skids to a halt beside him. Tom jumps into the passenger seat. He looks back through the rear window, toward the two SUVs. They aren't following. They can't. The survivors from the first vehicle are hurrying over to the other on its roof.

Tom moves his focus from the window to the woman. She looks back at him with scared doe eyes. The right side of her face is burnt, just like Louise's was in the picture. Unlike Louise, however, she still has both of her eyes. Her shoulders are trembling. Her shaking fists are balled on her thighs.

Tom turns back around. "Get us out of here," he says to Cindy.

"The girl?" Cindy says.

"We'll find out who she is," Tom says. "And if there's anything worthwhile she can tell us."

44

They take the mystery woman back to the launderette. She's shaking and crying. She can't speak.

"We need to check her for a tracker," Tom says as Cindy parks the car at the back of the building. He would've liked to have checked her earlier than now, but they needed to get clear, to make sure no one was following them. If he finds a tracker on her, they dump it here and keep moving with the woman, find a new safe spot and ask her some questions. "I don't know if she was just supposed to be a distraction for us out there, or if they're using her to find us."

"The picture of Louise," Chris says, leaning into the front, "the proof of life...was it faked?"

"I don't know," Cindy says. "It didn't look fake at first glance, but sometimes it takes a more in-depth search."

Chris goes silent. He swallows.

They take the woman into the launderette. Tom pats her down while Cindy tells Chris to go to the window and keep watch. Tom doesn't find anything. The woman stands very still the whole time, crying, trying not to make eye contact with anyone. She's like a beaten dog. She's too scared to move or make a sound.

"We need you to talk to us," Cindy says. "We're not going to hurt you, okay? Whatever happened to you, it's over now."

The woman inhales, and the breath shudders in her neck and chest.

"What's your name?" Tom says. "Can you tell us that?"

She swallows. Blinking, she manages to look at him briefly. "It's – it's Annie," she says, her voice quiet and strained, sounding like her throat is dry.

"How long did they have you for, Annie?" Cindy says.

"I – I – I don't know... I don't know..." She sobs.

"That's okay," Cindy says. "Do you need to take a seat?"

She looks down and shakes her head. "No," she says, very quietly. "I don't need to sit."

"Do you know someone called Louise Parton?" Tom says. At this, Chris turns away from the window.

Annie shakes her head. "I've heard her name," she says. "But I don't know who she is. We never met. I never saw anyone else. Just the – just the men, and, and – oh, *God*..." She covers her face with her hands, her body wracked with her tears.

"What did you hear about her?" Cindy says. "About Louise?"

It takes a moment for Annie to calm herself. She sucks down air, trying to regain her composure. "Just that – just that we were the same height and build. And that we both had this..." She points at the scarring on the right side of her face. "There weren't...there weren't any mirrors... How – how bad is it?"

Cindy's face is sympathetic. "It might not be as bad as you think."

"Why am I here?" Annie says.

"You were supposed to be someone else," Tom says.

"Oh," Annie says. It looks like everything is starting to make sense to her now.

"Do you know if Louise is still alive?" Chris says.

"I don't know," Annie says. "I'm sorry. But – but if they wanted to use me as a double, then maybe…" She trails off. She doesn't need to say it. They all know what she's thinking. "I just don't know why they would try to use me."

"Those are her clothes," Chris says.

Annie looks down at them. "I'm sorry," she says.

"What else did they say to you, Annie?" Cindy says.

"They said…they said that if I stayed quiet and played along, they'd let me go free."

Tom and Cindy look at each other. They glance at Chris. He's still by the window, but he's not keeping watch. All of his attention is on Annie. Tom motions for him to step away and he takes his place. It's clear outside. Tom listens to what is being said behind him.

"Annie, do you know where they were keeping you?" Cindy says.

"No – I was drugged when they took me there, and it felt like I was always in darkness. Then today, when they drove me away, there was a towel over my head. They didn't want me to see."

"Did you see anything at all before they put the towel on you? Anything that you would recognise if you saw it again?"

"I don't know," Annie says. "Maybe…maybe I was on a farm? It was hard to tell."

"Okay, that's good, that's something we can work with. Anything else? Anything at all?"

"I – I – There's nothing else, I'm sorry." She starts to cry again.

There's nothing outside. Tom turns back around. He sees Annie still standing, her hands over her face while her body convulses. Cindy looks like she wants to comfort her, but Annie has been through a lot. She's clearly been tortured. She's going to have PTSD. After all she's been through, they can't know if she wants to be touched. She'd have to make the first move on that.

She lowers her hands. Tears are rolling down her cheeks. She sniffs. "I think I'd like to take a seat now."

Tom's eyes narrow, staring at the right side of Annie's face. At her scarring. Something doesn't look right about it. He steps away from the window, closer to her. Cindy and Chris don't seem to have noticed.

"Of course," Cindy says. "We don't have any chairs, but you can just slide down onto the floor there."

"Hold up," Tom says.

Everyone looks at him. Annie does not sit.

Tom looks at her. His eyes remain narrowed.

"What's wrong?" Chris says. "Tom?"

Cindy doesn't say anything. She can pick up that he's noticed something. She doesn't question him.

Annie stares back at Tom. She's making eye contact now. "What?" she says, her voice shaky. "What is it?"

"I think you've overdone the crying," Tom says, reaching out.

She flinches, but she doesn't move back out of range of his reach. She knows there's nowhere for her to go.

High on her cheek, her scars are loose. Tom peels a strip off. Prosthetics. The skin underneath is pink, but it's fine. Tom holds the strip in front of Annie's face.

She looks at the piece of scarring, then at Cindy and Chris. They're looking at her differently now.

Annie starts to laugh.

45

'Annie' holds up her hands and shrugs, very *Aw, shucks*. "I've always been able to cry on demand," she says, her eyes still shining. She starts peeling off the rest of the prosthetics. "Makes me wonder why I ever gave up acting."

Knowing that the scars are fake, Tom can see past them now. In all of the pictures he's seen of her before this point, the pictures that Cindy has shown him, she's been dressed up. Very glamourous. Every inch the movie star. "Shannon Kennedy," he says.

She grins. "Pleased to make your acquaintance." She's unconcerned.

"Where's the tracker?" Tom says.

"What, you couldn't find it?" Shannon says, mocking. "I've heard so many things about you, Rollins. I keep waiting to be impressed. Although," she holds up a finger, "I *do* have to admit, I *was* impressed by that shooting back there."

Tom doesn't have the patience, and they don't have the time. He grabs her by the throat and pushes her up against the wall, sticking the Sig Sauer into her face. "Where's the fucking tracker?"

Shannon still appears unconcerned. She reaches into her pocket and holds it up. "Hard to find something when it's hidden in my hand, right?" She grins and winks at him. "Maybe I should try my hand at being a magician. What do you think?"

"We need to go," Tom says. "Right now."

"It's already too late," Shannon says.

Cindy goes to the window. "I see someone coming," she says. "A few vehicles, and they're coming *fast*."

Tom lets go of Shannon's neck. There's no time to bind and take her. Leaving her loose she'd be more of a danger to them in the vehicle, during the chase. "Let's go," Tom says, keeping Shannon covered with the gun. He waits for Cindy and Chris to get outside.

Shannon smiles at him. "Admittedly, you weren't supposed to realise so soon. So what happens to me? Are you going to put a bullet through my head? Ever so chivalrous."

Tom fires the gun around her head, tearing chunks out of the wall. She flinches, her eyes widen, but she manages to stand her ground. "Maybe I will," Tom says. "But that'll come later, when we have more time."

Tom leaves her behind, getting into the car. He pulls on the handbrake and spins it around and speeds from the launderette.

46

Tobin sees the Ford fleeing from the abandoned building.

"Floor it," he says. "We ain't losing them again."

Carter is driving. "Did you see them leave? There was three of them. No Shannon."

"I saw," Tobin says. He holds onto the handle above his head as the car jostles, mounting the pavement in their pursuit. Tobin pulls out his cell, calls Donkin. "Pull back – get into that launderette and see if Shannon is there." He hangs up before there's a response.

He watches the mirror and sees Donkin's vehicle peeling off from the convoy, heading to the abandoned launderette. There's still another car behind them, keeping pace. Three of them came here, following Shannon's tracker. All three vehicles are full. They collected Tobin and the others from the wilds after the brief shootout with Rollins.

"We need to end this," Tobin says. "This is a quiet area – if we're gonna make noise, it has to be now. Get me closer."

"I'm going as fast as I can," Carter says.

"Is your foot flat?" Tobin says. "You're not going as fast as you can – you're holding out because you're scared of the bends. Do they look scared to you? Don't be such a fucking pussy, Carter – fucking *jam* it."

Carter grits his teeth and does as he's told. Tobin pulls out his Glock. He puts down his window. It's late and it's dark, and the whole area is quiet and largely abandoned. If Tobin is going to fire, now has to be the time.

He leans out of the window and opens up, aiming for the rear tyres. He'd never fired a gun before he started as a bodyguard. Guns have never been his forte. His fists and his feet have always been his weapons of choice. Of course, they aren't always an option, especially at a distance. Tobin visits the shooting range once a month. He practises. His aim isn't perfect, but it's acceptable.

He's halfway through the magazine before he finally connects with the passenger side wheel. The Ford skids, scraping along the road, kicking up sparks. It causes the car to slow. Tobin has a clearer shot at the other wheel. He blows it out.

The Ford is out of control. It clips the nearest kerb and teeters over onto its side. It begins to roll. The side mirrors are smashed. The front and rear windows crunch and shatter. The Ford rolls off the road.

Tobin slips back into the car. "Stop driving – stop fucking driving!"

Carter slams on the brakes. The car behind does the same. The men jump out, FX55I0s raised, covering the car. It's come to a stop on its roof.

Tobin can see Cindy in the front passenger seat. She's dangling upside down, held in place by her seatbelt. She's unconscious. There's blood dripping from her temple. Tobin reaches in and drags her from the shattered window.

On the other side of the car, from the driver's door, Rollins has pushed his way clear. He's clearly dazed. There's blood running down his face, too. He reaches back into his waistband and pulls out a handgun, blinking blood from his eyes.

"Drop it, Rollins," Tobin says, holding Cindy in front of himself, a human shield. She's a dead weight, but she's light and easy to keep in place. Tobin presses his Glock to her head. "Drop it or I'll kill her."

Rollins sees him. He sees Cindy. He looks around at the other guns pointed his way. He drops the Sig Sauer. Tobin steps closer to him. He drops Cindy, letting her land on the ground. Rollins watches her fall. Tobin cracks him in the side of the head with the handle of the Glock. Rollins falls to his knees, bleeding from a fresh wound in the side of his skull. Tobin hits him again and he drops onto his side.

Tobin feels elation running through him, but he keeps it under control. "All right, grab them," he says to his men. He points at the Ford on its roof. "And don't forget the brother. Get everything out of the car that might be important. Anything that might contain ID. Move, move, move – let's get out of here ASAP."

47

Tom feels himself drifting in and out of consciousness, his body aching, everything catching up to him, unable to compartmentalise anymore.

Eyes flickering, he looks up, sees three men sitting above him, their boots upon him, holding him down into place. His vision is blurry, unclear, but his eyes drift enough for him to see that he's in the back of a car, stuffed into the footwell.

Blood is dried and flaking upon his face and the side of his head. He feels it matting in his hair, and making his skin tight. Tom blinks and braces himself, allowing his brain and body to calm and reconstitute themselves.

Tom feels the motion of the car. He hears the passage of the road beneath them. He tries to move and finds his wrists and ankles tightly bound – so tight that the tips of his fingers are tingling. Tom raises his head, though his brain swims and aches. He vaguely remembers the crash, and then seeing Cindy held captive by Tobin. Then? Then he had to give up his gun, and in turn Tobin hit him with his own.

And now here. How long has passed? Tom raises his head a little higher.

The man above him has been watching his movements. He's smiling. There's no mirth in it – only malice. He holds a Glock. He presses its barrel into the centre of Tom's forehead.

"Just go ahead and lie back down," he says.

Tom does. There's nothing else he can do in this confined space.

There's no sign of Cindy or Chris. He doesn't recognise the three men above him. He can't turn enough to see who is in the front of the car. He's going to have to lie back and wait.

"Not long now," the man pointing the gun at him says, as if reading his thoughts. "We're nearly there."

The constant rumble and thrum of the road beneath him changes as the car slows. Tom feels himself jostled, bouncing. The car has gone off-road. Beneath him there is crunching and grinding now.

The three men above brace themselves against their handles and the roof. They press their boots down firmer onto Tom to hold him into place as the car picks up speed and he bounces with it.

Tom closes his eyes and tries not to throw up. He clenches his jaw and breathes deeply in and out through his nose. Eventually – he loses track of the time – the car slows once again and, gradually, the journey comes to an end. The men in the front of the car get out first, and then the three from the back. They're not gentle with Tom's body. They stamp on him as they climb out.

From the passenger side of the vehicle, they cut the binds on his ankles and then drag him out by his legs and dump him hard on the ground. He's hauled roughly back up to his feet, a gun pressed into his skull.

Tom looks around, taking in the area. A compound, out in the middle of nowhere. It looks like it used to be a farm, once.

Tom sees Cindy and Chris, similarly bound, being pushed ahead of him. Both are unsteady on their feet, struggling to walk in straight lines. Off to his left, he sees Tobin. Shannon is beside him. She's peeling the last few pieces of stubborn prosthetics from her face. She grins at Tom.

"You didn't get very far," she says.

Tom spits at her. She's distant, and it lands far from her feet, but the intent is clear.

The gun at his skull is raised and cracks him across the back of the head, hard enough to hurt but not to knock him back into unconsciousness. He's pushed forward.

Behind him, he hears Shannon laughing. "Oh, he's feisty," she says. "We're going to have a lot of fun with him."

Tom is pushed ahead, surrounded on all sides, a gun pressed into him and others pointed at him. They're leading him toward the barn at the back of the property. Cindy and Chris reach it before him. They're pushed inside, through the open entryway.

Tom sees inside. Rows of cells on each opposing side of the building, most of them filled with people, dozens of them individually caged. Armed guards are at both ends of the barn, the large doors left open to let the air circulate. There's no one out here to hear the moans and sobs, or even screams, of the prisoners.

Cindy and Chris are thrown into two cells. The cells look like they would be used for large wild animals, but they've had bars inserted down the middle so they can hold more people. It's one person to a cell. Tom is forced into the one next to Cindy. The door is slammed shut after him and locked. The binds are cut from his wrists and he's forced toward the rear of the cage under threat of a cattle prod.

The man who held the gun on Tom stands close to the bars, smirking at him. "Y'know, you've killed a few of my buddies," he says. "I'd be happy to just watch you rot in this cage. It's the best place for a wild animal like you." He looks the cell over. "But I think you're gonna suffer well enough with what's planned." He winks at Tom and walks away with the rest of the transport team, only the guards left behind.

48

Tobin accompanies Shannon on her way back to the main house and her reunion with Guy. She throws herself into Guy's arms, laughing.

"How'd it go?" Guy says, stroking the red marks on her right cheek where the prosthetics have been removed.

"I overdid it a little with the crying," Shannon says, then kisses him. "It made the make-up start to peel, and Rollins noticed. Still – we *got them*!" She laughs again. "We got them, all three of them. They're ours. We can do whatever we want with them."

Guy is smiling, too. He's happy. He's finally happy.

Tobin feels some elation too, that they've finally captured Rollins and the others and put an end to their disruptive campaign. His elation, however, is somewhat dulled at the sight of Shannon in her husband's arms, the two of them smothering each other with kisses.

He clears his throat to get their attention. They turn slightly to look at him, but they don't let go of each other.

Shannon is looking at him with the same *Fuck me* eyes she was giving him out at the gym.

"You did well, Tobin," Guy says. "I wasn't happy about putting my wife in the line of danger, but it worked out."

"I didn't want Shannon out there either, but her build is so similar to Louise's," Tobin says. "She was our best, most believable option. Plus, it's not like we have many other women we could call on. In the end, Shannon is fine, and it all worked out in our favour." He pauses, then adds, "We have the prisoners out at the barn now. We've got them caged. What do you want me to do with them?"

"They're going into the labyrinth," Guy says.

"Until then."

"Keep them alive," Guy says. "From what I've heard about Rollins, I'm expecting he's going to put on a hell of a show for us. We need to drum up interest in this. Get some pictures and pass them onto our online team. They can do the rest. The incident out in San Francisco is still fresh in people's minds, too. That should help."

"We shouldn't take our time with this," Tobin says. "This Rollins, we don't want to keep him alive for too long. He's already caused us enough problems."

Guys nods and waves a dismissive hand. "Yes, yes. He's in the cage now. He's under guard. There's nothing he can do from there."

"I don't want to run that risk."

"Then it's up to you to watch him closely," Guy says, holding eyes with Tobin. "You did your job and you got him here, but your job isn't over yet."

Tobin nods. It's clear they're not taking his concerns as seriously as he'd like. "I'll go and get the pictures," he says. "And get the team to put the word out."

"We're expecting a big payday for this," Shannon says.

Guy grunts his agreement. "We need to make something back for the losses we've taken so far. Make sure Brad and the others know that."

"Right," Tobin says, taking his leave. Shannon and Guy are back at each other. He grits his teeth and leaves them to it.

49

Shannon kisses Guy and then pulls back to look at him. He grins. "It's over," he says. "We've got them. The problems are dealt with, and now we're going to make a hell of a lot of money from them." Guy studies her, and his smile fades a little. He cocks his head. "What's wrong?"

"I'm just thinking about Jilly," Shannon says.

"I know, I know, I get it. I miss her, too."

Shannon separates herself from him and goes to the sofa. She runs her fingers through her stringy hair. Since Tobin told them his plan, she hasn't washed it. She kept putting her hands through it to make it messy and greasy, to make it look believably like she'd been held captive. Her right cheek is still sticky where the prosthetics were. "I need a shower," she says.

"There's plenty of time," Guy says. "You don't need to change the topic. Do you want to talk more about Jilly?"

Shannon says nothing.

"We're going to have to find a replacement for her," Guy

says. "Someone else who can marshal our contacts and find our future stars."

Shannon frowns. "*Jilly* can't be replaced," she says.

"You know that's not what I mean."

Shannon falls silent.

Guy watches her, feeling like he may have said something wrong. "I didn't mean to be insensitive," he says. "I know how much she meant to you. She meant a lot to me, too. But we can't wallow in the past. We have to look to the future."

Shannon stares at him. "Do you really think that fixes what you said?"

Guy hesitates. "I suppose not. It maybe wasn't the best thing to say." He presses his thumb into his bottom lip. "I do have something you might like, though."

"What's that?"

Guy is smiling now. "Well," he says. "What has caused us all these problems to begin with? Or should I say, *who?*"

Shannon doesn't understand.

Guy wriggles his eyebrows and rolls his hands, trying to prompt her. "We have her brother in captivity right now."

"Oh," Shannon says. "Louise?"

Guy clicks his fingers. "Bingo."

"What about her?"

Guy holds out a hand for her. She takes it and he pulls her to her feet. He leads her through into their bedroom at the rear of the house.

And then Shannon sees. Louise Parton has been taken from her cage. She's been brought into the house. She's been cleaned up and put into a freshly washed white dress. She's in the corner of their bedroom, her wrists shackled, chained to the floor. Her mouth is gagged.

Shannon smiles and goes to her. Louise recoils from her touch, but there's only so far she can go. Shannon reaches out and strokes the right side of her face. There are no scars there. No burns. Just like Shannon, she was wearing prosthetics. They were all for the picture. All for the disguise.

"You're so very pretty once you've been cleaned up, aren't you?" Shannon says.

Louise can't respond through the gag. The skin around her eyes is red and raw from her tears. There are wounds upon her arms and legs. Cuts and scrapes. All superficial. They'll all fade and heal, given enough time. She won't get that time, though. She'll likely be dead before they can heal.

"You know, Guy," Shannon says, straightening and backing up, still staring at Louise. "You're right. This *does* make me feel better."

Guy is close behind her. He wraps his arms around her and kisses the back of her neck. "I thought it might. How desperate are you for that shower?"

Shannon places her hands upon his arms. "It can wait," she says, turning to him, her face close to his. "Especially since I think I'm about to get a whole lot filthier." They kiss. Guy slips his tongue into her mouth. She presses her body close to his. They go to the bed.

In the corner, Louise looks away. Guy notices. "Hey – *hey*!" he says, getting her attention, forcing her to turn back to them. "Eyes on us. *Hey*! Eyes on us. You look away, I'll take your fucking eyes out, you hear me? I'll scrape them out with my goddamn fingernails."

Louise watches. She has no other choice.

50

Tom wakes. Since they were caged with nowhere to go, and it was getting late, he figured he might as well catch up on his rest.

It's getting light outside the barn. The sun has come up. It's getting warm. The barn doors, front and back, are wide open, but there's no breeze. In the better light, Tom looks around at the other people in the cages. They're beaten, bruised, in some cases bloodied. Their clothes are filthy and tattered. They're broken. They either press themselves deep into the corners of their cells, like wild animals, or else they sit slumped on the ground, already defeated, awaiting the inevitable.

Last night, after their escort had left, Chris called out for his sister.

"Louise! Louise Parton! Is Louise Parton here?" Some of the other captives looked back at him blankly. Others acted like they didn't hear. "Does anyone here know Louise Parton? Has anyone seen her?"

A small voice called back from the other side of the barn,

down toward the rear door. "I know her," the voice, a woman's, said. "She was next to me."

Chris pressed himself against the bars. "Where is she now? Is she still alive?"

"I don't know," the voice replied. "They took her away maybe two days ago."

Someone else spoke up. A man, closer, opposite them. "When people get taken, they don't usually come back."

Chris sank back, deflated. He ran his hands through his hair, lacing them behind his neck, staring at the ground.

"Where did they take her?" Tom said. "Did you see?"

The man didn't answer. He didn't say anything more. No one did.

Chris hasn't moved since then. Tom looks through the bars of the cells toward him now. He's sitting at the back of his cell, head lowered, arms dangling useless between his legs, the backs of his hands flat on the ground. He's unmoving, but he doesn't look like he's asleep. Tom doubts he's slept at all.

Cindy is in the cage between them. She's curled on the ground, still unconscious. Tom doesn't disturb her. He looks around the barn. He spots security cameras dotted around the ceiling, covering every spot of the room. All of the cages are covered. The entrance and exit are covered. Tom spots the armed guards there too, occasionally strolling back and forth. One of them is smoking. They're armed with FX5510s.

Tom looks toward the opening at the entrance. He looks the compound over as well as he's able to see it. Toward the exit, there's nothing there. It's the rear of the compound, and it leads out into nowhere. There's nothing to focus on there.

Tom can see half of the main house. There isn't much activity, save for a handful of meandering armed guards.

There's a strange, small building that catches his attention. A tiny concrete block with a sloping roof. It looks like it leads underground. Tom hasn't seen anyone either enter or leave it.

Beside him, in her cell, Cindy begins to stir. Tom steps back from his bars and crouches down close to her. She blinks and pushes herself up, looking around. Her eyes settle on Tom. "Have you been awake long?"

"Not long," Tom says. "How you feeling?"

"Well," she says, turning herself around so she's sitting upright with her back against the bars. "Just fine and dandy, right here in my own private cage. Living the high life over here. When do you think we get our sponge baths?"

"Maybe for the cameras," Tom says.

"Do you think that's what they're planning to do to us?"

"I can't see why else they'd be keeping us alive."

Cindy looks at Chris. He hasn't moved. She doesn't try to talk to him. She leaves him alone. She speaks to Tom. "Have you seen anything worthwhile?"

Tom shakes his head. "Nothing that could help us get out. They have this place tightly locked down. Eyes everywhere."

"So what do we do? Sit and wait?"

"For now," Tom says. "Until we spot an opportunity. So be alert. Be ready." Tom straightens back up and leans against the bars again. Cindy drags herself up the bars and leans through next to him. "How's your head?"

"It's okay," Cindy says. "Crash knocked me straight out. Didn't feel a thing. Well, until I came round, anyway." She forces a laugh, rubbing the back of her neck. "How about you? You need cleaned up."

"Just a headache," Tom says. "And I'm not sure they're

going to give us a chance to clean. Unless they bring us that sponge bath you were hoping for." Tom sees movement outside, close to the small concrete block. It's Tobin, with a small team following him.

Cindy sees them, too. "Where do you think they're going? That building looks too small to accommodate them all. What is it – a storage room?"

"I think it goes underground," Tom says.

The men go inside. Tobin follows after them. The door closes.

"Do you think we want to know what's down there?" Cindy says.

"I think whether we want to or not," Tom says, "we're going to find out."

51

Tobin directs his team down into the labyrinth. He has other plans for today, plans he's more looking forward to, but first things first.

"We're gonna be making some big movies down here soon," Tobin says. "So get the rooms set up. Make sure the cameras are all functioning. Nice and clean and sleek, all ready to go."

The team get to work. Tobin leaves them to it. He's spent plenty of time down in the labyrinth. He knows his way around. He was here when it was planned and installed, using seven different construction teams, firing each one after the other and bringing a new one in. One construction company thought they were installing a pool, another thought an underground bunker, another thought a basement apartment, and so on. It was Shannon's idea. She said it was like the building of the Winchester house, or H.H. Holmes' Murder Hotel.

The lights down here are purposefully dim. The walls are concrete, plastered over and painted black. Everything down here is dark. The cameras are fitted with infra-red, so that nothing is missed.

There are scratches in the walls. Not everywhere, but there's enough of them. Seven years' worth of scarring. From blades, occasionally even guns, and in some places from fingernails.

It smells of blood down here. Even when it's clean, there's an odour of death lingering in the air. It's stronger in the rooms closest to the entrance/exit. These rooms are white tiled, and bright. The cameras in the wall here are hi-def. A doctor's chair is in the centre of the room, bolted to the ground, fitted with manacles and turned toward the main camera. Next to the table is another, smaller and taller, table. Right now it's empty, but soon it will be adorned with bladed weapons, depending on the client's preferences.

Tobin heads toward the back of the labyrinth. He's alone here. The rest of the team are closer to the entrance. When victims are brought here, they're told that if they make it to the exit, they can have their freedom. It's not true, of course. But it makes them fight. Makes them try harder. None of them ever reach the exit. Most of them can't even find the way.

Not everyone runs the labyrinth. Again, this depends upon the client's wishes. Sometimes there can be a few of them buying in, and they mask up and chase. For a lot of people, it's all about the chase. That gives as much of a thrill as the kill itself. Others prefer to take their time, and take it *all* with the victim. Hence the two torture rooms, with their manacled chairs. They can cut, and slice, and eviscerate to their heart's content. They can do whatever they fucking want. It's their money.

Tobin reaches the end of the labyrinth. If not for the

twisting walls, it would be a straight line opposite from the entrance/exit. The labyrinth is a square, and runs beneath the main house, the shed, and the barn. It's big. It took six months to construct. Guy and Shannon threw money at it to keep the construction crews working at all hours around the clock, for as long as they were employed.

Tobin presses his hand flat to the wall. He breathes deep as he makes his way slowly back to the exit, trailing his fingers through the maze. The walls are cool to the touch. Tobin smiles at the sense of a job well done. He *did* it. He captured them. He's brought them here. And now they're going to make a lot of money from it.

But more than that, Tobin feels a sense of excitement. He's met Tom Rollins briefly. They didn't have long together, face to face. Soon, however, they're going to have a chance to talk properly.

Tobin can't wait.

52

Tom has seen the men leave the small concrete block. That was a few hours ago now. Other than the guards watching the barn, he hasn't seen anyone else outside on the compound's grounds.

"How long do you think they're going to hold us?" Cindy says.

Tom doesn't answer. He doesn't know.

Chris has finally moved. He's standing now, leaning against the bars. They're all that's holding him up. They keep his defeated body propped. He hasn't spoken a word since he was told that Louise was taken away and hasn't been seen since. Tom knows what he's likely thinking. About how they didn't use her for the fake exchange – they used Shannon. They used Louise for the pictures, but then what? Did they just kill her and get rid of her body? Have they already made their little film? And what about the burns – were they real? Or were they just to help disguise Shannon?

Tom spots movement coming across the grounds. Tobin again, but this time he's heading for the barn. He's flanked by four men, all of them armed. They enter the barn, one of the guards from the entrance accompanying them. He has the keys.

Tobin stops directly in front of Tom's cell. He's smiling. For a moment, he doesn't speak. He looks into Tom's eyes, and he continues to smile.

"You and I are going to talk," he says.

Tom shrugs. "I'm not feeling very conversational."

"Well," Tobin says. "We'll see." He motions to the guard to unlock the cell. The four men with their FX551os spread out. Two of them point their rifles at Tom. The other two are pointing at Cindy and Chris.

Tobin is looking at Cindy. He looks her up and down. It's for show. He wants Tom to see what he's doing. "She's not really my type," he says, but he's not talking to Cindy – he's still talking to Tom. He turns back to him. "But there's something about her, isn't there?"

Tom glares at him.

The cell door is open. The guard steps back.

"Nothing stupid," Tobin says. "Step out and behave yourself."

The guard pulls out a plastic tie. Tobin holds up his hand.

"That's not necessary," Tobin says. "Rollins is going to behave himself. Because if he doesn't – you see my two men right here, pointing guns at your friends? They're going to stay right where they are, and if you so much as *look* at me wrong, they're going to open fire."

Tom says nothing.

Tobin nods. "That's right. He understands. Let's go. Out the cage."

Tom steps out. Tobin remains smiling, but he takes a step

back out of Tom's range. All of them do. They know they have him under control, but they're not going to take any risks on letting him get too close.

"Start walking," Tobin says.

Tom does. One of the men with a rifle gets ahead to lead the way. Tom feels the barrel of the other stuck into his back, above his heart, just to let him know it's there. Tobin follows behind.

Tom was able to get a good look at Tobin, up close for the first time. He's a lot taller than Tom. He has the slim, yet muscular build of a cage fighter. It's clear he works out. He wears tight tops to accentuate his muscles. They're not just for show. He can back himself up. He's a fighter. He knows how to handle himself.

Tom is led across the ground and toward the house. They don't go inside. They go to the garage down the side. This is a part of the house Tom can't see from his cell inside the barn. The garage door is already open. There's no car inside. It's not used for storage, either. It's a very bare room, save for the chair in the middle.

Tobin indicates for Tom to sit down. He does so. The room is concrete. The floor is flat and smooth. The walls are exposed blocks of grey. The garage is not in keeping with the ranch style of the house itself. It's clearly a later addition, despite the fact it's not being used for anything. The house is made from wood. In here, in the garage, it's hard and grey and unforgiving. It is, however, cool. As the sun gets higher, Tom doubts this will remain the case. It will get hot in here. It will be like a sauna. Tom wonders how long they're planning on keeping him in here. If it will be long enough to make him sweat.

"I've been looking forward to seeing you up close," Tobin

says. He remains standing, looming over Tom. The two men that have accompanied him are flanking him, their rifles still pointing at Tom. "It's a shame you're not feeling very conversational. You had an awful lot to say on the phone when we spoke."

"You caught me at a good time," Tom says. "Now isn't such a good time."

Tobin smirks. "You're gonna want to try and perk yourself up, Rollins – or should I call you Tom? Which would you prefer?"

"I don't care."

Tobin laughs. "I like Rollins. It flows better, doesn't it? Tom is so *dull*, so abrupt. When I fought, on the marquee, it never had our first names, and if it did they were in small text. It was always surnames. Klinghoffer v. Chavez. Klinghoffer v. Broadrick."

"Klinghoffer's a mouthful," Tom says.

"It's German," Tobin says. "What about Rollins? Where's that from?"

"Germany, England, Scotland, Scandinavia. We got around."

"From what I've heard and read about you, you're still a wanderer. Is that right?"

Tom shrugs.

"You should *really* talk to me, Rollins," Tobin says. "It's not in your interest to play this so disinterested."

Tom shrugs.

Tobin takes a step back and leans against the wall, folding his arms. He stares at Tom for a long time without speaking. Tom stares back. It's difficult to tell what Tobin is trying to do here. If he's trying to intimidate him into talking, though Tom isn't sure what it is he wants to talk about. He hasn't asked any questions yet.

"My first fight," Tobin says, a seeming non sequitur, "this was, hell, a long time ago now." He thinks. "I think I was maybe seventeen. I could've still been sixteen, I'm not sure. My trainer had set it up. He had high hopes for me, and he wanted to see how I handled myself, especially against a bigger, older, more experienced opponent.

"Now, this was before MMA had taken off the way it has. This fight wasn't in any cage, or an arena. It was the parking lot of a dive bar. There was a ring, though. We weren't rolling around the asphalt like savages. My first opponent – he was a soldier. He'd gone AWOL and he was taking these underground fights to make money while he was in hiding. So, y'know, sixteen- or seventeen-year-old me, I was intimidated. I won't deny it. This guy was in his late twenties, and he was *built*, and he was a literal *killer*. He had these scars all over him. You could see that he'd been shot through his left thigh. He'd been *shot*. What could I do when a goddamn *bullet* couldn't keep this guy down?

"But I went out there. I didn't back down. I knew that if I didn't fight, if I walked away, I'd be walking away for my whole life. My trainer wouldn't have been impressed. He would've disowned me. I wouldn't be able to train with him anymore. All of his energies would go into someone else. So I went out there. I knew I couldn't lose. I couldn't afford to. And I kicked that soldier's ass. I beat him bloody until the referee stepped in and ended it. And you know what I realised in that moment? Sure, the guy was a soldier, and he was a survivor, but he wasn't a *fighter*, not really. Not the way that *I* was – and am – a fighter. After that, nothing and no one could stand in my way. No matter who I was confronted with, and how they were presented, I knew I could beat them."

Tobin pauses. Finally, he adds, "You were a soldier, weren't you, Rollins?"

Tom doesn't answer.

"Fighting isn't just about pounding on your opponent's face until they're bloody and exhausted and ready to submit. It's about picking them apart, and you don't do that physically. That's all up here." Tobin taps the side of his head. "It's about figuring out how to take your opponent apart, and then going ahead and doing just that. It's as much mental chess, as it is physical."

Tom looks back at him. He's unimpressed. "Jesus," Tom says. He holds up his hands. "Whatever you wanna know, just ask. I can't listen to you talk anymore."

Tobin isn't smiling now. He breathes in deeply, and makes an annoyed sound when he exhales. "Do you think you're funny, Rollins?"

"Not particularly."

Tobin's eyes narrow.

Tom circles a hand in the air, motioning for Tobin to wrap things up.

"All right," Tobin says. He pushes himself off the wall. He begins to pace, slowly, in front of Tom. "You were working your way toward us," he says. "Investigating us. You managed to get in touch with some of our people. You killed them. We know that you spoke to Mandy and Freddy Bliss. Who else did you talk to?"

Tom says nothing.

Abruptly, Tobin stops pacing. "Who have you spoken to?" he says. "Who have you told about us, about anything you know about us?"

Tom says nothing. He understands why he's here now. It makes sense. They're worried if Tom and the others have spoken to anyone else, have told them what they've found out. They're worried about someone else carrying on their investigation, and potentially exposing the Kennedys and their operation.

"You said you were ready to answer," Tobin says.

"I was ready for you to shut up," Tom says.

Tobin glares down at him.

"Why don't you beat me, Tobin? Wasn't that the point of your little story? That you think you can hurt me?"

"Maybe I can't hurt you, Rollins. Have you been tortured before?"

Tom doesn't answer.

Tobin is smiling again. He parts his lips to speak, but he pauses, revelling in it. "Has Cindy?"

Tom keeps his expression blank. He reveals nothing.

"I'm not going to beat you, Tom. I don't think that would accomplish much right now. You can take it, right? Hell, I know you can. Look what you went through just to get here. I could break your bones. I could rearrange your face. You still wouldn't answer me. But Cindy... She's never been a soldier. She's never done the things you've done. So maybe I'll talk to her. Or, shit, maybe I'll make a call and have her brought up here right now, and we'll bind you to that chair after all. And you can watch. Would you like that, Rollins? Would you like to watch as I break her bones? But maybe it would take more than that, right? Maybe I'd have to break another part of her. You know what I'm talking about, Rollins. You know I liked what I saw. She's not my type, but I know I'm gonna be thinking about her for days. I should just get her up here and indulge myself."

Tom's face isn't so blank anymore. He's gritting his teeth. His arms are folded, but his fists are balled tight and he knows it's making his arms tense and shake. He stares at Tobin. Imagines charging him, slamming him into the wall and tearing his throat out with his hands.

Tobin laughs. "There we go, Rollins," he says. "I don't need to break *you*. I break *her*."

"No one else knows anything," Tom says. "Everyone we've talked to is dead."

"Are you sure about that? Think long and hard."

"Jilly Beck is dead," Tom says. "Ricky Buxton is dead. *You* killed Mandy and Freddy Bliss. Anyone else that Cindy or Chris tried to talk to either didn't take them seriously, or didn't get back to them. No one knows about you, or what you're doing here."

"We have Cindy's laptop," Tobin says. "It's just a matter of time before my men get into it. If we find that she's been spreading stories online, if we find that she has hidden files ready to be released by a certain time or date, I can bring the two of you right back out here and we'll pick up right where we're leaving off. I'll follow through on my promise."

"You won't find anything," Tom says.

Tobin stares, and then he smiles. "Good," he says. He gets close to Tom. He pats him on the cheek. "That really didn't need to be so difficult, did it?" He steps back and motions to the two men with the rifles. "Take him back to the cage. I'm sure his friends are missing him."

"How long are you going to hold us for?" Tom says.

"Longer than you'd like," Tobin says. "But when the time comes, you'll see it was shorter than you wanted." There's a gleam in his eye.

"Are you going to film it?"

"Of course," Tobin says. "If there's an opportunity to make money, we're always going to take it. You should see the kind of money we're already pulling in from the Mandy sequel. People are eating that shit *up*."

Tom gets to his feet. He doesn't leave the garage straight away, despite the rifle poking into his back. He looks at Tobin. "You're going to see what it's like to run," Tom says. "You're going to see what it's like to be scared."

Tobin snorts. "Sure," he says. "Let me know when you've had *that* dream. You'll have to tell me how it ended." He waves a hand for the men to remove Tom from his sight.

53

A few days go by. Tom keeps himself loose in the cage. There's not enough space for push-ups, but he squats and he stretches, ready for whatever is coming next. He does pull-ups using the roof bars.

Cindy does the same. She tries to keep pace with Tom, but she doesn't have the stamina he does. She pushes herself, though. Pushes until she's sweating and exhausted and close to vomiting. The prisoners in the other cages watch them, but they don't join in. They've already lost hope. Calisthenics aren't going to make them believe they can escape.

Chris doesn't speak much. Doesn't join in with their exercises. He stands at the cell door and he stares out, across what he can see of the compound, as if hopeful he might catch a glimpse of his sister, or at least find out whether she's living or dead.

The guards bring them bread and water. Everyone gets the same portion. It's not much, but it's enough to keep them alive. It's no wonder the other people in the cages look so gaunt and hungry.

Tom is sitting cross-legged on the floor. He breathes deeply, meditating, his eyes closed, keeping his mind calm now for when it needs to be alert later.

He's noticed that most of his wounds from San Francisco have healed. His more recent injuries have scabbed over. The time in the cage is giving his body a chance to rest and recuperate. He's sure this is the opposite of what Tobin and the Kennedys want from him. They won't want him and Cindy to be working out, either, and taking turns keeping watch on the open barn doors, but so far they haven't said anything about it. No doubt they're watching, all hours, through their cameras.

Cindy is keeping watch. She taps the bars to get Tom's attention. He opens his eyes and looks at her. She nods toward the entrance. Tom gets to his feet. The Kennedys and Tobin are approaching, accompanied, as usual, by a few armed guards.

They come straight for Tom, Cindy, and Chris. Tom isn't surprised. While they've been held captive here, they haven't seen anyone approach the other captives, save to feed and water them. Most of the activity has been localised in front of these three cells. They're the biggest deal at the minute.

Guy and Shannon stand close together, their arms around each other. They look at Tom and the others. Tobin stands to the side. Tom notices how he watches the Kennedys out the corner of his eye. How he seems to grimace a little at the sight of them. Or, more precisely, at the sight of Guy Kennedy. At his arm around his wife.

Guy is staring straight at Tom. He lets go of Shannon and

steps forward, closer to the cell than he should. If the armed guards were not nearby, he wouldn't risk it. Tobin has made sure Cindy and Chris are covered again.

"We've had a lot of interest in *you*," Guy says, looking Tom over. "I assume you're familiar with the Aries Group?"

Tom is, though he's surprised to hear their name. A mercenary group. He had a run-in with them up in Colorado. The members out there were all killed. He doesn't explain any of this to Guy. He doesn't say anything at all.

"Because," Guy continues when he sees Tom isn't going to respond, "they've offered us a *substantial* amount of money to keep you alive until they can get here." He grins, hoping to elicit some kind of a reaction.

Tom doesn't give him one.

Guy falters.

"Ah, he's no fun," Shannon says. "Just tell them what we're going to do to them. That's always good for a giggle."

Guy is able to smirk again at this. "We've had to turn the Aries Group down, unfortunately. While they offered a lot, they couldn't offer *enough*. We stand to make so much more from you through our streaming service."

"I assume it's private," Cindy says.

Guy laughs. "Do you think we're stupid enough to broadcast it to the world? How would we make any money from that? It's a *very* exclusive service, and it costs more than the three of you could afford combined."

"Should we be impressed?" Cindy says.

"I don't need you to be impressed. I just need you to die."

"Oh, it's not so blunt as *that*," Shannon says, stepping forward. "It's not simply a case of just *dying*. We expect more from you than that. Our clients pay good money. Sometimes, our clients just want to kick back and see young men and women get tortured and killed – maybe throw in a little rape, too. Hell, maybe they want to *do* the raping. But *sometimes*, they want to see the cattle run. And in this instance, there's going to be a run."

"What does that mean?" Tom says.

"You'll find out soon enough," Shannon says. "You and Mr. Parton there. There was already some interest in dear Chris – he's a very pretty boy, after all – but once people found out about the brother-sister connection – well, let's just say the interest level *spiked*. So you, Mr. Parton, and you, Mr. Rollins, you're going to run."

Shannon takes a step to her right, in front of Cindy. She reaches out as if to stroke Cindy's cheek through the bars, but Cindy flinches back out of her reach. "I'm not part of the run?" Cindy says.

"Oh no, not you, Cindy. You don't have to run. There's been a *lot* of interest in you. The highest bidder can do whatever they want with you."

"You're sick," Cindy says. "You're all sick."

"We're also very good at what we do," Shannon says.

"And because of that," Guy says, "we're very rich."

"When are we going for this run?" Tom says.

Shannon taps the side of her nose. "We're just letting you know what to expect. We're not going to tell you *everything*, Rollins. You wouldn't want us to spoil all of the surprises, now, would you?"

"We just wanted you to be prepared," Guy says. "And we were curious about this Aries Group. But it feels like you don't have an explanation for us."

"I'll tell you once I'm out of this cage," Tom says.

Tobin laughs. "I see you're still dreaming, Rollins."

Guy and Shannon both laugh. They slip their arms

around each other. Tom sees how Tobin involuntarily winces at this.

"The three of you should feel honoured," Guy says. "Do you think the rest of these people get this kind of treatment?"

"The rest of them weren't recently in the news," Shannon says, looking at Tom. "They're not quasi-celebrities. We can make money off them, sure, but not the same kind of money we're going to make with all of you."

Guy winks. "We'll see you all again soon, I'm sure."

The Kennedys and the guards start to leave. Tobin holds back.

"Oh, by the way, Rollins," Tobin says before parting. He points toward one of the security cameras. "We've seen how you and the girl are keeping in shape. That's good, that's real good. Our viewers always like a fighter. Especially when they've kept it *tight*." He winks, then turns to leave with the others.

"What's your play, Tobin?" Tom says.

Tobin stops. He looks back, frowning. "What?"

"What's your plan? With the Kennedys."

Tobin turns back to him, not understanding.

"I mean, I assume it's Shannon, but maybe it's Guy," Tom says. "Which one is it you're jealous of, Tobin? Which one is it you want?"

Tobin's face drops a little.

Tom leans through the bars. "What are you going to do about it, Tobin? Or maybe you're not gonna do anything at all. You're just gonna pout across the room and think about what could've been."

It takes Tobin a moment to respond. "I'm sure you think

you're real smart," he says. "See how smart you feel once you're in the labyrinth."

"A labyrinth, huh?" Tom says. "Is that what's under that concrete block over there?"

Tobin doesn't answer. He glares at Tom, then turns and leaves the barn.

54

The airstrip is private. It's in the middle of nowhere, a half-hour away from the compound. Tobin drives to it, and tries not to think about what Rollins said to him. It was two days ago now, but it still bugs him. The fact that Rollins noticed anything at all eats at him. How obvious has he been? Shannon said she'd noticed. That's why she came onto him. And what did *that* mean? More importantly, though, has Guy noticed?

Tobin has manged to avoid Shannon alone since then. He's kept himself busy with his men. Even when he's in the gym, he makes sure there's someone else with him, ostensibly as a spotter or a sparring partner. Shannon hasn't had another opportunity to get close.

Tobin isn't driving out to the airstrip alone, though he's alone in the car. There are two more cars flanking him, along with a minivan. Plenty of seats for the people they're on their way to pick up.

The airstrip is owned by the Kennedys. Like everything else they own around here, it's registered through a fake name. Their official home is still out in LA. Neither of them has been there in years.

The flights are in. The various private jets and light aircraft have landed. Tobin waited until they'd all landed in Lubbock before he and his men left the compound. He saw some of the aircraft descending, watching from the farmhouse.

The Kennedys own a plane of their own, but it's not a jet. They have a Cessna 208 Caravan. Tobin has ridden in it many times. It's much more enjoyable, and comfortable, than flying coach. They could have gotten a jet, but when Guy found out they don't come with parachutes, he baulked at the idea. Guy is afraid of flying. More specifically, he's afraid of heights. Private jets, if they have an issue and start to go down, can't be jumped out of. Well, they *can*, but the jumper will soon end up in the propellors or the engines. Guy wanted to know that if they started to go down, he had a chance of escape. And, so, they settled on the Cessna 208 Caravan.

The airstrip comes into view. The convoy of vehicles race toward it, slowing only as they pull up onto the tarmac runway. There are currently a lot of planes parked upon it. They're parked to the side, near the tower, so as not to block the strip. Tobin can't remember the last time he saw it so full. The run with Rollins and Chris, and the private encounter with Cindy, they're all proving to be a big deal. There's a lot of interest. A lot of eyes.

A group is gathered in the hangar bay. All men this time. For privacy, no names are given, but some of these people are public figures. They're known.

There's the rockstar, and his bodyguard. The football player, and *his* bodyguard. Businessman one, two, and three.

There's the sheik, and his small retinue of two bodyguards. And, finally, there's the politician. The politician will be spending his time privately with Cindy. The others will be hunting Rollins and Chris. Eleven men, all told. They're all from out of state. They've all had to travel to be here.

These men have paid the highest. They've covered the expenses for their bodyguards to accompany them. Tobin looks them over. The football player is a big guy. He's Black, wide, and thick with muscle. The rock star has long hair, dyed black. He's tall, but he's thin and pale. His skinny arms are covered in tattoos, and there are nautical stars around his left eye. The three businessmen stand close together. They arrived together. They know each other in their everyday lives. They wear expensive suits. Under them, it looks like they work out. Spend most of their free time in the gym.

The sheik similarly wears an expensive suit. He's not a small man, but he's dwarfed by his two bodyguards. All of the bodyguards are big. They look like they're on steroids, every one of them. The rock star's bodyguard is white, the football player's is Black, and the sheik's are both Middle Eastern.

The politician is in his mid-fifties, and though he clearly keeps himself in shape, he looks older. Tobin has heard that he has a heavy cocaine habit. Judging from the way he sniffs and brushes at his nose, the way he laughs hard at something the rock star has said and the intensely focussed look in his eyes, Tobin can believe it.

Tobin waves them in, flanked by his men. There are only three of them – the drivers of the vehicles that followed him here. "You all know why you're here," Tobin says. He smiles for them. He's welcoming. These men are distinguished guests. They're important. "So I'd just like to say, on behalf of the Kennedys, we're very glad to have you, and we hope you enjoy your time. If you'd like to accompany me to the vehicles, my men here will bring your bags."

The politician sniffs. "How long until we get down to what we paid for?"

"Not long," Tobin says.

"I think I speak for us all when I say we're itching to get into it," the politician says. The others are nodding, agreeing with him.

"When we get to the compound, the Kennedys will be there waiting to greet you, and they'll be ready to answer any questions you might have." Tobin gestures toward the vehicles. "We *are* going to have to ask you to be blindfolded for the journey."

"Why?" the rockstar says. "We all know why we're going out there. We know what we're gonna do. We're all in this together now, right?"

"It's important to us to be careful," Tobin says. "The Kennedys are very adamant on this point. No blindfold, no ride. You can turn around and get back on your jet, because you won't be coming with us. Oh, and no refunds."

The rockstar holds up his hands. "Let's not get hasty," he says. "It was just a question."

"And that was the answer."

No one else has anything further to say about the blindfolds. Tobin motions toward the vehicles again. Without another word, the party follow his direction.

55

"The convoy's on their way back," Tom says.

Cindy gets off the ground of her cell and stands near him at her door. They see the distant dust cloud drawing closer. "They haven't been gone long," she says. "Just over an hour."

Tom nods. They watch as the vehicles – three cars and a minivan – come toward the compound. Glancing back, Tom sees that Chris is at his cell door, too, watching.

The vehicles stop close to the main house. A couple of moments pass. Tom can see movement inside the vehicles, but it's hard to tell what's happening. It's as if they're removing things from their faces. Finally, men start getting out of the vehicles. From the lead car, Tom spots Tobin. From the others, he sees men he hasn't seen before – heavies that are unfamiliar, who don't work for Tobin. Thickset, steroid-pumped gym goers. One is white, one is Black, and two are Middle Eastern. The way they carry themselves, the way they look around – while blinking their eyes against the sunlight – Tom thinks they're bodyguards.

Soon after, other men start to get out of the vehicles.

"Holy shit," Cindy says. "I recognise that guy."

She's talking about the skinny pale guy, long black hair and stars tattooed on his face. A rockstar. Tom recognises, vaguely, some of the others. A football player. A politician.

Of the others, three men in suits huddle close together and look around the compound. They point out the barn and laugh among themselves. There's another man, flanked by the Middle Eastern bodyguards. A sheik, perhaps. Maybe a prince. When they spoke to Jilly, she made references to both.

Chris clears his throat. Tom and Cindy look toward him. "What does this mean?" he says.

Tom thinks he must already have a good idea. "It means that something is going to happen soon," he says. "I think these are the people we've been waiting for. It could happen today, it could happen tonight, it could even be tomorrow. Whenever it is, we need to be ready."

56

Tobin leads the paying killers into the living room of Guy and Shannon's home. The Kennedys are standing at the far end of the room, arms around each other, waiting for their guests. They separate once everyone has entered, and Guy claps his hands together. He shakes hands with the politician. He's paid the most to be here. He nods at the rockstar.

"I'm a big fan of your work," he says.

The rockstar grins. "I can say the same about you."

Guy looks up to take everyone else in. "I assume you've all had an enjoyable journey here? The ride was comfortable, yes?"

The gathering mumbles in the affirmative.

"I'll keep this brief, because I'm sure you're all eager to get into things," Guy says.

Further mumbles, but more excitable this time.

"So, first of all, we'd like to thank the three of you for your generosity." He holds out both hands toward the three businessmen. "We know you requested a female of Louise

Parton's calibre, and we're very grateful that you've agreed to share her with us all."

One of the businessmen holds up a hand, like it's no big deal. "That's fine. We're happy to partake in the others."

Another of the businessmen grunts. "I don't make much of Chris, but I'd like to take a swing at Rollins. I've heard impressive things."

"I saw him on the news," the third says.

"Rollins might be too much for y'all," the football player says, grinning. "You might wanna leave him for me."

"Then it seems we've come for the same man," the sheik says. He indicates his bodyguards. "I've come prepared."

"You can soften him up for me," the football player says, nudging his own bodyguard with his elbow.

"There's plenty to go around," Guy says, motioning for calm, for everyone to pay attention to him. He gets the situation under control. The men are grinning at each other, lightly ribbing, but it could only be a matter of time before things turn serious, and potentially nasty. They need to know that they're all on the same team.

Tobin steps up. "Don't take Rollins lightly," he says. "The last thing you want to happen is you end up getting yourselves killed because you're all arguing over who's going to make the killing blow against him."

They fall silent at this. They watch Tobin.

"He's been caged, but that doesn't make him any less dangerous. You all need to be very, *very* aware of the kind of man you're stepping into the labyrinth with."

Guy places a hand on his shoulder. "Thank you, Tobin," he says. "I think they understand now."

Tobin nods and steps aside.

"We begin filming tonight, at nightfall," Guy says. "Here's

how things will work – our friend here," he indicates the politician, "will be in his own private room, and so a lot of what I'm about to say doesn't apply to him. For the rest of you, however, when we're finished here Tobin will escort you to the labyrinth so you can get acquainted. He will show you your positions for the evening. After that, you pick out your masks, and your weapons. You've all seen the films and the livestreams – you know what to expect down there, and you know that nothing is off limits. You can do whatever your heart desires, whatever your own imagination can conjure. You can make this as long or as short as you like. You've paid, and now it's all up to you. The people at home are getting a show regardless, but we know our fans are usually partial to a slower kill."

"Then they ought to enjoy what I've got in mind," the politician says.

This gets some chuckles from the gathering.

"All right, I think that just about covers everything here," Guy says. "After Tobin has shown you around the labyrinth, and you've picked out your accoutrements, we'll reconvene here for a few hours before the show begins. We'll be providing dinner, and I'm sure you'll all be satisfied with it. My wife is a spectacular cook."

Shannon waves like the queen at this.

Guy claps his hands again. "All right, I'm sure many of you have looked forward to this moment for a long, long time. Please follow Tobin to the labyrinth for the tour. Enjoy yourselves and remember, the main thing tonight is that you all have *fun*. If you have fun, the viewers have fun – we *all* have fun."

There's a brief smattering of applause from the gathering, and then Tobin motions for them to follow his men out of the house.

Shannon places a hand on Tobin's arm before he can leave. "Make sure they all know their positions," she says. "And where they need to be with regards to Louise."

Tobin nods. "Don't worry," he says. "I've got it."

Shannon's hand lingers upon his arm. Her eyes are locked on his. She's smiling at him. Her finger rises and strokes his bicep slightly.

Guy turns and sees them. Shannon lets go of Tobin's arm. Guy doesn't say anything. Doesn't make it clear if he realises what was happening.

Tobin leaves the house.

57

Night is falling. Tom is ready. He stands by the cage door, bouncing on the balls of his feet. He watches the entrance to the barn.

There's an electric atmosphere in the air. Everyone is picking up on it. There's an anticipation. People saw the new arrivals. They know what this means. They know what's coming next. Most of the other prisoners are watching the cells of Tom, Cindy, and Chris. They're probably silently hoping and praying that they're right, that it's these three that the new arrivals have come for, begging for one more day's respite.

Tom spots a group approaching the barn. "Here we go," he says. "Be ready."

It's the Kennedys, accompanied by Tobin and a handful of his armed men. The men who arrived earlier in the day aren't accompanying them. They stop in front of their cages. Tom can almost hear the sigh of relief that passes around the rest of the barn.

Guy is smiling. It's a shit-eating grin, and Tom would like

to stomp his teeth down his throat. "Are you prepared?" he says. "You look prepared. It's a big night, and the three of you are our star attractions."

"Or should that be four?" Shannon says.

The way they look at each other, the way they bounce off each other, Tom thinks they've rehearsed these lines, this moment.

Shannon turns to them now. "I'm going to need the two of you," she points at Tom and Chris, "to listen very closely, because this is important. We're going to take you into the labyrinth. From there, what happens next is up to you, but this is the part you need to be aware of – Louise is down there."

Chris straightens at this. He pushes himself against the bars. "Alive?"

"Of course she's alive!" Shannon says. "She's been keeping my husband and me company. It's been nice having her in the bedroom, like a pet sleeping at the bottom of the bed. I'm going to miss her."

"What happens if I find her?" Chris says. "Will you let us go?" He knows they won't. He's grasping, desperate.

Shannon holds out her hands. "Only one way to find out." She turns to Cindy now. "And *you*," she says.

Cindy stares back at her. She doesn't speak.

"All we need from you is to look pretty," Shannon says. "That won't be too difficult, now, will it?"

"Get them out of the cages," Tobin says to one of his men. "Start with the girl. She goes down first."

Cindy's cell is unlocked. She's handled roughly, dragged out. She looks back at Tom. Tom looks back at her. They don't speak. There's nothing they can say. They just have to hold on for each other. They just have to survive.

"Chris next, then Rollins," Tobin says. Cindy is out of the barn, now. With a gun in her back, she's directed toward the small concrete block. Tom watches her go as Chris is removed from his cell.

The rifles are levelled at Tom as the guard unlocks his door. Chris stands to the side, held in place. He looks like he wants to get going. It's the most animated he's been since they were first brought here. He wants to find his sister. He *needs* to find her.

"Behave yourself, Rollins," Tobin says.

"Don't I always?" Tom says. He grins at Tobin.

Tobin looks unnerved. "All right, step on out. Nice and slow."

Tom does as he's told. The guard who unlocked the door is standing close. He clips the ring of keys onto a belt loop.

Tom makes a move. He's fast, striking like a rattlesnake. He grabs the guard with the keys and pulls him forward into a headbutt, dazing him. He grabs at his waist, as if he's reaching for a gun. He's not going for the gun.

Tobin is fastest to react. He strikes Tom from behind, rocking the back of his skull with a quick jab. He follows through with a kidney blow, knocking Tom to his knees. A guard steps up with rifle raised, but Tobin shoves it aside. "No!" he says. "What are you thinking?"

As Tom suspected – they won't kill him now. They need him for their little film. It's about to begin. Men have paid good money to be here. They wouldn't be happy if Tom's brains were splashed across the barn floor before they had a chance to get at him.

Tobin takes a step back and motions to a couple of his men. Tom is on his hands and knees, looking up, defiant.

"There's still too much fight in him," Tobin says. "Probably best if he's tenderised first. Stomp him."

The two men eagerly step forward and lay into Tom with their boots, weakening him for the labyrinth. Tom balls up. He covers his head. He takes it. He can always take it.

In his hand, concealed, balled tight in his fist, he has the keys.

58

It's dark in the labyrinth. It takes a moment for Cindy's eyes to adjust. The two men who escorted her here stand by her sides, holding onto her arms. One of them looks back toward the entrance where they came down the stairs, waiting for something.

Eyes narrowed, Cindy looks around. Down the corridor, she sees bright light coming from a room, illuminating the black wall opposite.

Cindy can see some of the cameras. They're concealed in the walls, perhaps easy to miss at first glance, but they're not exactly hidden. Some are mounted on the walls, too. They're here to capture everything.

It's hot, and it smells like death down here. Like a charnel house. It has recently been cleaned with bleach, she can tell, but the tinge of blood still hangs in the air, overriding everything else. She wonders, briefly, how many people have died in this place. It could be about to claim more lives, though Cindy can only hope those lives don't belong to her, Tom, or Chris. Or Louise, if it's true that she's down here somewhere.

There's movement on the stairs. Cindy spots Chris first as he's pushed ahead. He's taken forward, down through the heart of the labyrinth. After him, Tom is brought down the stairs. Cindy sees how he clutches at his ribs, how there's some blood coming from his mouth. He's been beaten.

She wants to call out to him, to cry his name, but she bites her lip and stops herself. It wouldn't accomplish anything. They need to be focussed. They need to survive down here, by any way they can.

Tom is turned to the right, separated from Chris and in the opposite direction from Cindy. She watches as they disappear down the dark corridor.

"All right," one of the men holding her says. Cindy realises he's talking into a radio. "They're heading into position. We're putting Cindy in the room now."

They start moving, dragging her toward the well-lit room down the corridor. She digs her heels in. She's not going to make it easy for them.

The two men are stronger, though. They force her into the room. It's very white. The light bounces off the walls and hurts her eyes. In the centre of the room there is a doctor's chair. It has restraints. Binds for the ankles, and, threaded through the top of the chair, manacles for the wrists. Next to this, there is a small table with surgical implements arranged on top of it. Cindy feels the spit dry in her mouth. Her throat constricts. The men are taking her to the chair.

There is a camera in each wall. Cindy remembers what Mandy told them. It's a different layout, but it's similar enough. In the wall at the foot of the chair, the camera there will be pointing directly to her. Next to it, there is a monitor. It shows the inside of the labyrinth in infra-red, cycling through all of the cameras, waiting to be tuned to something specific.

Cindy fights against being placed into the chair. She manages to hit one of the men with her elbow, but the other cracks her across the jaw with the butt of his rifle. It doesn't knock her down, or out, but it's enough to daze her and make her easier to handle. Her head swimming, she feels them lift her onto the chair. Feels them clamp her tightly into place.

She blinks hard, shakes her head, forcing herself to come around and to remain alert. Her arms are above her head. When she pulls to the right her left arm rises higher, and when she pulls to the left her right rises. She pulls on both simultaneously, but they don't budge. They're tight on her wrists. She can't slip free.

The two men leave the room. Cindy is alone. She looks around, searching, but there's nothing to help her. Everything is out of reach. On the monitor, she sees Chris deposited into the labyrinth. He's kicked in the back of the knee and clubbed in the side of the head. The men who have escorted him leave him behind, same as Cindy. The view changes, and she sees a big man walking slowly down a corridor. In the dark, something gleams in his right hand.

The door to the room opens again. Cindy looks toward it. A masked face appears around the frame, staring back at her. It's a grinning face. Its eyes are hollowed and unblinking. It stares at her for a long time, and then the rest of its body follows it through. He's wearing a doctor's smock. It's creased and dirty. He comes closer and strokes the side of her face. His hands are uncovered. His skin is rough and aged. Cindy tries to bite at his fingers.

The man in the grinning face mask laughs. "Oh, you're

feisty," he says. His voice is aged and gruff. "I could tell you would be." He circles her, stopping next to the table of tools. His head turns toward the monitor. When he looks back at her, he's giddy, like he can barely contain his excitement. "We're going to have a lot of fun together, you and I," he says. "We're going to have a night neither of us will ever forget."

59

Tom is dumped in the labyrinth. He allowed the men to carry him, pretending he was still limp from the beating in the barn. He watched out of the corner of his eye, though. Tried to map the route they took him. It was difficult. The walls all look exactly the same. There are discerning marks, however. Signs where people have been harmed. He counted footsteps. Made notes of left and right turns.

The two men leave him and hurry away. Tom pushes himself up and takes a deep breath. He pockets he keys he swiped from the guard in the barn. He's careful in his movements. He's spotted the cameras.

He breathes deeply and listens, acclimatising himself to the labyrinth. He doesn't have long. They took Cindy, and he needs to find her. He needs to find Chris, too, and Louise. There's no time to waste.

He closes his eyes. Once again, he compartmentalises all of his various aches and pains, both old and new. He listens.

There are ominous noises coming from throughout the

labyrinth. Ringing footsteps. The scraping of weapons against walls. Maniacal laughter. Sounds obviously intending to instil fear and panic. Tom stays calm.

But he can hear whimpers, too. Tears. Sniffing. A woman, crying out, as if struck. It doesn't sound like Cindy. It could be Louise.

Tom doesn't rush into anything. His back against the wall, he uses it to push himself up to his feet. He hears footsteps, but they're all distant. The laughter is distant. Everything is distant. No one is near to him. They could be coming this way, but their sounds are still too far off to be sure.

These people are amateur killers. Wannabes, in fact. They're untrained. They get off on torture and murder. On destruction. Tom doesn't have anything to fear from them. To them, this is all a big game. They don't realise they're about to become the hunted.

Tom breathes deeply, one more time, then pushes himself from the wall. He starts to run. He can orientate himself on the way. He heads for noise. Noise means people. People are his key to escape.

The only way out is through.

60

Guy and Shannon are alone in their bedroom. They sit close at the foot of the bed, the widescreen television attuned to the happenings in the labyrinth. They don't need to flick camera to camera. Their tech team out in the shed is doing that for them, finding the best angles for every occupant underground. The Kennedys are watching the same live feed as their viewers at home.

"Rollins is moving fast," Shannon says, watching the screen. "Was he playing possum, when they dragged him out there?" She bites her lip. "I don't think I've ever seen anyone running *toward* the danger before. Maybe Tobin and his men should have worked him over a little more."

Guy waves it off. He's unconcerned. "He's not going to get far," he says. "He'll see a mask and a machete and he'll shit himself. He'll turn and start running in the other direction. They always do."

Shannon thinks about the masks. Some good choices have been made. The politician is wearing the grinning face.

The rockstar wears the mouse, and his bodyguard is Nixon. The football player is the bear, and *his* bodyguard is Reagan – a coincidence with two bodyguards choosing presidents that everyone seemed to enjoy. The three businessmen chose the clown, the kabuki, and the pig respectively. And, finally, the sheik wears the bat mask, and his bodyguards are Santa and an oni. They'll all make for great visuals.

"Have we ever had so many people down in the labyrinth at one time before?" Shannon says.

"Not that I can remember," Guy says. "It's a momentous occasion. Once in a lifetime, perhaps. Well, certainly *their* lifetimes." He points at the screen and he laughs.

Shannon watches Rollins intently. He's still running, making his way through the corridors. He pauses only to listen, and then he starts moving again. The cameras are sticking with him.

"He's outnumbered," Guy says, seeing how she continues to watch. He leans closer to her, brushing his lips against her neck. "And the football player is twice the size he is. Rollins is going to meet his match when they run into each other." He chews on her earlobe.

Shannon relents to his advances. "You're right," she says, turning to him and biting his bottom lip. "I know you're right."

"I always am," Guy says, placing a hand between her legs. He starts to rub. "Now let's just enjoy the show," he breathes into her ear. "I think it's going to be a good one."

61

Tom runs. He hears a pained grunt. The sound of flesh slapping hard against flesh. The grunt was male. Chris's, potentially. Tom goes to it.

Chris is on the ground. There are three men above him. They wear overalls and masks. Two of them look like the steroid freaks Tom spotted arriving earlier in the day. They're armed with a knife and a crowbar. The third man, the smaller, is kneeling on Chris's throat. Through dark-adjusted eyes, Tom can see how Chris's own eyes are bulging, rolling back into his skull, as the oxygen is forced out of him.

Tom goes to the man on the right, the man with the knife. He creeps lightly. The man doesn't hear his approach. Tom grabs for the knife and snaps the man's wrist in the process. As the other two register the noise, Tom spins with the knife, driving it into the back of the other standing man's thigh, all the way to the hilt. He screams and drops the crowbar. Up close, Tom can see the masks they're wearing. The man with the knife was wearing a Japanese oni mask. The man with the crowbar was Santa Claus. The smaller man is a bat.

The bat rises, removing his knee from Chris's neck, realising that the two bigger men have been incapacitated. He tries to flee. Tom is blocking his exit. He slams a fist into the centre of the bat mask, crumpling it. The bat stumbles back, tripping over Chris's body and hitting the wall.

Tom picks up the crowbar. He smashes the bat across the face with it. He goes down and lands flat on his front.

The big guy in the oni mask holds his broken right wrist to his side and grabs at Tom with his left hand. Tom strikes his ribs with the crowbar, backing him up, then jabs the end into his sternum, lifting him a foot off the ground. Tom lets go of the crowbar and the man falls onto his side.

The other man, Santa Claus, is on the ground. The knife in the back of his thigh has hit something important. He's bleeding out.

The bat is on his front, trying to push himself up. Chris has pushed himself across the ground away from him, giving Tom space. Tom stomps down hard on the back of the bat's head, driving it into the concrete floor. Something cracks. The bat lies very still.

Tom offers Chris his hand and pulls him to his feet. Chris looks down at the bodies on the floor.

"We keep moving," Tom says. "I've heard a woman. Could've been your sister."

"I heard her, too," Chris says. "It sounded like Louise for sure. I was going there when these three jumped me." Chris is bouncing, eager to go.

"I have keys," Tom says, leaning close to him, not sure if the cameras also have microphones on them. He has to assume they do. The kind of people watching this shit, they'll want to hear it, too. "We get Louise, we find Cindy, and then we hope one of these keys opens a door out of here."

Chris is nodding along.

"Stick close to me," Tom says. "It looks like they have close-combat weapons – things to stab, and things to bludgeon. I don't think they're going to have guns, but we can't just assume that. We need to be careful."

"Got it," Chris says. "I'm on you."

Tom places a boot on the chest of the oni mask and yanks the crowbar out of him. He turns and starts running. If it was Louise crying out, she's silent now. Tom heads to where he heard her last. If his sense of direction is correct, they're going to the centre of the labyrinth.

Suddenly, all noise is disrupted by a mechanical roar. From the end of the corridor, a tall, skinny man in a butcher's apron with a mouse mask steps into view, revving a chainsaw. Tom sees the tattoos running up and down his bare arms, and his long, black hair at the back of his head. It's the rockstar. Beside him, wielding a hammer, is Richard Nixon. Or, more precisely, a steroid-pumped gym monkey in a Nixon mask.

Tom grabs Chris by the back of the collar and they head down another corridor. Behind them, the rockstar and his bodyguard pursue. Tom takes a left turn and presses himself flat against the wall close to the corner, holding Chris in place so he does the same. He glances at Chris and sees how sweat pours down his face.

Tom braces himself, gripping the crowbar tight. The two are approaching, following them, getting louder. He hears the rockstar calling, his voice a high screech to be heard over the revving chainsaw. "Come out, come out, wherever you are!"

He and Nixon continue down the corridor, past Tom and Chris's hiding spot. They pass by. The rockstar presses the chainsaw to the wall, throwing up sparks.

Tom motions for Chris to stay where he is, then he moves. He attacks, lodging the hook of the crowbar into Nixon's trapezium, burying it between his neck and his shoulder on the right side. Nixon cries out. His body twists in pain. He drops the hammer with a clatter. The rockstar hears the combination of sounds and whirls toward them, chainsaw raised.

Tom has control of Nixon with the crowbar. He twists left and right, Nixon moving with him, grabbing at the crowbar, desperate to alleviate his pain. The rockstar jabs with the chainsaw, but his thickset bodyguard is blocking his swipes.

The rockstar is getting desperate. Tom can see the cornered look in his eyes through the mouse mask's holes. His bodyguard is out the picture, and now he's alone, and he has no clear shot with the chainsaw.

"Face me!" he says, crying the words, his voice breaking. "Face me, you fucking coward!"

Tom rushes him, pushing the bodyguard ahead. He spooks the rockstar. The rockstar does the only thing he can – he points the chainsaw in front of himself to ward off the attack.

The chainsaw rips through the bodyguard's torso. Blood sprays the walls and the mouse mask. Tom continues to push him forward, avoiding where the chainsaw bursts through the bodyguard's back. He twists so the vicious, spinning teeth don't catch him, and he pushes the bodyguard on top of the rockstar, crushing him. The chainsaw stops running.

"No!" the rockstar screams. "No – this isn't right! Get him off me! This isn't how it's supposed to go!"

Tom plucks the crowbar out of the bodyguard's shoulder. He looks down at the rockstar, looks right into his terrified eyes. "And how's it supposed to go?"

The rockstar can't answer this.

Tom drives the length of the crowbar down through the rockstar's wide right eye, through to the back of his skull, scrambling his brains. The rockstars goes into convulsions. Tom pulls the crowbar back and retrieves the fallen hammer. He calls Chris out of hiding and hands him the hammer. Chris surveys the gruesome scene before him. He's heard it from his hiding spot, but this is his first time seeing it. "Jesus Christ," he mutters.

Before he can say anything else, there's a scream. A woman's scream.

Chris's head snaps toward the sound. "Louise," he says.

Tom stops him from racing off. "They have to know we're close after all of this," he says, pointing to the chainsaw. "They could've made her scream on purpose, to draw us out, to make us rush in without thinking."

"I'm not rushing anywhere," Chris says. "Like I said – I'm on you."

Tom nods. He leads the way toward the sound, bloodied crowbar held tight.

As Tom suspected, the sound leads them to the centre of the labyrinth. It's a large space, a wide circle. Nowhere to hide.

There are three men, and one woman. A clown, a kabuki, and a pig. The woman is in a white dress that, despite being dirty and stained, almost glows in the darkness here. She's shackled to the wall. It's Louise.

The first thing Tom notices is that her face is not burnt.

The man in the pig mask is behind her, holding her away from the wall. He presses a knife to her throat. The clown is armed with a baseball bat, and the kabuki has a machete. They hold back. They don't attempt to rush Tom and Chris.

Tom soon finds out why.

A deep, guttural laugh approaches from the darkness of an adjoining corridor. A man steps into view, still laughing. He wears a bear mask. From his build, he can only be the football player. Beside him is an equally large man, wearing a mask of Ronald Reagan.

"You made it," the bear says. He's carrying a meat cleaver. "And fast. Here I was starting to worry that maybe I was gonna miss all the fun." He turns to Ronald Reagan. "You get the pretty boy. Rollins is mine."

62

The bear approaches. The cleaver is raised.

By Tom's count, these are the last five men in the labyrinth. He counted eleven men arrive earlier today. One of them must be with Cindy.

Tom thinks of Cindy. Wherever she is, wherever they're holding her, whatever is happening to her, he needs her to hold out. He'll be there as soon as he can.

The bear swipes the cleaver and Tom rolls through to avoid it, while Ronald Reagan grabs for Chris. Ronald Reagan is armed with a pipe. He swings it like a baton. Chris backs up, avoiding its lethal arc.

The bear strikes with the cleaver again, narrowly missing Tom's scalp. Tom dives to the side, toward Ronald Reagan. He swings the crowbar to his left, embedding its hooked end into the back of his right knee. Reagan seems to trip over himself, the crowbar lodged in his knee. Chris swings the hammer. He destroys the mask and shatters Reagan's jaw. Teeth shatter and fly through the air, skittering across the ground.

Tom turns back to the bear, unarmed. The bear sees what he's done. Tom yanks on the crowbar. It's lodged tight, but he manages to get it loose. As the cleaver comes down, he swings the crowbar and deflects it, knocking it from the bear's hand. The bear clutches his hand to himself, pained from the reverberation. Tom turns the crowbar sideways and jabs its length into the bear's throat. The bear stumbles back, choking. Tom slips the crowbar down his hand, holding it at the end, and swings it upward, burying the hook into the bear's crotch.

The bear can't make a sound. He's in too much pain. The crowbar's hook has split his testicles. Tom turns to Chris and holds out his hand for the hammer. Chris tosses it to him. Tom catches it, spins, and brings the hammer down on top of the bear's skull.

He turns to the three remaining. The clown and the kabuki look at each other.

"Fuck it," the clown says, and he attacks with the baseball bat.

As he gets closer, Tom jabs the hammer into his face. The clown's head snaps back. Holding him by the front of his coveralls, Tom bludgeons him with the hammer until he's stopped moving, then shoves him to the ground.

The kabuki holds the machete two-handed, but it's clear he's shaking. The tip of the blade is trembling uncontrollably. "Oh shit," he says. "Oh shit, oh shit – fuck this."

He drops the machete and he turns and starts to run. Tom picks up the baseball bat and throws it at his legs. It tangles in the kabuki's feet and he goes down, his face skidding across the ground, destroying the mask. Tom makes eye contact with the pig while he crosses the space toward the kabuki. The pig is shaking, too. He holds tight to Louise, the knife at her throat. Tom notices how he's slipped at some point, nicked her. Blood is running down her neck, and has stained the front of her white dress.

Tom picks up the bat. The kabuki rolls onto his back. He looks up at Tom through the half-ruined mask. He's not anyone Tom knows. He's not a public figure. He's just another rich asshole.

"Please," the man says.

"How many people do you think have begged for their lives in this place?" Tom says.

The man closes his eyes tight. He squeezes out a tear.

"You're just another one of them," Tom says, and he brings down the bat, over and over, until the mask and the face are both destroyed.

"Stop, *stop!*" the pig is crying. "Stop it, or I'll kill her, I swear to God!"

Tom turns to him, shouldering the bloodied bat matted with hair and matter. "There's no God here," Tom says. "And you're not going to kill that girl."

Behind the mask, the pig is crying. "I will – I'll kill her, I mean it."

"You hurt her, and I'll destroy you," Tom says. "Same as I've done to everyone else here. You're the last one standing, piggie. There's no one coming to save you. Drop the knife and step out. You won't like the alternative."

The pig knows Tom is right. He does as he says. He drops the knife and he steps out from behind Louise, his hands raised in surrender.

Chris hurries toward Louise with the hammer. He works at the shackles, smashing them to get her free.

"Take off that mask," Tom says to the pig. "You look ridiculous."

The pig hesitates. He looks toward the cameras in the walls. The mask is hiding his identity.

"It's too late to care if you're recognised," Tom says.

The pig removes the mask, defeated. He drops it to the ground. Again, Tom doesn't recognise him, other than having seen him earlier in the day.

"Where is Cindy?" Tom says.

The pig sniffs. "They were taking her to the torture room," he says.

"And where's that?"

"It's in the labyrinth. At the exit."

"Where's the exit?"

"Same place as the entrance – it's the same thing. As you come down the steps, to the left, down the corridor – that's where the torture room is."

"You've been a big help," Tom says. He nods at Louise and Chris standing behind the pig.

With a screech, Louise drives the knife that was at her throat into the pig's back. He stumbles forward, his face twisted in a rictus of pain, his arms twisting back to get at the knife lodged in him. He falls forward onto his face.

Louise is shaking, looking down at her bloodied hands. Chris holds her arms, clutching her tight to him. He's finally got her back.

But getting her back is not enough. Now they need to get free. There's no time for their reunion while Cindy is still out there. She's in the torture room. She could be going through anything.

"We're not clear yet," Tom says, and he starts moving again. Behind him, Chris and Louise follow. They stick close. They don't want to get lost down here.

63

Shannon has to get Guy's attention so he sees what's happening in the labyrinth. He pulls his face up from between her legs and turns his head to see. "Oh my God – *look*," she says.

Guy takes it in, his body going rigid. There's plenty of death and destruction up on the screen, but it's not the *right* kind of death and destruction.

"*Shit*," he says, wiping his mouth with the back of his hand and hurrying to his feet. He grabs at his scattered clothes and Shannon does the same, watching Rollins making his way back through the labyrinth, followed by Chris and Louise. They got her back. They were never supposed to get her back. She was just a lure. The bait on a fish hook. She was supposed to die in there with them, and instead everyone *else* is dead.

Guy gets on his phone. He calls Tobin. He has it on loudspeaker while he pulls his clothes on. Shannon can hear the conversation.

"Have you seen what's happening?" Guy says.

"I see it," Tobin says, his tone grim. "I've been watching with Brad."

"You need to get in there," Guy says. "Get a team, and –"

"I've already done it," Tobin says, cutting him off. "I've sent in a team. They're all armed. It might be an anticlimax, but we can't afford to let them get any further."

"I don't fucking care – just make sure this goes our way."

"It will," Tobin says. "He got lucky with the close-combat weapons, but it doesn't matter how fast he is, he can't pull those fancy moves against our guns."

Shannon buttons up her shirt and watches the screen. She hopes Tobin is right.

64

The man in the grinning face mask has been taking his time. He hasn't dived straight into physical torture. Instead, he started with the mental variety.

"Why don't we see how your friends get along?" he said, flicking through the various cameras on the monitor. "And if you see anything that upsets you, don't be afraid to cry. You can scream and thrash – you can do anything you want. I don't mind." The way he looked at her, Cindy could tell he was smiling under the already smiling mask. "I want to see the hope leaving you."

The cold metal manacles bit into Cindy's wrist. While the man followed the happenings in the labyrinth, Cindy has worked at the manacles, trying to free herself. She's focussed on her left hand. The manacle scrapes at her skin, scraping and bloodying it. She didn't have to worry about the noise she made. The man was engrossed in the monitor, and he *wanted* her to make noise. When she whimpers, he looks back at her and she can see from the way his shoulders rise and fall that he enjoys the sound. When he turns, watching her, Cindy stops what she's doing and hopes he doesn't notice how she's bleeding from her left wrist.

He's been leaning closer to the monitor. Cindy looks and sees why. Things are not going the way he expected. Tom is the reason. He's killing his way through the labyrinth. He has Chris and Louise with him.

The man stands. He turns to Cindy. She stops working at the manacle. "Is that all of them?" Cindy says, laughing at him. The laughter comes as much from the pain as anything else.

The man in the grinning face mask doesn't respond. Cindy can see how his chest rises and falls. He's breathing hard. He's worried.

"You should run," Cindy says. "If there's no one else in his way, Tom is coming straight here. He's coming for me, and he's coming for *you*. If you're smart, you'll leave this room right now and you'll run, and you won't stop, and you'd better hope Tom isn't able to figure out who you are."

The man starts to laugh. "Are you kidding me?" he says. "I'm not going anywhere. I paid a lot of money for you, and I intend to get my worth."

"It's your funeral," Cindy says.

"No." The mask shakes side to side. "Tobin will deal with him. Tobin and his men. They'll cut Rollins and your other friends down before they can get anywhere near here. You'll see. You'll see it all up there on the monitor. *But.*" He reaches out to the table of tools and brushes his fingers lightly over them. "I've maybe wasted enough time. I think we'll get down to work, mm? Give the people at home something they'll really enjoy."

Cindy grits her teeth. She works at her left hand again,

pulling down, trying to slip free. The manacle is bloody, but it doesn't provide enough grease. It's too tight.

She thinks of Mandy. She thinks of her story. Of what she had to do to escape. Of the sacrifices she was prepared to make in order to survive.

The man is looking the tools over, touching each of them in turn. He lingers upon a bone saw. He's deliberating.

Cindy pulls on the manacle. There is a little give. Space for some of her hand to get through, but not all of it. She's trapped because she's scared to sacrifice. She has to do what Mandy did. She looks at her wrist. Sees how it's already cut and bloody.

The man settles upon the bone saw. He nods to himself, as if this is the correct decision, and he grips its handle.

Cindy braces herself. With her right hand, she grabs at the chain and pulls on it, holds it tight. Holds it so there's no give on the left.

The man straightens. He turns to her.

Cindy bares her teeth. She feels her hair sticking to her forehead and temples, slick with sweat. She breathes hard and fast, preparing herself. The man pauses, looking at her, seeing how tensed she is. He assumes it's for the saw. He chuckles.

Cindy screams. The skin around her wrist bunches up and tears. She wrenches her left hand free of the manacle. Hot blood splashes her face.

But her arm is free. She stares at it, red from fingertips to elbow. The blood is still pumping from her. Experimentally, she wriggles her fingers. They still work.

The man has taken a step back, startled. He holds the bone saw up, as if he's forgotten what to do with it.

Cindy gasps. She feels like she could throw up. There's

no time to waste. The man won't remain startled for long. With her free hand, Cindy grabs at the table of tools. She wraps her hand around a scalpel. Covered in blood, it's hard to keep a good grip.

The man realises what she's doing. He steps forward. Cindy slashes at him with the scalpel, cutting him across the palm of his left hand and slicing through the fingers of his right, wrapped around the saw. He drops it and clutches his hands back to himself. They're cut deep. He tries to take a step back, but Cindy drives the scalpel down into his right thigh.

She hits something important. The femoral, perhaps. Blood begins to spray from the man's leg. He makes a panicked, choked sound in the back of his throat as he stumbles, painting the wall bright red, his hands clamping at his thigh. He hits the wall and slides down it. He's already lost a lot of blood. He's not going to last much longer.

Cindy frees her right hand. She holds her left to her chest. It burns. It screams in agony. She grits her teeth against it, tasting bile rising at the back of her throat. She reaches down and frees her ankles with her right hand.

As she slides off the chair, the door to the room opens.

65

Tom leads the way toward the exit, Chris and Louise following. Chris keeps hold of his sister. She's barefoot and weak. He keeps her from falling.

Tom had to double back to where he was first deposited in the labyrinth. He knows the way from here, following the wall that he was carried along. He starts to hear voices throughout the labyrinth. This doesn't surprise him. Tobin will have sent his men in to clear up the mess.

As they round a corner, Tom spots two of the men up ahead, armed with their FX5510s. They look like they're listening to their radio, being given directions toward Tom and the others. He sees them look up as Tom is nearly upon them, no doubt warned that he's on his way.

The men can't react fast enough. Tom swings the baseball bat at the man on the left, closest to him. He shatters his jaw with the swing, then jabs it into the chest of the man on the right, stunning him, before bringing it down on the top of his skull. The force of the impact is so great that it breaks the bat. Tom uses the jagged handle to jab into the side of the neck of the man on the left. Both men dead, Tom takes their weapons, passing an FX5510 and a Glock to Chris. He takes one of each for himself. He uses the Glock to shoot out all of the cameras he can see, and then they press on, Tom still blasting cameras as they go.

Tom spots light coming from what must be the torture room. The door is wide open. This isn't a good sign. Tom feels his speed increasing, legs pumping, fearful of what he will find inside.

The first thing that confronts him is blood. A lot of it. It's sprayed upon the walls, painting them a bright red, and on the ground is a deep pool, still spreading outward.

There's no sign of Cindy. He steps deeper into the room and sees the source of the blood. A dead body crumpled in the corner, initially obscured from view by the doctor's chair. The grinning face mask is slumped to one side. Tom spots the bloodied scalpel on the ground, gleaming where blood does not coat it. He sees the wound on the man's thigh where the blood has pumped out of him, filling the room.

Tom turns to the monitor, catching a glimpse of movement. Tobin, at the exit. He's directing his men to cover the way out. There's someone beside him, held tight. It's Cindy. Once Tobin has his men arranged, covering the exit, he drags her out of the labyrinth.

Chris is watching, too. "How are we supposed to get past that?"

Tom doesn't answer straight away. He flicks through the monitor, checking the rest of the labyrinth. There are other men moving through it, searching for them. Shooting out the cameras has made it difficult for them to get a track on them. Now that they're in the torture room, and Tom has left the cameras alone thus far, he sees how the men check their radios and start turning around, coming back this way. Tom notices how the men, Tobin's men, are all dressed the same. It's a basic uniform – black trousers, black long-sleeved T-shirts.

Tom turns away from the monitor. "We need to double back to the men I just killed," he says. "We'll have to take the long way to avoid the group blocking the exit. I have a plan."

66

Tom continued to kill cameras on the way, making it difficult for them to be found. He went off down corridors to destroy more cameras, so as not to create an obvious route. He worked fast, knowing that Cindy had been taken.

They get back to the two men killed. There's blood on their clothes, but in the dark it's hard to tell. Tom and Chris quickly switch out what they're wearing for the all-black uniform of the dead men. They take off fast toward the exit, holding Louise between them as if they've captured her and they're dragging her along. They can only hope that in the chaos the men won't see their faces and realise who they really are until it's too late.

The exit comes into view. The men blocking the way are two rows deep. There's eight of them. They peer into the darkness, looking on edge. Tom's shooting out of the cameras has spooked them. While they were moving through the labyrinth, he heard how his own gunfire set off the men deeper inside, set them to firing at the noises, shooting at shadows.

"Don't shoot," Tom calls, making his voice deeper, gruffer, disguising it, though he's not sure if it would matter.

The men turn toward them, rifles raised, but they don't fire. They wait, trying to work out if this is truly a pair of colleagues.

"We got the girl," Tom says. "The two men are still out there."

"Who are you?" one of the guards says. "Don't come any closer – namecheck!"

They're close enough. Tom and Chris let go of Louise. They open fire on the men.

They catch them by surprise. The guards are able to loose off a couple of rounds in retaliation, but their shots are wild. Tom and Chris mow them down. Tom runs up, putting an extra bullet in each body, making sure they're all dead. Last thing they need is a shot in the back on their way out.

Tom continues to the surface. He doesn't wait for Chris and Louise. He knows they'll follow. He kicks the door open and drops to a knee, shouldering the rifle. Luckily, due to the darkness of the labyrinth, it does not take his eyes long to adjust to the darkness of the night.

There are some spotlights illuminating the compound, but they're in front of the buildings. Tom scans the area. It's not as wild up here. The door behind him opens, but Chris and Louise hold back, not wanting to crowd him.

In the distance, speeding away, Tom sees a vehicle racing away across the scrubland, headlights illuminating the way ahead of them, wheels kicking up dust behind. It tears through the chain-link fence surrounding the grounds.

Men approach from the right, the direction of the main

house. Weapons raised. Tom turns on them and guns them down. They fall without firing a shot.

"Over there – they're heading to the barn," Chris says.

Tom sees them. Three men. They're armed, and they're running. To the cages. There's no sign of Tobin and Cindy. No sign of the Kennedys. Tom surmises the three men are heading to the barn to eliminate anyone left over.

"Put them down," Tom says. "But leave the one on the right to me."

He and Chris open fire. Tom targets the man on the right. He aims low, strafing the back of his legs at his calves and ankles. Chris blasts the other two men in the back.

Before going after them, Tom turns and checks the ring of keys he swiped. Each of them is marked with a small white square with a black character upon them – either a letter or a number. There is one with an L. Tom pushes the labyrinth door closed and pushes the key inside. It turns. He locks the door, leaving the men still in the labyrinth locked within.

He runs to the man he dropped. He's screaming in pain, reaching for his bloodied lower legs. Tom can see bone sticking through. It's doubtful he'll ever walk again, but he's not going to be alive long enough to find out.

"Hands up!" Tom says, drawing down on him, FX5510 aimed at his chest.

Weeping with pain, the man complies.

Tom drops to a knee beside him. "Tobin had Cindy," he says. "Where have they gone?"

The man gulps air. He's going into shock. Tom slaps him, hard.

"Answer me!" He doesn't have time to waste.

"They'll go – they'll go to the – the airstrip," the man says, swallowing.

"An airstrip?" Tom says. "Private? They have planes?"

The man nods.

"Where are the Kennedys?"

"With them."

"Where's the airstrip? Which way?"

"It's a – it's a straight line that way," the man says, pointing, and Tom can see the escape car in the distance. It's heading the direction the man says the airstrip is. Cindy must be in that vehicle. "About twenty minutes, a half-hour, give or take. Please, you need to help me."

Tom doesn't have any further questions for the man. He stands and shoots him dead, already turning as he does so. He tosses the ring of keys to Louise. "Free the people in the cages," he says. "Chris, I need you with me."

Chris looks at his sister. He bites his lip. Hesitates for just a second, not wanting to leave her, then he hands her the Glock. "If you need to use it, just point and shoot," he says.

She takes the gun from him, nods once, then turns and heads toward the barn without a word. She's not steady on her feet, but she forces herself on, driven by a determination to help the people captive in a situation she knows all too well.

The vehicles that arrived earlier in the day are still parked next to the main house. Tom notices the minivan is gone. He heads to them. He jumps in behind the steering wheel of the vehicle at the front. There's no keys. He hotwires it. Chris jumps in beside him as the engine roars into life. Tom slams his foot flat to the accelerator and races from the compound, heading into the night across the scrubland, following the cloud of dust he can dimly make out in the distance ahead.

67

Carter is driving. Tobin tells him to go faster. Tobin is in the back of the minivan, holding tight to Cindy. Brad is in the front passenger seat, clinging onto the handle overhead as they bounce over the terrain. The Kennedys are in the back with Tobin and Cindy, holding onto each other.

Tobin calls ahead to the airstrip. Two of his men, pilots, are already there. They won't be expecting to fly tonight. They'll be expecting an easy night, watching over the planes. When they answer, Tobin shouts into the phone. He has no time for conversation. "Fire up the Cessna," he says. "*Immediately* – we're on our way and we're coming in hot." He hangs up and radios back to his men at the compound. He's been trying for a while. There hasn't been any answer yet. There still isn't.

"*Fuck*," Tobin says, trying one more time. If his men don't answer, he knows this isn't good.

"What's happening back there?" Guy says.

"That's what I'm trying to find out," Tobin says, snapping.

He has no patience. He radios again and finally gets an answer. It's Neil.

"They've locked us in the labyrinth!" he says.

"What? They got out?"

"They've killed everyone you had blocking the exit. Holy shit, Tobin, what are we gonna *do*?"

Tobin ignores the question. "What about on the compound?"

"I don't know – we're locked in the fucking labyrinth!"

Tobin throws the radio to the ground in frustration.

"He won't stop coming for you," Cindy says. Tobin spins on her. She's smirking, despite the obvious pain she's in. She holds her left wrist to her chest, cradling her elbow with her right hand for support. "You might as well just give up now and make it quick for yourselves."

"I know he's coming," Tobin says through gritted teeth. "It's the only reason you're still alive right now, bitch. You're collateral. If he wants you back alive, he's gonna have to cool his fucking warpath."

"Do you really think he's gonna talk to you?" Cindy says.

"Shut your goddamn mouth," Tobin says. "Don't talk me out of keeping you breathing."

Cindy is grinning still, but she's silent now.

"Tobin, what do we do?" Shannon says, leaning toward him.

"We get in the air, and we get out of here," Tobin says. He sees how Guy has already stiffened at the prospect of flying, how his face has blanched, but there's no other option available to them. They need to get clear. If they want to stay alive, and free, they need to get out of here right now. There won't be any regrouping. Most of their people are dead now. Their operation is in tatters. There's no coming back from this. Their only hope now is to escape.

Brad is leaning toward the side mirror, looking into it. "Um, I think I see something," he says.

"What is it?" Tobin says.

"Another dust cloud," Brad says. "Another set of lights, coming up fast."

Tobin twists to look out of the rear window. He sees what Brad sees. As he turns, he sees the knowing look Cindy gives him. She's enjoying this. Enjoying seeing them squirm.

"He won't catch up," Tobin says. "We'll be in the air by the time he gets here." Tobin points ahead, through the windshield.

Coming into view is the airstrip. The Cessna is already running.

68

Tom races through the scrubland. He's seen the minivan stop. He can see the airstrip, and the figures that race to board the Cessna. The group have dumped the minivan. It's still running, idling at the side of the runway.

"We're not gonna reach them," Chris says.

Tom doesn't answer. There's no alternative. No other option. They *have* to reach the airstrip. He's pushed this car too hard to give up now.

They speed toward the airstrip. The Cessna is already running, but it won't be able to take off immediately. Tom has a couple of minutes' grace.

The Cessna begins to roll as Tom reaches the runway. He pulls on the handbrake and the car skids sideways to run parallel to the small plane. The group have seen them coming. They haven't closed the door yet. Tom sees Tobin and another man trying to get it shut. It opens upward. They pull on a bar to bring it down into place.

"Take the wheel," Tom says. He starts climbing over the top of Chris, who ducks under him to take control of the car. "Put your foot down – don't slow. Get me in close, under that door."

"Oh, Jesus," Chris says through gritted teeth, but he does as he's told, mashing his foot to the ground.

The car has a sunroof. Tom smashes it with the handle of the Glock. Chris slows slightly as shattered glass rains around them.

"Don't slow!" Tom says. "Go, *go!*"

As the car speeds back up, Tom pushes himself up through the sunroof, Glock still in hand. He fires toward the open door of the Cessna. Tobin pulls himself back into cover away from the shots, but bullets find the other man. He clutches his chest and falls from the plane. The car thuds over him on the runway and Chris almost loses control. He grips the steering wheel tight and forces the car to straighten.

Tom climbs out of the car, onto the roof. "Get me closer!" he shouts down. He keeps the door covered with the Glock. He glances at the plane's wheels. It's starting to rise.

The car is as close to the open door as it's going to get. If Tom waits any longer, if he hesitates, it's going to rise and get too high. The Cessna will get away, Tobin with it, the Kennedys with it, Cindy trapped inside.

Tom jumps.

He lands hard inside the doorframe as the Cessna takes flight, and he feels a lurch as it begins its ascent, leaving the ground. He slips back, falling out of the door. He scrambles, and manages to lodge his arms against either side of the frame, holding himself in place. He loses the Glock. It slips back past him, out of the plane. Looking back, he sees the airstrip receding behind them. Sees Chris skidding the car to a halt before he runs out of runway.

His ears pop as the air pressure changes and the wind whips around him. Straining, he drags himself into the plane. Over the wind, he can hear people shouting and screaming. He turns and braces himself, boots on either side of the open door, and grabs the bar for the door. He pulls it down, sealing it into place. The Cessna is suddenly much quieter. Next to the door, Tom sees parachutes. There are a lot of them. Enough for everyone on board.

Tom turns. Tobin is standing, pointing a Glock at him. Behind him, Tom sees the interior of the plane. It should usually seat eight – ten including the pilot and the seat beside him, potentially for a back-up pilot. Tom is directly behind the pilots. Instead of eight chairs in the body of the Cessna, there are only four. The others have been removed to create extra space. The Kennedys are at the rear. Guy is ghostly pale, clinging to the arms of his chair and staring at Tom like he's some kind of apparition. Shannon stares too, but there's still colour in her cheeks. She holds onto her husband's arm.

In front of them is Cindy. Beside her, a short, overweight man with a balding head and a short goatee holds her into place, but he looks uncomfortable doing so. He stinks of cigarettes. Tom can smell him from here. He swallows at the sight of Tom.

Cindy turns to Tobin. "I told you," she says.

"Shut up," Tobin says, gun pointing at Tom.

Tom smiles at him. "Are you really going to risk firing that in here?" he says. "And with me so close to the pilot?"

Tobin's eyes flicker toward the two men at the front. He knows Tom is right.

He lowers the gun. He's smiling. He hands the Glock to the man next to Cindy. "Look after this for me, Brad," he says. "This shouldn't take long."

69

Tobin attacks. Tom braces for him. In the confined space of the Cessna, even with half of its chairs removed, it's not going to be possible for Tobin to unleash his kicks, especially not with the force he'd like, and still so close to the pilot. Tom does not underestimate him, though. He's no doubt effective at close-quarters grappling. Tom has seen enough MMA fights to know that most of them take place in close quarters, rolling on the ground, wrestling for the advantage.

Tobin strikes with short punches, aiming at Tom's face and head. Tom covers up, but Tobin shifts his attack and aims now for Tom's unprotected torso. Tom pushes through, keeping his head covered. He can take the shots to his ribs and abs. They sting, but they're too close to do any real damage. His head is more important than his torso.

He gets in close and Tobin grabs at him, attempting to wrest control. He raises knees, aiming for Tom's face, but again Tom is able to keep them at bay with his forearms and elbows. He pushes Tobin back, but Tobin manages to kick him in the midsection and double-leg tackles him to the ground. Tom lands hard and he feels the Cessna lurch with the impact.

"Wrap it up, Tobin, wrap it up!" the pilot calls back.

"Do as he says, Tobin!" Guy cries, his voice cracking.

Tobin mounts Tom, attempting to lock in a hold on his right arm, but Tom locks his fingers in an S-grip and is able to fight him off. He keeps him at bay, jabbing at Tobin's face and neck. A rabbit punch catches him under the left eye and instantly raises a mouse. In retaliation, Tobin drops his weight across Tom with an elbow strike, slipping through his defences and hitting him above his left eyebrow. It splits and Tom feels blood running across his forehead and down his temple.

Tobin sees the blood and grins. He presses Tom to the ground, his weight on his chest. Tom's legs, however, are free. He brings up his right knee and drives it into Tobin's spine. Tobin cries out, but Tom brings it up again and again, knocking the air out of him, twisting his body. Tobin's right hand grabs at Tom's face, aiming for his eyes. Tom catches it and wrenches back his index finger, snapping it. Tobin grunts, but Tom doesn't let go. He grips the index finger tight in his right fist, and with his left he encloses Tobin's middle finger. He tears them apart.

The two fingers split down the centre of Tobin's hand. There's a spray of blood. Tobin screams. He pushes himself back from Tom, looking down at his ruined right hand. He hurries back to his feet as Tom stands, and it's clear that Tobin is worried. He's underestimated Tom. He's scared now.

Tobin looks toward the Kennedys. More specifically, he looks toward Shannon. She looks back at him, biting her lip. They're all worried. Tobin was their last line of defence.

"It can be us, Tobin," Shannon says. Her husband looks at her. "Kill him, and it can be us. Just you and me."

Tobin swallows. He nods. He turns back to Tom. His right hand is held close to him. He angles his body toward Tom with his left side. His mutilated right hand drips blood to the floor. Tom raises his fists. He waits.

Tobin sweats. He takes a tentative step forward. Tom doesn't move. Tobin kicks at him. It's nothing fancy. Not a side kick or a heel kick. Just a front kick, like he's trying to force Tom back toward the door and out of the plane.

Tom catches it with ease. He smashes his forearm into the side of Tobin's knee. It dislocates. Tobin goes down. Helplessly, he looks up at Tom. Tom holds him by the neck. He brings the point of his elbow down onto his nose, shattering it, then he smashes him across the jaw, rendering him unconscious.

Tom turns to Brad. He holds out his hand. "Give me the gun."

Brad does so instantly.

Tom motions for Cindy to stand. She joins him. Tom notices how her left arm is bloody. How she's wounded at her wrist, and she holds it against her chest. "Put on a parachute," he says. "And pass one to me."

Cindy does so. Tom shoulders the parachute, looking the plane over, gun raised.

"You said – you said you shouldn't shoot that in here," Guy says. His teeth are chattering.

"I said *Tobin* shouldn't shoot it in here," Tom says. He opens fire, shooting Brad through the heart. Shannon shrieks. Tom steps closer to the Kennedys. "This is going to be brief," he says. "But I want you to know what your victims felt. I want you to feel even just a *modicum* of the fear that they felt."

"What are you going to do?" Shannon says. She's trying to be defiant, but she's failing.

Tom kneecaps them both. They scream in agony, clutching at their legs. Tom didn't think it was possible, but Guy gets paler.

The two men at the front have turned, hands raised. "You don't need to hurt us," the pilot says. He looks at the parachutes. "You need me. You don't need to jump. I can land this plane anywhere you want."

"I'd rather jump," Tom says, and he shoots both men through the heads. He fires upon the control panel, emptying the magazine into it. Instantly, the Cessna begins to descend. If there was anything left of the panel, warning alarms would no doubt be sounding. Instead, it just sparks.

Cindy pushes the door open. "You ever done this before?" Tom says to her.

"Nope," she says.

"Just pull this cord," Tom points at it, "when I do."

Cindy swallows. She nods.

Tom grabs the rest of the parachutes and throws them out of the plane. The Cessna is plummeting fast. The wind pressure screams through the cabin. On the ground, Tobin begins to stir. Tom looks back at the Kennedys. He sees the pain and the terror on their faces.

He turns, takes Cindy in his arms, and they jump.

70

Tom and Cindy walk through the scrubland, arms around each other, keeping each other up. The sun is beginning to rise. It has been a long night of walking.

They saw the Cessna crash. Saw it explode in the distance after they'd landed, briefly lighting up the night. The fire was still burning as they walked away. They'd waited, and watched, and made sure no one emerged. There were no survivors.

About an hour after the crash, they saw emergency vehicles heading toward the site. They were able to easily avoid them. They didn't want to talk to anyone. They just wanted to leave. They walked on, heading toward the airstrip.

As they arrive, it's currently still clear. The police have not yet reached it, though it's surely only a matter of time. There's no sign of Chris, but no doubt after Tom jumped onto the Cessna he raced back to the compound and his sister.

The minivan that had been left running is out of gas.

Tom finds another car parked behind the airstrip's hangar. The keys are behind the sun visor. Tom starts the engine.

"Tom," Cindy says. They haven't spoken during the walk through the scrubland. They're too tired. They've been through too much.

Tom looks at her.

Cindy looks back. Her left wrist is pressed to her chest still. She reaches out and places her right hand on the back of his. She doesn't say anything further. She doesn't need to.

71

The story of the Hollywood couple and their snuff movie business in Lubbock, Texas, dominates the news. Arrests are occurring across the country, and though no names have yet been given, the government is reaching out to nations with whom they have extradition treaties in order to bring in some of the Kennedys' fans from further afield.

Tom and Cindy returned to Lubbock and have laid low in Cindy's apartment. Tom disinfected and dressed the wound to Cindy's left wrist. It's heavily bandaged now. She can still wriggle her fingers and grip things, and Tom thinks this is a good sign. It means no nerve damage. It's going to leave a nasty scar, but it could have been worse.

No one has come looking for them. A few days have since passed. They've watched the news. Cindy has monitored online chatter. The death of the Kennedys has been reported. No one knows what caused their flight to crash yet, though the dumped parachutes have been found out in the scrubland. The investigation is ongoing. The explosion and subsequent fire may disguise the fact that the bodies have bullets in them, but Tom isn't sure.

Tom stands at the window, looking down at the streets below.

Cindy watches him from her desk. "Uh-oh," she says. "I know that look."

Tom turns to her.

"You've been in one place too long," Cindy says. "How long are you planning on staying around?"

"Until I'm certain you're safe," Tom says.

"I appreciate that. But I think everyone is either dead or under arrest now."

Tom looks around her apartment. The smell of burning flesh is gone, but the scarring from the battles that have occurred here remain. "Are you going to move again?"

"I don't know," Cindy says. "Would it matter? This feels like an outlier. They didn't find *me* – they found Chris. It was him they were following. I'm not sure I need to. I guess this place will do until, y'know, I'm ready to give it all up and join you on the road."

Tom smiles. "It's an open invite. Just say the word."

Cindy looks at him. It's like she's thinking. Deliberating.

Before she can speak, her buzzer rings.

Cindy goes to it. It's Chris Parton. Cindy buzzes him in.

He comes up to her apartment. He's not alone. Louise is with him. She looks better than when Tom saw her last. She's cleaned up. She's in jeans and a blouse. Her hair is tied back. Her face looks fresh and clean. She hugs Cindy, and then she hugs Tom. She squeezes each of them tight.

"You're looking well," Cindy says, inviting them to sit down on her sofa. The siblings do. Cindy sits on a chair close to them. Tom remains standing.

Louise nods. "It's the best I've felt in a long time," she says. She smiles broadly. "Sometimes I pinch myself and make sure this isn't a dream. Like, a near-death dream, and I'm imagining that I got away."

Chris squeezes her hand. "It's real," he says. "You're really here." He turns to Cindy and Tom. "Thanks to them."

Tom shuffles uncomfortably. He doesn't need to be thanked. He can see it's the same for Cindy. "We did what we could," she says. "We did what we hope anyone would do." She clears her throat and changes the subject. "How's everything else? How are you sleeping?"

"There's still some nightmares," Chris says, talking about his sister. "But we're hopeful they'll fade."

"Therapy could be your friend," Cindy says.

"We've already made a booking," Chris says. "It's for Louise, but I'll be sitting in, too."

"I want him to," Louise says.

"I'm sorry I wasn't at the airstrip to pick you both up," Chris says. "I wasn't sure what to do. I figured getting back to Louise and the others was the best idea. I went back and we called the cops. I saw the plane crash. I didn't know if you'd been able to get off. We went back in the car and drove around the scrubland but we couldn't find any sign of you. We didn't know whether you were alive or dead. We only came here today on a whim. You can't begin to imagine how relieved I was when you answered the buzzer."

"What did you tell the cops?" Tom says.

"Everything," Chris says. "Everything we knew."

"You told them about us?" Cindy says.

Chris nods. "Shouldn't I?"

"I'm just surprised we haven't heard from anyone yet,"

Cindy says. "Especially with Tom being something of a national celebrity at the minute." She grins.

"Well, when I mentioned his name, I could see that they recognised it," Chris says.

Louise laughs. It's a good sound to hear from someone who's been through so much. "You should've seen the looks on their faces – they were like, *Tom Rollins? The San Francisco guy?*"

"They struggled to believe you were the same person," Chris says.

"He gets around," Cindy says. She holds her hand out. Tom takes it. She pulls him in closer and puts her arm around his waist.

"I have something for you, actually," Chris says, looking at Tom. "It's out in the car. If I'd known you were going to be here, I would've brought it up."

"What is it?" Tom says.

"Your backpack."

"Oh really?" Tom says. "Where was it?"

"It took the cops and the ambulances about an hour to turn up. While we were waiting I took a look around the compound. I found it in the main house. I recognised it, and when I looked through it I found your gun and knife, and the picture of you and Cindy, so I knew for sure. They must've taken it after they ran us off the road." Chris starts to stand. "I'll go get it."

Tom steps forward. "I'll come with you," he says.

Cindy follows them out of the apartment. Louise remains on the sofa. Tom holds back while Chris hurries ahead. Cindy gets Tom's attention. "Are you going to come back up here?"

Tom pauses. He looks down the corridor. "Probably not."

"I hope you weren't going to give me any of that Irish goodbye shit."

"You know I wouldn't. But you're here now. I don't need to come back."

There's a pause. Neither of them says anything. They look at each other.

Tom breaks the silence. "Like I said, it's an open invite."

Cindy breathes deeply. "I know," she says. "And...and part of me wants to come, more than anything else. But I know that when I walk out of here with you, out onto the road, that's it, isn't it? It's you and me, all the way 'til the end of the line. That's our life."

Tom waits for her to continue.

"And that wouldn't be a bad thing," she says. "It's what the biggest part of me wants. But there's still a part of me that's *here*, in Lubbock. It's with my friends. I have...relationships here. I'm not ready to walk out on them just yet. I'm not ready for everything to be you and me. And I dunno – maybe I never will be. Maybe I'll never take that step. Sometimes I lie awake and I think about you out there, alone, and I think, if anything ever happened to you, if you were killed or in some kind of accident, would I even know? Would I find out too late?" She bites her lip. "But I'm still not ready. Not yet. I can't go with you, not today."

Tom nods. He understands. He wraps his arms around her.

Cindy holds him tight. "Make sure you come back to me," she says.

"I always do," Tom says, then he lets go of her and walks away. He doesn't look back.

ABOUT THE AUTHOR

Did you enjoy *Choke Hold*? Please consider leaving a review on Amazon to help other readers discover the book.

Paul Heatley left school at sixteen, and since then has held a variety of jobs including mechanic, carpet fitter, and bookshop assistant, but his passion has always been for writing. He writes mostly in the genres of crime fiction and thriller, and links to his other titles can be found on his website. He lives in the north east of England.

Want to connect with Paul? Visit him at his website.

www.PaulHeatley.com

ALSO BY PAUL HEATLEY

The Tom Rollins Thriller Series

Blood Line (Book 1)

Wrong Turn (Book 2)

Hard to Kill (Book 3)

Snow Burn (Book 4)

Road Kill (Book 5)

No Quarter (Book 6)

Hard Target (Book 7)

Last Stand (Book 8)

Blood Feud (Book 9)

Search and Destroy (Book 10)

Ghost Team (Book 11)

Full Throttle (Book 12)

Sudden Impact (Book 13)

Kill Switch (Book 14)

Choke Hold (Book 15)

The Tom Rollins Box Set (Books 1 - 4)

Printed in Great Britain
by Amazon